THE REALMGATE WARS
GHAL MARAZ

THE REALMGATE WARS

GHAL MARAZ

JOSH REYNOLDS
GUY HALEY

BLACK LIBRARY

A BLACK LIBRARY PUBLICATION

Ghal Maraz first published in 2015.
This edition published in Great Britain in 2016 by
Black Library,
Games Workshop Ltd.,
Willow Road,
Nottingham,
NG7 2WS, UK.

10 9 8 7 6 5 4 3 2 1

Produced by Games Workshop in Nottingham.
Cover illustrations by Aleksey Bayura and Mac Smith.

See Black Library on the internet at

blacklibrary.com

Find out more about Games Workshop
and the world of Warhammer 40,000 at

games-workshop.com

Printed and bound by CPI Group (UK) Ltd, Croydon, CR0 4YY

From the maelstrom of a sundered world, the
Eight Realms were born. The formless and the divine
exploded into life.

Strange, new worlds appeared in the firmament, each one
gilded with spirits, gods and men. Noblest of the gods was
Sigmar. For years beyond reckoning he illuminated the realms,
wreathed in light and majesty as he carved out his reign. His
strength was the power of thunder. His wisdom was infinite.
Mortal and immortal alike kneeled before his lofty throne.
Great empires rose and, for a while, treachery was banished.
Sigmar claimed the land and sky as his own and ruled over a
glorious age of myth.

But cruelty is tenacious. As had been foreseen, the great
alliance of gods and men tore itself apart. Myth and legend
crumbled into Chaos. Darkness flooded the realms. Torture,
slavery and fear replaced the glory that came before. Sigmar
turned his back on the mortal kingdoms, disgusted by their
fate. He fixed his gaze instead on the remains of the world he
had lost long ago, brooding over its charred core, searching
endlessly for a sign of hope. And then, in the dark heat of
his rage, he caught a glimpse of something magnificent. He
pictured a weapon born of the heavens. A beacon powerful
enough to pierce the endless night. An army hewn from
everything he had lost.

Sigmar set his artisans to work and for long ages they toiled,
striving to harness the power of the stars. As Sigmar's great
work neared completion, he turned back to the realms and saw
that the dominion of Chaos was almost complete. The hour
for vengeance had come. Finally, with lightning blazing across
his brow, he stepped forth to unleash his creations.

The Age of Sigmar had begun.

TABLE OF CONTENTS

WAR IN THE HIDDEN VALE

Josh Reynolds

PROLOGUE

In the Garden of Nurgle

Gardus ran.

He did not run alone. Ghosts kept pace, maybe a hundred or more: souls trapped in Nurgle's garden or perhaps memories given a twisted half-life by Gardus' will and the madness of this place. They ran with him, or stumbled in his wake, no more substantial than the stinking murk that rose from the ground beneath his feet.

Some were familiar, most were not. Nonetheless, they all clung to him with whispy fingers, shapes thinning and fading as he struggled out of their clutches. Men and women and children, all victims of plague and illness, all caught in the garden, unable to escape. He wanted to call to them, to comfort them, but he could not. He was helpless here, able only to run, to flee that which followed.

Help us...

Garradan, help me...

Healer, where are you...

Healer...

Garradan...

'Gardus, why do you run?' echoed the hateful, burbling voice of his pursuer.

The ghosts momentarily scattered, only to return all the more insistently as Gardus stumbled and sank to one knee in the mire. He thought again of turning to face the daemon as a true Stormcast, hammer in hand. But something told him to keep running. A voice... a whisper of song... some compulsion to which he could not give name drove him on.

And so he ran, through the very seat of Nurgle's power. Signs of it were everywhere he looked. Strange, unnatural plants loomed on all sides, their fleshy leaves dripping with mucus and their pale blossoms weeping pus. He could hear heavy forms floundering in the murk, but could not see them. He could barely see his own hand in front of his face. His lungs burned with foulness and his armour was crusted with grime and mould. Whenever he stopped for breath or fell, the mould began to grow, creeping across his silver sigmarite. It was as if the garden were seeking to take him into itself, to make him part of it.

He had seen what such a fate meant – had seen the twisted, moss covered boles with silently screaming faces, and trees bent in agonised, almost human postures – and had no wish to experience it himself. Only the faithful, he thought, as he pushed himself to his feet.

'Still repeating that phrase, as if that'll help you,' came the rumbling taunt. 'Your thoughts hang heavy on the perfumed air of the Grandfather's garden. It disturbs the flies, Gardus – or should I call you Garradan?'

So far, Bolathrax had kept itself at a distance, seemingly more interested in the chase than the kill. That was the sole reason he still lived, Gardus knew. The garden of Nurgle was populated by more than the stinging flies that crawled across his armour. Great beasts, brawling daemons and cackling, pestilential sprites had all shown themselves at one point or another. Most crept out of the dripping undergrowth to watch his flight. Others tried to stop him, but were warded off by a roar from Bolathrax or else fell to Gardus' hammer and sword. The deaths of these creatures were greeted by a rumbling from the poisonous clouds above.

He ignored those clouds now, after the first time, when he'd looked up and they'd briefly cleared to reveal a grin as wide as the sky itself and two pus-cream eyes as big as moons. This was Nurgle's realm, and nothing happened here that the God of Decay did not see and approve of. Gardus did not look up now, or to the side. He kept his gaze to the fore and ploughed on, trying to ignore the exhaustion that clawed at his mind.

'Tired, aren't you, Garradan?' Bolathrax gloated. 'But not as tired as you were that final night in Demesnus Harbour, eh? When the skinstealers at last crested the walls and the hospice of Grand Lazzar came under attack, you had been awake for three days, tending the wounded and dying. Was that why you picked up those candlesticks as they butchered your patients? White robes gone red, Garradan… That's what you dream of.'

The ghosts redoubled their efforts to gain his attention as Bolathrax spoke. He saw the faces of lepers and wounded soldiers, of starvelings and nobles alike, mingling with the howling, scarred features of skinstealers. He brought his hands up.

Garradan... help me...
So sick...
Help us teacher...
Burning up...
Can't move...
Help us...
Garradan...
Garradan...

Gardus stumbled on, driven by a resolve as hard as steel. Sigmar would sustain him. He was faithful.

He swept his arms out, trying to drive the ghosts away, but it was no use. He could see faces in the surface of the waters he waded through, and in the murk before him. All of them cursing him, begging him for help, screaming his name. The ground trembled beneath his feet as Bolathrax continued to follow and to chortle grotesquely.

'Where are you going, Garradan? The garden is boundless and you will never breach its walls. Stop, give in, and Bolathrax will be merciful...'

'Only the faithful,' Gardus said, driving himself forward. He was not Garradan the healer, not anymore; he was Gardus, the Stormcast Eternal. He was no mere mortal, he was Sigmar's lightning made flesh. And he *would not stop.* 'Only the faithful... Only the faithful...'

The words were less a prayer now than a mantra, a chant to keep him sane in this mad garden of horrors. He scraped the thick shroud of mould off his helm, clearing his vision, and blinked in shock as a brilliant glimmer of light flickered through the haze ahead.

'What?' he croaked. A trick? A trap? Or something else?

He heard a rumble from above and risked a look. The mouth in the clouds was no longer leering, but instead… frowning. Hope blossomed in his chest and he took a trembling step forwards. It was so beautiful. He took another step. His breath caught in his throat.

Wherever that glow originated from, it could not be of this hideous realm. The song in his head, the whisper of sound that pulled him on, swelled to a crescendo as Gardus ploughed on. At last, he knew where he was going. Weapons in hand, he pressed forward, wading towards the swelling, lambent light…

CHAPTER ONE

To silence the dirge

The sound of the Dirgehorn hung over everything.

Here, so close to the source, it was almost a physical pressure, beating upon the minds and souls of the Storm-cast Eternals who fought their way through the crooked, fungus-slick trees and overgrown fen of Rotwater Blight.

The call of the Dirgehorn was *in* everything, reverberating from every stone and stump, quavering in the fly-blown air like an unending groan. The hideous sound of it rolled on and on, each note slithering into the next. It was a wave of pure discord, sluggish and flat, carrying with it despondency and gloom. It was a constant drone that shivered along on the wings of flies and miasmic breezes, withering trees and cracking rocks. Where it passed, green leaves turned black and the very stones sprouted quivering boils and buboes.

The sylvaneth had been put to flight by its mournful note, clutching at their heads with palsied fingers as their bark-like flesh grew cracked and pale. Those who had made Rotwater Blight their home fled deeper into the forests to escape it, and the land echoed with the sounds of their flight. Dryads shrieked and wailed as they staggered through the swampy forest, adding to the already horrid din, and squealing forest spites filled the air, flickering like fireflies as they hurtled away from the maddening pulse.

But while the treekin fled, the Stormcasts plunged into the teeth of that droning sound, determined to silence it or perish in the attempt. Retinue after retinue, brotherhood by brotherhood, they slogged on, through stinking mire and dying glade, pitting lightning-forged hearts and souls against the blaring call of Nurgle. Liberators and Retributors marched in ordered phalanxes along the mould-spotted trails and were guided by winged Prosecutors, who braved the fly-choked air to steer their kin to firmer ground. The Decimators' weapons glowed with cold fire as they carved a path towards the Dirgehorn's call, hacking through thick vines that sprayed viscous sap and clutching branches that writhed like serpents as they fell.

The Steel Souls, a Warrior Chamber of the Hallowed Knights, led the way. Their panoply of war gleamed silver and rich gold, while their shoulder guards and heavy shields were of deepest regal blue. The Steel Souls were not alone in their march – others shared their burden. Warrior Chambers from the Astral Templars and the Guardians of the Firmament both fought their way through Rotwater Blight alongside the Hallowed Knights, their Decimators joining those of the Steel Souls at the point of the spear.

The Stormcasts had borne the wailing call of the artefact known at the Dirgehorn for many miles and days of marching, braving horrors undreamt of. They had struggled through belching quagmires and hillocks of dead insects. The bubbling morass of the Greenglow Lake stretched to the west of the armoured host, splitting the land like an open wound. To the east, the thick forests of the Blight rose wild and forbidding. The sky overhead was the colour of an infected wound, and a choking wind blew from the east.

Everywhere Lord-Castellant Lorrus Grymn of the Hallowed Knights looked, it was as if the land was dying. He strode alongside the column, accompanied by the furry, feathered shape of his loyal gryph-hound, Tallon. His heavy halberd lay across one broad shoulder, and he kept a firm grip on its haft, ready to swing it into position at a moment's notice. He held his warding lantern high, casting its light across the ranks of warriors as they marched. The fortifying glow burned off the layers of filth that caked the armour of his brethren, returning it to a glorious lustre, as was fitting.

The Hallowed Knights had been the fourth Stormhost to be founded, the ranks of their Warrior Chambers filled with the faithful of the Mortal Realms. Their only commonality was that each had called upon Sigmar's name in battle and had been heard, and that each had shed his mortal flesh in the name of a righteous cause. The Steel Souls were the best of them, tried and tested and found worthy in the fires of war. But not without cost, Grymn thought.

Yes, the Steel Souls had paid a heavy price. Lord-Celestant Gardus, the one who had given them their name, was gone, lost through the realmgate known as the Gates of Dawn, leaving his warriors bereft of his leadership. It had been Gardus who had led the first strike into the wilds of Ghyran so that a permanent path to Azyr might be opened. It had been Gardus who had been sent to ensure that Grymn and the rest of his Warrior Chamber might descend upon the Jade Kingdoms to reinforce their brothers. It was not to be, however.

Despite the aid of the Astral Templars, and the last minute intervention of the warglades of the mysterious sylvaneth, Gardus had been forced to destroy the realmgate and had perished in the act. Damn you, Gardus, Grymn thought, not for the first time. It was even as the Lord-Relictor of the Steel Souls, Morbus Stormwarden, had said. The sage had seen Gardus' fall in his dreams and had come to Grymn with his concerns. But too late.

And now Gardus was gone. The best of them. The one who had been, up to this point, Grymn's only equal on or off the field – a man with whom he had been proud to stand shoulder to shoulder against the foes of Sigmar.

The Steel Soul had not died as a Stormcast ought and returned to the great forges of Sigmaron, there to be remade by the hands of the God-King himself. Instead, Gardus had thrown himself into the Realm of Chaos, locked in combat with a greater daemon. No soul returned from those hell-realms.

Not even one made of steel, Grymn thought. Angry now, he turned his thoughts to the present. They had a duty to fulfil and they would meet it no matter the cost. The Dirgehorn would be silenced. Of this Grymn was confident. But he knew that while the artefact had sorely afflicted the inhabitants of these wooded realms, it was not the sole cause of their pain.

Flies droned and swamp-sludge bubbled as rotted boughs creaked in the unnatural pall that marked the places where

Nurgle's influence had eclipsed that of the Realm of Life's rightful ruler. Chain-throttled oaks moaned wordlessly about them and forest spirits struggled helplessly in the mires of Nurgle's making. The Stormcasts who fought across the ever-shifting landscape of Ghyran were doing what they could to free the Jade Kingdoms from the clutches of the Plague Lord, but they could not do it alone. Sigmar had sent representatives to find the Lady Alarielle, in her seclusion, and re-establish old ties, but as far as Grymn knew they had all returned to Azyr empty-handed.

Alarielle had, like Sigmar himself, existed for untold aeons, and there were murals in Sigmaron dedicated to her. The largest and greatest of these showed Sigmar waking the Radiant Queen from her centuries of slumber, and the two throwing back the forces of darkness together. Once, she had been the God-King's ally. Once… but not for many years, since the powers of ruin had swept through the Mortal Realms and the great celestine Gates of Azyr had slammed shut, sealing the Realm of Heavens off from the rest of the Eight Realms. Now those gates were open once more, and Sigmar had stretched forth his hand to old and new allies alike, so that together they might throw off the chains of monstrous tyranny.

A good dream, if as yet unproven, Grymn thought.

'Lord-Castellant!'

Grymn looked up as the silver swooping form of Tegrus of the Sainted Eye, Prosecutor-Prime of the Steel Souls, gestured towards the shore of the lake. Grymn cursed as he saw several Stormcasts stumble towards the dark waters.

'Tallon – go!' he said urgently as he hurried towards the warriors. The gryph-hound chirped and bounded away. The animal slid between the Stormcasts, snapping and shrieking, stopping them in their tracks long enough for Grymn to reach them. 'Back, you fools, get away from the water,' he roared.

As he caught hold of a stumbling Stormcast's shoulder and pulled the warrior back, the still waters of the lake erupted in a storm of lashing, mouth-studded tendrils. Several of the Stormcasts were snatched up before they even had time to cry out. Tallon flung himself upon one tendril, severing it with his beak and freeing the warrior it held.

'Back,' Grymn roared again, hooking his lantern on the blade of his halberd and extending it out over the water. The light of the warding lantern shone across the frothing lake, and the tendrils retreated as if burned. In the darkness, something wailed like a damned soul, and Grymn heard heavy bodies flopping and thrashing.

'Tegrus,' Grymn called out to the Prosecutor swooping overhead. 'Drive these beasts back into the depths!'

Overhead, Tegrus led his winged warriors out over the water. They hurled their celestial hammers at the vast shapes that dwelled beneath the murk. The monsters plunged deeper into the waters to avoid the barrage, leaving behind only a sour smell and the shooting blue light of those warriors they had managed to drown before Grymn had stymied them.

'Away,' he snarled, gesturing back towards the path. 'Get back. Move!'

Grymn turned his attentions to the warrior he'd saved. The Liberator stumbled against him as they moved away from the water, half-torpid, weapon and shield dangling from his grip. He was an Astral Templar, clad in amethyst and gold.

'Awaken,' Grymn said, shaking the Liberator. The warrior

slumped, and Grymn grunted as he caught him. 'Awaken, I say – do not give in. Heed me!' He set his halberd so that the light of his lantern caught the warrior full. As the light bathed him, the Liberator struggled upright, gaining strength from the healing glow of the warding lantern.

'I just… I just wanted to clean this filth from my war-plate,' the Stormcast said, his voice slurred. 'To wash myself clean of the taint of this place. To drink…'

'Yes, brother, there is no shame in that,' Grymn said urgently. 'But this place devours warriors as surely as any beast. You must keep to the road. Stay in the light.'

Some among the Stormhost were beginning to succumb to the waking nightmare of this realm, their spirits sapped by the relentless blare of the Dirgehorn and the miasma that clung to the land around them. Their war mantras were drowned out by the growing cacophony of the horn, denying them succour, and every day saw more warriors sent back to Azyr in a blaze of blue light. Rotwater Blight was as much their enemy as the servants of Nurgle.

'I can… I can hear it, Lord-Castellant,' the Liberator said. 'It's… burrowing into my mind… my soul.' He reached up as if to tear his helmet off, and fumbled with his weapon and shield, nearly dropping them. 'It's echoing in my head!'

Grymn seized the warrior's hands.

'Stop,' he snarled, shouting to be heard over the shriek of the Dirgehorn. 'You are Stormcast. Remember what that means, brother.'

'I have him, Lord-Castellant,' a voice said.

Grymn looked up and saw the heavy shape of the Lord-Celestant of the Astral Templars. Zephacleas had been a big man, even before his Reforging, and he loomed over Grymn now, his amethyst armour scorched in places and scored with the marks of claws and fangs. Now he caught the Liberator by the shoulders.

'Arcos, isn't it? You stood with me at the Lake of Screaming Reeds, when that toad dragon hurled itself at the shieldwall of our brothers. I nearly broke my blade on its blubbery hide and you were there, shielding me from its vile spew. And at the Grove of Blighted Lanterns, did you not raise your hammer in defence of your brothers, as the jabberslythes screamed? Stand tall, Arcos. We are the Beast-Bane, slayers of the Black Bull of Nordrath, and we shall not allow a mere winding tune to break us.'

The warrior nodded wearily and allowed his Lord-Celestant to urge him back towards his brethren. Zephacleas watched him go, and then turned to Grymn.

'Death is a high price, but not without its allure,' the Lord-Celestant said, watching the lake.

'Is your resolve so fragile, Beast-Bane?' Grymn asked harshly.

'No, but this hellish landscape has worn us down, Grymn. For some among our warriors, to return in failure is beginning to seem preferable to slogging through this foulness for even a single hour more,' Zephacleas growled. 'Even the air attacks us.' He clutched at his head for a moment. 'And that blasted wail never ends! It gnaws at us every moment, digging into us. I can't even hear myself think.'

'We must press on. We are close,' Grymn said. 'The horn grows louder, and we are assailed more frequently. We are close, Zephacleas. And only the faithful shall prevail.' He thumped the other Stormcast on the shoulder. 'Much is demanded...'

'...of those to whom much has been given,' Zephacleas finished. 'Gardus says – said – that often.' He shook his head. 'I wish that he were here.'

'As do I,' Grymn said. 'But we must–' A cry from above interrupted him. He looked up, saw the Prosecutors circling a high, sloping hill that overlooked the lake and said, 'Tegrus has found something.'

'The enemy?' Zephacleas asked.

'Better, I think,' Grymn said. 'Come, we must alert the others.'

CHAPTER TWO

The land itself

In the light cast by his lantern, Grymn looked out over the cluster of bubbling springs surrounded by lush green vegetation and took a deep breath.

'The air is cleaner here,' he said. The Prosecutors had led them up the hill and to the crest, where amidst the crags they had discovered this quiet oasis. Grymn, determined to investigate before he risked his warriors, had led his vanguard in.

'It could be a trick,' Zephacleas said.

'It is a trick,' Ultrades of the Broken Spear said. Like Grymn, the Lord-Celestant of the Guardians of the Firmament was stoicism given form – a warrior of iron will and determination, who had earned his name by killing an enemy warlord with a broken spear blade torn from the Stormcast's own bloody side. 'Another ploy of the enemy. They could not bring us down by force, and so they seek to gull us with a safe haven in a landscape of horrors.' He shook his head. 'We should press on.'

'Our warriors require rest,' Grymn said, glancing back at the vanguard of Decimators and Retributors who had followed them to the hill's summit. The bulk of the Stormhost still waited on the slopes below, grateful for the pause. All save Tegrus and his retinue of Prosecutors, who had flown on to see what could be seen of the trail ahead.

While Stormcasts had incredible endurance, Zephacleas had been right – they were all worn down. The Rotwater Blight had sapped even the hardiest of them of their strength. Grymn had been able to keep the worst of it from his Warrior Chamber thanks to the light of his lantern, but even they skirted the edges of exhaustion. The other Warrior Chambers had lost brothers to the mire and sucking loam, as well as the myriad dangers that lurked on the fringes of their path.

'We need rest,' he said again. 'And this place could provide it,' he added. He lifted his hand. 'Listen…'

'I hear nothing,' Ultrades said.

'Exactly,' Grymn said. 'The drone of the Dirgehorn has receded. Listen!'

'He's right,' Zephacleas said, as he looked around. 'I can barely hear it.' He laughed. 'I almost forgot what my own voice sounded like.'

'And more, there's fresh water – no flies, no steaming clumps of filth or poison,' Grymn said, as he started towards the closest spring. Ultrades caught his arm.

'What are you doing?'

'One of us must test it. We have been without pure water for days. If this is truly a trap, better to lose one than many. I am Lord-Castellant of the Steel Souls. It was given to me to be the shield for my brothers, and so it falls to me,' Grymn said. He pulled himself free of Ultrades' grip, and took off his crested helm of office. 'Do not fear, my brother. I have faith and Sigmar watches over me, even here.'

'As he watches over us all,' Zephacleas said.

Grymn turned and went to the closest spring, where he dropped to one knee, leaned his halberd against his shoulder and made to scoop out a handful of the clear water bubbling there. He hesitated, considering Ultrades' suspicions as well as his own. Then he plunged his fingers into the water and brought a handful of spring water to his mouth. At his side, Tallon watched intently. The gryph-hound cocked his head, and clicked his beak interrogatively.

'Easy,' Grymn murmured, ruffling the beast's neck feathers. He took a drink, closing his eyes as the cool water rushed down his throat. After a moment, he cracked one eye and looked at Tallon. 'Well, the water's clean, all right.'

He drank again, relishing the taste of it. He felt as if a warm, golden light were filling him, and his fatigue sloughed away, as if it had never been. Tallon ducked his head and began to lap at the water with eager chirrups as Grymn turned to the others. For the first time since his Reforging, a broad smile split his face. Zephacleas stepped back.

'By Sigmar, it's poisoned him,' he said.

'I'm smiling, you slack-jawed oaf,' Grymn laughed. He waved a hand at those Prosecutors hovering above, signalling them to alert the rest of the Stormhost that it was safe to climb to the summit. 'Get in here and drink, all of you. It looks as if we've found the only pure water in this land.' He paused, and added, 'Better than pure.' He examined his gauntlet and the crystal-clear droplets glittering on his palm.

'It seems our allies have not deserted us. And perhaps this land is not entirely lost, after all.'

He closed his hand, and looked to the north, where another hill rose sharp and foul from the forest that clung to its slopes, like a cankerous tooth. That was where his scouts had marked the sound of the Dirgehorn as emanating from. That would be where they would meet the enemy, and set it to flight once more.

You started this fight, Gardus, and now I shall finish it. The steel in your soul is now in ours, and we shall not fail, he thought.

He turned around and watched as the Stormcasts knelt to drink, or to splash the clear waters across their filth-stained armour. He could hear the newfound hope in their voices, and the bitter outrage. They had been tested in the Blight, and it had not been easy., but they had persevered. The Hallowed Knights shall not falter, he thought, as he set his helm back over his head. I shall see to that, if nothing else.

'Their faith has been renewed.'

'Aye, Morbus. That it has. It has been sorely tested, these past few weeks. With Gardus gone...' Grymn looked at the Lord-Relictor. Morbus Stormwarden was an imposing figure, his weapons and armour replete with icons of faith, death and the storm. It fell to him to keep the souls of his fellow Hallowed Knights from the gloom of the underworld, should such a fate loom close.

'Gardus is gone,' Morbus agreed. 'But we yet stand, to carry on in his name.' He touched one of the icons on his chest-plate. 'When I saw... what I saw, I never truly imagined that it would come to pass.' Morbus had seen Gardus' demise in a dream, and though both he and the Lord-Castellant had sought to warn their Lord-Celestant, they had been too late. 'I never truly thought that the Steel Soul could fall.'

'Nor did I,' Grymn said. Why did you have to do it, he thought. But he knew the answer well enough. Gardus was the sword, and Grymn the shield. It was the sword's way, to thrust itself into the enemy's heart, even if it shattered in doing so. 'If only...'

'We did not know,' Morbus said, watching over the Storm-casts solemnly. 'A vague premonition of doom is of little importance in times like these, when all of reality shudders beneath the weight of war. And Gardus was... Gardus.'

'That he was, my friend,' Grymn said. 'And we are left to carry on.' He cocked his head. 'Tegrus,' he called out, as he glimpsed a familiar silver-clad shape circling above.

The Prosecutor-Prime swooped low over them. 'We are close, Lord-Castellant. No more than a few hours' march,' Tegrus said, anticipating his question.

'And the enemy?'

'Beastmen,' Tegrus said, dropping to the ground before them. 'From what we could see through the trees, we are outnumbered. A dozen of them for every one of us – ungor and gors, some in armour. Bullgors as well.'

'They gather in strength,' Morbus said, leaning against his reliquary staff.

'More enemies means more glory,' Grymn said. He stroked Tallon's narrow skull. 'What of the Dirgehorn?'

'At the summit of the tor, I believe. Although even I couldn't get close enough to see for sure. They're clustered up there as thick as fleas, and they sent a hail of arrows my way,' Tegrus

31

said, gesturing with one of his hammers. 'We shall have to fight our way up.' He looked at Grymn. 'It will be bloody.'

'Good. I am in the mood for it,' Grymn said.

'As am I,' Tegrus said grimly. 'Would that Gardus were here to share in this battle.' He crossed his hammers and bent his head. Grymn and Morbus bowed their heads as well.

'Would that he was. But he is not, and so we must fight in his name. We will teach the enemy that the Steel Soul is not so easily broken. We will teach them, Tegrus.'

'So we shall, Lord-Castellant,' Tegrus said, rising into the air with a snap of his wings.

Morbus watched him go, and said, 'What next, Lorrus?'

'We are owed a debt of pain, Morbus. I intend to collect it.' Grymn lifted his lantern high, so that its light was reflected from the sigmarite that armoured his warriors, and threw back the shadows. 'Who are we?' he asked, his voice carrying to every ear. 'Who are we?' he said again, thumping the ground with the haft of his halberd. 'We are the tempest-borne, the warriors of lightning, and the sons of Sigmar himself. We are Stormcasts. Who will be triumphant?'

'Only the faithful,' came the reply, from hundreds of throats.

'They almost made us forget that, in these days and weeks of horror. They have drowned us in filth, but we still stand, brothers.' He thumped the ground again. 'We are Stormcasts! Who will stand, when all others fall?' Grymn cried.

'Only the faithful!' the Hallowed Knights roared. Astral Templars and Guardians of the Firmament added their voices to the cry.

'They thought to defeat us with noise, with ambushes. They

thought to make us despair. These are the tools of a coward,' Grymn said. 'Who knows no despair, save in failure?'

'Only the faithful,' the Stormcasts cried as one.

Grymn swung his halberd up and pointed north.

'Listen, brothers. Hear the wailing of their horn and know that it is the scream of a frightened beast. They thought to make us fear, brothers... Let us return the favour.'

CHAPTER THREE

The blighted glade

Light. All around him, light and something else… the voice, the song, swelling in his head, drowning out all thought. Gardus staggered on, limbs heavy with the weight of ghosts, and the light grew brighter, until he thought it might blind him.

In the light, in the song, he heard and saw things… the future? The past? Images of islands in the sky, and a heaving foulness thrashing in once-clear waters. Of great roots stretching towards the pale sun as rats gnawed at them. Of a valley, reflected. And, finally, a face composed of branches and leaves, of spider-silk and moonlight… a woman, with eyes like flickering green suns, not human, but a queen. She spoke in a voice like distant thunder. At first her words made no sense, but then, like turbulent waters grown still, everything was clear.

Yes, he thought. Yes, I know what I must do. Then, all at once, both light and song were gone, and he heard stone scrape beneath his feet and felt acrid air burn his lungs. His armour was covered in filth and his cloak was slime-slicked, but he was free. Coughing, he staggered and wearily sank down to one knee. His stomach roiled and he toppled forwards, vomit spewing from the mouth-slit of his war-helm. His stomach heaved as he purged himself of the sour taste of Nurgle's garden. Free, he thought.

Once his stomach was empty, he used his hammer and sword to shove himself to his feet. He could hear fighting in the distance. He could smell fire and war, and knew that he had returned to the Mortal Realms. Gardus looked around. He stood upon the cracked stone dais of a realmgate. It flickered luridly behind him, the tall, fungus-covered archway still aglow with the now-fading energies of its activation. The realmgate occupied the centre of a clearing, surrounded by trees on all sides. The ground below the lip of the dais was hidden by an eerie green mist. It stank of rotting meat and worse, though not as badly as Nurgle's garden.

The trees around him had been infested with grotesque fungi, and they dripped slime and mould. Foul, fleshy blossoms clustered in hollow trunks, and a throbbing canopy of moist, spore-ridden tendrils spread across the upper reaches of the forest, blocking out the weak sunlight. Where the mist was thin, Gardus could see bubbling mounds of black ooze that rose from the forest floor like boils on the flesh of the afflicted. Somewhere amidst the trees, he heard the frantic clanging of gongs and a squealing, as if from the throats of giant rats.

'Only the faithful,' he said hoarsely, his throat scraped raw. He stepped down off the dais, weapons in hand, and began to follow the noise of battle. Though the song had fallen silent, still its melody remained in him, and he knew what he must do. Ghyran suffered a blight, and it was up to him to help cleanse it. Whatever afflicted this glade would be first.

Gardus picked up speed, the ache in his muscles and the burning in his lungs forgotten as he followed the screams of the dying and the splintering of wood. A discordant blaring of horns sounded from the southern edge of the clearing, sending a tremor of disgust through his soul. He had heard that sound before, in Nurgle's realm. He swept out his hammer, smashing a toppled branch thick with maggoty fungus from his path. The servants of Nurgle were close, and Gardus would see them pay for all that he had endured. He struck a rotting, fallen tree with his shoulder, reducing it to a cloud of splinters. Then he was half-staggering into the midst of a battle, surrounded by noise and slaughter.

Heaps of dead skaven lay everywhere, and mingled amongst them were the shattered bodies of sylvaneth dryads. Hordes of ratmen clad in filthy robes scuttled through the trees towards the retreating dryad-groves. Nearby, a fallen treelord groaned and collapsed into a pile of rotting wood and rancid sap as a skaven, larger than the others, struck him with a smoking censer-ball. Gardus took a half-step forward, but as the treelord's dying groan swept through the clearing, he saw hulking warriors force themselves between the fungus-riddled trees on the glade's southern edge. The bloated blightkings charged towards the dryads with glottal war cries. Axes and scythes hacked down treekin and spilled ruddy sap into the muck.

Already in disarray, the treekin recoiled in obvious panic.

More dryads fell to the skaven; frenzied plague monks stabbed rusted blades into supple bark, tearing festering wounds in their foes. The blightkings added to the tally of the fallen with single-minded brutality.

Gardus plunged towards them, ploughing through a swarm of ratmen who, having noticed his arrival, sought to drag him down. The skaven came at him in a scrabbling rush. Gardus killed the first to reach him with a blow from his hammer, and decapitated the second. Soon, however, he was surrounded by hairy forms. Rusty blades scraped against his armour, digging for a vital spot. He swept out his arms, flinging broken bodies through the air. With the last of the ratmen twitching out their death-agonies in the mud, he moved towards the servants of Nurgle, intent on lending aid to the sylvaneth.

As he ran, Gardus saw a single branchwraith, gnarled and weathered by age and war, tear one of the swollen warriors messily in two with a flurry of lashing vines. Even as the halves of the body slopped to the ground, the branchwraith hunched forward and thrust her clawed hands into the earth. A green shimmer blazed about her inhuman form, growing brighter and brighter, until she suddenly tore her claws free and dragged them upwards. A tangle of roots and vines came with them, and the ground ruptured as thorny tendrils burst from the murk to ensnare the blightkings.

But the brutes could not be stopped. They stomped and hacked at the lashing tendrils, fighting their way towards the branchwraith and her retinue. Gardus roared in fury as he pounded towards the blightkings, and one of the warriors hesitated and turned towards him, pox-marked blade raised. Gardus didn't slow.

'Who will be victorious?' he bellowed, as he brought his hammer down on the blightking's skull. Such was the force of his blow that he ripped the warrior's head from its blubbery neck. 'Only the faithful,' he continued, whipsawing around and slashing his sword across the throat of a second foe. He kicked the dying blightking aside. '*Only the faithful!*'

Divine lightning crackled across him as he clashed his weapons. 'Turn, plague-dogs, *turn*,' he roared. 'Turn and face me!'

His blade smashed down, cleaving a blightking from skull to sternum. Gardus tore the blade free in a snarl of lightning, and spun to cut the legs out from under another of the pox-warriors. He drove his boot into the fallen blightking's skull hard enough to crumple the rusty helm the warrior wore. Smoke rose as the white fires that crawled across the Stormcast burned away the daemonic slurry that befouled his armour.

As he fought, he caught glimpses of the battle swirling about him. He saw dryads tear through skaven ranks and a massive treelord overturn a bubbling, poison-spewing plague furnace with a roar, crushing those plague monks unlucky enough to be close by. He spilled the rotten guts of another opponent, preventing the warrior from smashing the skull of a wounded dryad. The remaining blightkings forgot about the branchwraith and her followers as Gardus continued his rampage. The bloated warriors hurled themselves at him in growing desperation. Axes scored his armour but he refused to fall. He swung and slashed, chopped and crushed, littering the ground with the dead. He reared back and kicked a blightking in the chest, sending the brute staggering into the talons of the branchwraith, who caught the warrior's head with her vines and crushed it, helm and all.

Gardus met her inhuman gaze. For a moment, Stormcast and sylvaneth stared at one another. Then the branchwraith threw back her head and shrieked, vines lashing. Her dryads echoed her cry and plunged past Gardus, hurling themselves back into the fray to aid their kin. Gardus followed them, his weapons slick with bile and spoiled blood.

Together, Stormcast and sylvaneth fought against the enemies of Life itself. Squealing skaven and groaning blightkings met them in the centre of the clearing, and Gardus roared out the battle-cry of the Hallowed Knights until his voice became a strained rasp. He left a trail of the dead and dying behind him as he fought to keep pace with the branchwraith and her sisters. The white fire thatwreathed him burned brighter and brighter as he pushed himself past the point of exhaustion. Despite the pain of his wounds and the fatigue that poisoned his muscles and numbed his mind, Gardus was determined to see the glade cleansed of its affliction.

As he fought, he saw the branchwraith stride through the swirling ashes thrown up by the plague furnace's destruction to confront a shrieking skaven. The skaven, swathed in foul robes, its hairy flesh puckered with scars and buboes, chattered a challenge. Gardus made to step forwards, but the branchwraith threw an arm across his chest, stopping him.

'No,' she said, in a voice like branches crackling on a fire. 'Our sap runs hot, son of Sigmar. But Thellembhol's runs hotter still.'

Gardus looked past the skaven, and saw an immense shape loom out of the smoke. The treelord that had upset the plague furnace rose up over the foul creature. The skaven whirled about, claws raised, eyes glowing as verminous lips writhed in the beginnings of a croaked incantation. Thellembhol raised one massive foot and slammed it down, stamping the life from it.

Gardus looked around; the battle was over. If any of the skaven had survived the wrath of the dryads, they had fled. The blightkings were all dead, their bodies dissolving into rancid sludge. His limbs felt heavy, and the fires which had seared his armour clean began to gutter and fade. He staggered and sank to one knee. Thick vines caught him before he fell, their thorns clattering almost gently against the plates of his armour.

'You are tired almost unto death, son of Sigmar,' the branchwraith said, looking down at him, her inhuman features twisted into an expression of what he thought was concern. 'Know that you have the thanks of the sylvaneth and the Lady of Vines, war-hand of the Radiant Queen.'

'Lady,' Gardus said, as he pushed himself up, 'I have waded through a sea of horrors to return to this realm… I must get back to my brothers. I – I must tell them of what I have seen. I have seen the Hidden Vale, and Alarielle. I can lead them…'

He trailed off as he suddenly recalled to whom he spoke. The Lady of Vines had stiffened at his words, and he felt the treelord approach, a rumbling growl slipping from its bark-maw.

'Fear you to tell your tale, son of Sigmar?' the Lady of Vines hissed. 'You have learned a dangerous truth, it seems.' The vines about him tightened, and he tensed, ready to fight his way free. Then, with a rattling sigh, the branchwraith released him. 'Then, perhaps your coming shall bestir my mother from the darkling dreams which do assail her. Be not afraid, son of Sigmar – we shall take you to your brothers.'

Gardus sagged, relief flooding him. Then, with reserves of strength he did not know he possessed, he pulled himself upright. He met the branchwraith's flickering gaze and nodded. 'Thank you,' he said. 'Lead on, O Lady of Vines... and I shall follow.'

CHAPTER FOUR

Blare of the Dirgehorn

'Forwards!' Grymn roared, as he raised his halberd high, casting the light of his warding lantern across the blasted expanse of Profane Tor. Thunder snarled overhead, and a cerulean rain pounded down on faithful and foul alike. Strobing lightning revealed a gore-streaked tableau. 'Forwards, for Sigmar… for Azyr… and for the Steel Soul,' Grymn bellowed, fighting to drown out the drone of the monstrous Dirgehorn.

The Steel Souls had battled their way to the top of the tor through herds of slavering beastmen and the wailing of the horn. Somewhere in the clearing below, Zephacleas and Ultrades were bellowing orders to their respective warriors as they fought to give the Hallowed Knights time to silence that diabolical moan.

The Dirgehorn sat curled about the trunk of a great hag tree, amongst piled weapons and trophy skulls. The tree was a towering nightmare, looming over the tor, its branches stretching everywhere. It stank of rot and death, and noose-throttled corpses and spiked cages dangled from its crooked branches, twisting in an unnatural dance to the Dirgehorn's song. A beastlord of immense size, with a crown of curved horns, put its slobbering jaws to the mouthpiece and blew again and again, as if to urge its warriors on to greater feats of madness.

Lightning streaked across the sky as the Stormcasts forced themselves forwards at Grymn's command. With every echoing whine of the daemonic horn, skin blackened and metal tarnished, and men were forced to fight to prevent being bowled over by the sheer, abominable force of it. Beastmen swarmed across the tor from all sides, leaping over the great roots of the hag tree and flinging themselves onto the invaders.

'Fight, Stormcasts,' Grymn snarled. 'Only the faithful shall be victorious. Only the faithful shall see the spires of Sigmaron again. Fight. Fight! *Fight!*'

With every flash of lightning, Grymn could see silver-clad Hallowed Knights doing just that as they battled the servants of the Ruinous Powers. Liberators locked shields with frothing, goat-headed gors; Judicators launched volley after volley at the gigantic beasts prowling the misted eaves of the tor; wailing bray-shamans cast curse after curse upon the heads of the Stormcasts; and armoured champions of Chaos hacked a path through the ranks of their foes.

It was the latter that occupied Grymn's attentions, and he smashed his way towards the bloated warriors, followed closely by Tallon. A two-headed beastman lunged into his path and he drove the end of his halberd through the creature's gut. As it bent over, he brought the blade of his weapon down on the stretch of flesh between its necks. Black blood gushed and a pair of agonized screams rose up from the creature's twin throats. Grymn ripped his halberd free and shoved the dying creature out of his path. A second beast-man charged towards him, axe held over its horned head, but Tallon pounced on it. It fell with a strangled bleat as the gryph-hound's beak tore out its throat in a welter of gore.

Grymn reached the obese Chaos champions a moment later. They were an unpleasant sight, even when considered beside their own diseased kind – the split-bellied axemen wore rusty, brine-crusted armour, and they had patches of pallid flesh that bulged around the straps and plates. At their head was a monstrous warrior with a horribly distorted body. Fully half of it was rent asunder and from the gaping wound emerged the snapping beak and twisting tentacles of some vile sea-beast.

Grymn knew instinctively that this was their leader. He set his feet and swung his halberd out, letting the haft slide through his hands as he did so in order to gain reach. The blade smashed into the marred flesh that marked the champion's mutated side, and Grymn was rewarded by a spurt of inky blood.

The champion wheeled, smacking his halberd aside. The force of the blow almost tore the weapon from Grymn's hands, but he recovered quickly.

'Foul play, shiny-skin,' the betentacled champion roared as he drove Grymn back with a sweep of his great axe. 'Only fair to introduce yourself first. I am Gutrot Spume, Lord of Tentacles, Master of the Rotwater, and various and sundry other titles of importance. Who are you?'

'Your death, abomination,' Grymn said.

'Ha! Heard that before, aye,' Spume cackled. 'You aren't the first, and won't be the last. Come on then, if you're of a mind.'

The champion spun his axe in his human hand, and chopped out at Grymn, almost quicker than the latter's eye could follow. Grymn jerked to the side, avoiding the bite of the immense blade, and thrust his halberd out like a spear. The spike at its tip slammed into Spume's shoulder-guard, rocking the champion on his wide feet.

'That's the spirit, shiny-skin,' Spume said, as three of his tentacles snagged the haft of the halberd and held it in place as Grymn tried to pull it free.

'Tallon,' Grymn barked. The gryph-hound lunged, his iron-hard beak snapping shut on the sinewy appendages and tearing them apart. Spume staggered back with a bellow, slashing out at the gryph-hound, and the animal bounded away. Grymn spun the halberd between his hands and swung it out. Spume blocked the blow, and for a moment Grymn's world narrowed to the clash of blades as they traded blows back and forth. Their duel was not a graceful one; instead, it was a thing of strength and sheer bloody-mindedness – two things that Grymn had in abundance, and that marked him for leadership, alongside the Steel Soul.

Damn you, Gardus, he thought. Sigmar had made Gardus his sword, and Grymn his shield. But now he's gone, and I must be both. The thought drove him, as always, to fight all the harder. Gardus had been his greatest rival, the one whom he tested himself against. But now Gardus was gone, and only Grymn was left.

As lightning flashed, he could see that he and his opponent were not alone in their struggle. He saw a slavering bullgor tear away a fallen Stormcast's armour, only to howl in thwarted rage as the dying warrior evaporated in a burst of blue. He saw lightning hammers blast through barrel chests and storm axes lay open spines. As he parried a blow from Spume, he saw Tegrus swoop low in the corner of his vision and smash the head from a blightking's shoulders.

Spume's laughter faded as they duelled back and forth through the rain. The battle swirled about them, men and beasts rising and falling in untold numbers, but they remained locked in combat, neither warrior able to best the other.

Grymn parried a sweep of his opponent's axe and replied in kind.

He roared in anger and chopped down on Spume's head. His blade glanced off the champion's featureless helm. Spume staggered. Grymn saw an opening and took it. He spun his halberd about and stabbed it forward, catching the champion in the gaping beak-maw that had replaced his armpit.

The maw closed on the sigmarite head of Grymn's halberd, and the yellowed fangs cracked and shattered. The abnormal growth shuddered, and Spume's tentacles stiffened and drooped, forcing him to drop his axe. As he fell back, Grymn saw his paladins, led by Machus, his Decimator-Prime, chop down the last of Spume's warriors. Before he could call out to them, Spume lunged for him, tentacles flailing.

The axe-wielding Machus beheaded the last of his opponents and kicked the body aside.

'Lord-Castellant, I am coming,' Machus said, hacking down a beast that leapt into his path.

'Machus, take out that damnable horn,' Grymn shouted, as he forced Spume back. The Decimator-Prime chopped through a second bloat-bellied beast and hesitated. Grymn cursed. 'Forget about me, fool – destroy that horn!' he roared, crunching the sigmarite-bound haft of his halberd into his opponent's bloated throat.

'Should have let him aid ye, shiny-skin,' Spume croaked, as he grabbed Grymn's throat with his human hand. With a grunt, he hurled Grymn backwards across the clearing. The Stormcast slammed hard into a moss-encrusted menhir and fell, wracked with pain. His vision blurred as rainwater ran into his eyes through the slits of his helm, and he slipped and fell as he tried to push himself to his feet. Things grated inside him and he coughed blood. He stretched out his hand, trying to reach his halberd where it had fallen. Damn you, Gardus, he thought. You were always too reckless. Why did you have to die? It should be you leading this attack. You were the sword. I am the shield.

'Now I'll be for chopping your head off and nailing it to my mast,' Spume wheezed as he staggered towards Grymn. He had recovered his axe and dragged it behind him. 'It'll be Gutrot Spume who's the wormy apple of Nurgle's eye, and not some jumped up Ghyranite who got a bath in the Pit of Filth and decided to turn coat...'

His muttering broke off abruptly into a scream as Tallon caught hold of one of his trailing tendrils and dug in with his paws, yanking Spume off-balance.

The champion whirled, the gryph-hound leapt, and they both fell over. As they struggled, Grymn saw Machus hurl his great double-bladed axe towards the repugnant horn and its bestial wielder. The weapon slammed into the beastlord and pitched him backwards into the instrument, hard enough to crack the twisted curve of bone. The horn split along its length and the artefact's great drone rose to an agonised scream. The magical energies of the horn roiled out of control, consuming the beastlord's twitching body before exploding with an earth-shaking rumble, taking the hag tree with it. A thousand sharp daggers of oak and bone filled the air, eviscerating every warrior nearby not blessed enough to be clad in holy sigmarite.

As the smoke cleared, and his senses with it, Grymn saw Tallon trotting towards him, a writhing tendril clasped tight in his beak.

'Good hound,' he said as he got to his feet. He grunted in pain as he retrieved his halberd and lantern. Spume was gone. Whether he was dead or had fled, Grymn couldn't say, and didn't much care. He looked about. Beastmen lay broken and bloody all around. Machus strode towards him through the smoke, his axe in hand. 'Do you yet live, Lord-Castellant?' he called.

'No, I'm a ghost,' Grymn spat, shaking his head. 'Of course I live. And next time I tell you to do something – do it!'

Machus bowed his head. Despite his chastisement, Grymn could tell the Decimator-Prime was relieved. He shook his head.

'Rally the others, Decimator-Prime,' he growled. 'There's red work yet to be done.'

'Aye, Lord-Castellant,' Machus said, hastening to obey.

Grymn watched him go, and turned to see Morbus making his way towards him, accompanied by a number of others. Zephacleas and Ultrades walked with the Lord-Relictor as he stalked through the wreckage of battle, his reliquary staff glowing softly with a silver light.

'We must redress our lines,' Grymn said. 'The enemy have been beaten here, but they will return in strength. We must find a proper defensive position, as well as another realmgate.'

'Wait – look,' Zephacleas said, pointing towards the slopes below the tor. 'Look!'

Grymn caught sight of a glow moving through the smog-shrouded reaches below. It grew in intensity as it wound through the trees and the shattered remnants of the cursed menhirs, and Grymn became aware of the sound of creaking wood and rustling leaves.

'Sylvaneth,' Morbus murmured. Grymn knew he was correct. He had glimpsed the treekin often enough since arriving, and knew the sound of them well. Like a forest caught in a windstorm, the march of a warglade was an eerie chorus of creaks and groans.

'Yes, but are they coming as allies… or enemies?' Grymn said. Tallon growled softly and snapped his beak. The gryph-hound sensed his master's unease, and Grymn reached down to stroke the animal's feathered ruff. 'Easy, my lad. Easy…'

'We should take up a defensive position,' Ultrades said, one hand on the hilt of his runeblade.

Grymn shook his head.

'Too late for that,' he said. 'They're all around us. Can't you hear them?'

'All I hear are the trees creaking in the wind,' Ultrades said. Grymn snorted.

'There is no wind,' he said. He turned his attentions back to the light, and realised that he could make out figures within it. The tall, unnatural shapes of dryads stalked forward, carrying something – a throne of tangled branches and stiff vines – on their shoulders. The glow emanated not from the treekin, but instead from the figure slumped on the throne. A figure that was not unfamiliar…

'*Gardus…*' Zephacleas whispered.

Grymn started.

'Gardus,' he said, in disbelief. He took a step. Then another. 'Gardus,' he said again, unable to believe his eyes. A slow, flat smile spread across his face as he descended to meet his Lord-Celestant.

'You have no idea how glad I am to see you.'

CHAPTER FIVE

The Despised One

Torglug the Despised One looked out over the Glade of Horned Growths and heaved a sigh. 'The rats are failing. Gluhak is failing. Spume is failing. Only Torglug stands, Grandfather...' Down below, fungus-riddled trees shed their bark as the rot-fog of the skaven faded. The master of the Brotherhood of the Red Boil, the plague-priest Kratsik, was dead, squashed flat by a vengeful treelord. Something maybe to be thanking them for, Torglug thought, as he leaned on the haft of his axe and stared out at all of the nauseating green. He didn't care for the skaven. They were too tricksy by half, and always seeking an advantage over their betters.

'Not Torglug alone,' a harsh voice hissed. The Despised One didn't turn.

'You are still living, then, Vermalanx? I was thinking you are dead at the Ghyrtract Fen,' Torglug said. The blight-flies had brought word that one of the lightning-men had killed the rat-daemon at the Gates of Dawn, when boisterous Bolath-rax had underestimated the hardiness of their enemies with predictable results.

'I am harder to kill than that, Woodsman,' the vermin-lord said, as he crouched atop the shattered standing stone behind the Chaos champion. The rat-daemon used the name by which he was known in Nurgle's Manse. The daemons there called him Ironhood the Woodsman, for he had hacked down life-trees by the hundreds, in order to better fuel the blessed decay spreading from the open gates of Grandfather's garden.

'Your servants are not saying the same,' Torglug said. Even as the lightning-men had silenced the Dirgehorn, the treekin, led by the pestiferous Lady of Vines, had launched a long-anticipated assault on the Glade of Horned Growths. Now the lightning-men were readying themselves to march anew, though just where he couldn't say.

'My servants are a fecund folk. You have no need to worry on their account,' Vermalanx hissed. 'And in any event, enough of them remain to see to Nurgle's needs in this bit-ter place. Your own blightkings suffered below as well. Look to them, rather than mine.'

'My warriors are being very hardy, rat-king, hardier than your vermin,' Torglug said. He hefted his axe and set it on one wide shoulder as he turned to face the verminlord. The rat-daemon was larger than the Despised One, a thing of rangy muscle and mangy hair. It clung to the stone, fleshless head cocked, and eye sockets glowing with a sickly light. Its tail lashed at the implied insult. 'And hardier especially than your drowned men, Spume,' Torglug continued, looking past the stone and its occupier.

Vermalanx hissed and turned. Several figures made their way through the ring of broken stones and heaps of piled bodies. Gutrot Spume, tentacles coiling in agitation, spat a salty oath at Torglug's words.

'At least my blightkings fought an army – yours fell to a lone warrior,' Spume growled. He swung his axe out and shattered a nearby stone.

'One not even Bolathrax could bring low,' said the sorcerer Slaugoth. His jowls wobbled in amusement. 'I should have liked to have seen that great bowl of jelly waddling after our silver-skinned friend. Old Bolathrax has never been run so hard in his life, I'll warrant.' The master of the Rotfane chuckled at the thought.

'You are finding this funny, Maggotfang?' Torglug demanded, turning his bleary-eyed glare on the sorcerer. He threw out a hand. 'They are ruining things, these newcomers. How soon until they are coming for your Rotfane? Or the world pimple?'

The lightning-men had come far, or so buzzing blightfly and scurrying pox-rat had claimed. They had fought their way through the quagmires of Rotwater Blight from the Ghyrtract Fen. They had slain fat old Ga'Blorrgh the toad dragon at the Lake of Screaming Reeds. They had survived the horrors of the Grove of Blighted Lanterns and the Greenglow Lake, before they had shattered the Dirgehorn atop Profane Tor.

And now, the vile treekin had been roused to war. It was as if the Realm of Life were preparing itself for a final battle. Foolishness… arrogance, Torglug thought. Why do they fight? Can they not see that the Grandfather only wishes to take care of them? To take away their pain, their uncertainty. He shook his head. He had fought, as they fought, once upon a time. He did not like to think of that time, for it shamed him to remember how he had resisted Grandfather's kindness. He had been ungrateful. Rude, even. His grip on his axe tightened, and the ancient wood creaked, as if in pain.

But the Grandfather had opened his eyes and made him see that the world was not as he had believed. And with each day that followed, Torglug tried to earn the kindness and patience that the Grandfather had shown him. His axe had reaped glory for his new patron. He had poisoned the lifewells he had once fought so hard to defend, and brought the blessings of pestilence to his people, in their ignorance. And soon, his past transgressions were but a thing to be chuckled over by both disciple and divinity.

He knew, deep in the core of him, that the lightning-men represented something dangerous. Something that even the Grandfather feared, in his way. A power long forgotten, rising anew. Drums sounded in the deep realms, the skies boiled with strange lightning, and the whole of creation seemed to be holding its breath. None of the others seemed to understand, which only made it all the more infuriating.

'Be at ease, Despised One, we're all children of the garden,' Morbidex Twiceborn gurgled, stroking the mottled hide of his pox-maggoth. The Twiceborn resembled nothing so much as an overlarge nurgling, squeezed into rusty armour. He grinned toothily into the face of Torglug's annoyance. 'Some days, you just have to laugh.'

'And some days are for being serious, Twiceborn,' Torglug growled. His axe dropped from his shoulder and embedded itself in the soft loam at his feet. Morbidex's maggoth shifted uneasily, and the big beast gave a grunt of warning. Torglug glanced warily at it. The maggoth was like some unholy combination of ape, plaguebearer and giant, with a temperament to put all three to shame. 'You are silencing that beast, or else...' Torglug said.

'Easy, Tripletongue,' Morbidex murmured. He patted the monster's fang-studded muzzle. 'He didn't mean it, my sweet.' He looked at Torglug. 'Did he?'

Torglug grunted and placed his axe back on his shoulder. 'Now is not the time for laughing. You are thinking maybe the Glottkin will be so amused?'

'And who are you to speak for us then, Woodsman?' Otto Glott said, spinning his scythe like a child's toy as he stepped out from the trees, trailed by his brothers. Ethrac leaned on his staff, his robes stiff with grime and his face hidden beneath a cowl. Ghurk shoved a tree over as he followed Otto and Ethrac, his enormous lumpen features slack with disinterest. 'Think you're the wormy apple of Grandfather's eye now, Despised One? You haven't found the Hidden Vale any more than we have, so don't go getting ideas above your station.'

Torglug glared at Otto, but said nothing. He did not like the brothers, but he knew better than to challenge them openly. Otto scratched his chin and grinned. Then he gave a satisfied sniff and gestured to his brother, Ethrac. 'Now that we're all here, any ideas what Sigmar's whelps might be looking for, second-most-beloved sibling?'

'Same thing we are, brother from my mother,' Ethrac said with a shrug. Torglug grimaced beneath his helm. *The Hidden Vale,* he thought. The secret bower where the so-called Radiant Queen, Alarielle, had hidden herself away when Grandfather's grip on her kingdoms had become too much for her frail soul to bear. He, the Glottkin, Slaugoth and a host of others had spent centuries searching for it, even as they warred with the ferocious treekin and the few remaining free tribes of Ghyran. It had become something of a game for them, all except Torglug. He knew Grandfather's mind better than any, and he knew how serious a matter Alarielle's capture was, whatever the Glotts thought.

'Yes, kinsman-mine,' Otto countered, brushing flies from his open gut. 'Even Ghurk knows that and he can't count to one, bless him.' He reached up to pat the muscular arm of the third Glott brother, who loomed behind him. 'But since we don't know *where* that is, it might behove us to learn, don't you think?'

'I am open to suggestions, Otto,' Ethrac said. He looked at Torglug. 'What about you, Ghyranite? What sort of ideas are percolating in that sour brain of yours?'

Torglug hesitated. Then, with a grunt, he gestured to Vermalanx.

'The rats,' he said. 'Let them be earning their keep.'

Vermalanx hissed, startled. Then, slowly he nodded.

'Yes-yes, my folk can do that. I know just the rat,' the verminlord murmured. If bare bone could take on a cunning expression, Vermalanx had one. The rat meant treachery. They couldn't help it. It was in whatever passed for their blood. Torglug extended his axe, so that the edge just brushed the verminlord's chin.

'You are thinking carefully,' Torglug said, his voice deceptively mild.

'Now now, Torglug, no need to threaten our furry ally,' Otto said, stepping forward, his scythe held lengthwise across his shoulders. 'I'm sure he'll do just what we ask, won't you, my fine, bare-tailed friend?'

Vermalanx hesitated. Then he nodded. 'Of course, yes-yes. We all serve the Great Corrupter, do we not?'

Torglug lowered his axe. Despite his suggestion, he didn't trust the rat-daemon to do anything but seek its own advantage. He didn't trust any of them, in fact. They were all competing for the Grandfather's affections, in their own way.

But only one of them was truly worthy.

And soon, Torglug thought, I will prove it.

CHAPTER SIX

A soul returned

Tegrus of the Sainted Eye, Prosecutor-Prime of the Hallowed Knights, stood at the top of Profane Tor and looked down into the clearing at his newly-returned Lord-Celestant and the host of Stormcasts who surrounded him.

'How can this be?' he murmured. He wondered still if it were an illusion. It would not be the first such shade that had appeared to lure unlucky Stormcasts to their doom. And surely this was not truly Gardus sitting upon the dryad-borne throne like some Ghyranite saint of old. 'Aetius, Solus… are you seeing this?' he asked his companions.

'Hard not to, given the clamour,' Solus said. The Judicator-Prime of the Hallowed Knights was a man of few words, who had an internal serenity that Tegrus could scarcely fathom. He sat on the bole of a toppled tree and ran a cloth across the gleaming blade of his gladius. His boltstorm crossbow sat at his feet. He and Aetius had, along with Tegrus, volunteered to oversee the retinues engaged in destroying the foul icons and symbols that littered the top of the tor. None of it could be left standing, and the air rang with the sounds of the Retributors' hammers and the Decimators' axes as they smashed idols and chopped apart the crude gibbets that had once hung from the hag tree.

'It cannot be him – it must be a trick,' Aetius said. The Liberator-Prime was not a man to whom trust came easily. 'No one, Stormcast or otherwise, returns from the Realm of Chaos.' He tightened his grip on his hammer.

'But it is,' Tegrus said. 'Grymn and Morbus are down there already, with Zephacleas and Ultrades.' He looked at his fellow Stormcasts. 'We should be down there as well.'

Ever since Gardus' disappearance in the final moments of the battle for the Gates of Dawn, Tegrus had wondered if there was anything he could have done differently to have prevented what happened, and had come to no good conclusion. Nonetheless, he had been unable to shake the sense of his own failure. He had not been fast enough, observant enough... Somehow, somewhere, he had failed his Lord-Celestant. But now Gardus had returned and Tegrus felt angry, confused... joyful.

'After you,' Solus said. He extended his gladius and peered down the length of the blade. 'If it's him, and not some trick of the light, he'll find us in his own time.' He looked at Tegrus. 'But then, you've never been the patient sort, Tegrus.'

Tegrus laughed. 'No.' He looked at the Liberator-Prime. 'Aetius?'

'Someone must stand sentry,' Aetius said, gesturing to the still-smoking remains of the Dirgehorn. 'Gardus or no, I'll not shirk my duty.' He hesitated, and then added, 'But Solus is right. You are not so bound.'

He looked at Tegrus, and the Prosecutor-Prime could see the unspoken plea in the other man's eyes. Aetius rarely saw eye to eye with his fellow commanders in the Warrior Chamber, but he was their brother nonetheless, bound by oaths and bearing the same Reforging scars on his flesh. And he too had known Gardus, and flourished under the ever-patient Lord-Celestant's command.

'You're right,' Tegrus said, clapping Aetius on the shoulder. Then, with a snap of his great wings, he was hurtling out over the tor. As he left the ground far behind, he was tempted, as always, to simply keep flying. To rise and swoop forever, lost amongst the untold glories of the heavens. But the green skies of Ghyran were not the blue horizons of Azyr, and there was no peace to be found in these clouds. Blight-flies and worse things choked the air even now. Where the servants of the Ruinous Powers went, the world sickened and changed.

Tegrus had seen it often enough, and as a result, was always ready to cast down the worshippers of the Dark Gods wherever they were found. But in order to smite the foe, one first had to find him – a skill which Tegrus had honed in the Nihiliad Mountains during the cleansing of Azyr. He had rained blazing arrows down upon the Chaos warbands that had infested the crags, and exposed their positions to Sigmar's armies. Those had been good days. He had learned his true purpose there, swooping through rumbling thunderclouds to bring fire and fear to the enemies of the Celestial Realm.

Indeed, he had been so good at it that Sigmar himself had offered Tegrus a place as one of his trusted hunter-assassins.

A high honour for any Stormcast, but Tegrus had refused it – his place was with his Warrior Chamber.

He swooped low over the crowd of Stormcasts gathered about the foot of the tor, huddled in the cleansing light of Lorrus Grymn's lantern. With a snap of his wings he dropped from the air to land in a crouch before the newly returned Lord-Celestant. As he stood, other Stormcasts backed away.

'Is it you, my lord?' Tegrus asked as he stepped forward.

Gardus turned towards him and Tegrus felt his heart swell as he examined the face of the man before him. Gardus held his helm beneath his arm, as if to reassure his fellows of his identity.

Then, is that not what Gardus would do? Would he not reassure us, and speak kindly to us?

Some maintained that Gardus was too soft-hearted to lead, but Tegrus knew the truth of it – Sigmar had zealots aplenty, but the Stormcast Eternals must be more than swords… they must be heroes. And that Gardus surely was.

'If it was not, I expect you would be the first to divine it, my friend,' Gardus said. He extended his hand. Tegrus hesitated, then clasped his Lord-Celestant's forearm in a warrior's greeting. Gardus pulled him forward into a brief embrace before releasing him. Tegrus peered into Gardus' eyes.

'Where did you go, Steel Soul?' he asked. 'What did you see?'

'The Gardens of Nurgle, my friend, and horrors without end,' Gardus said softly. 'I ran for weeks, pursued by things too foul to name…'

'Weeks… but you've only been gone a few days,' Tegrus said.

Gardus closed his eyes, and his body tensed, like that of an animal fearing the lash. The last vestiges of Tegrus' bitterness fled as he saw the pain in Gardus' face.

What happened to you, my friend? he wondered. He made to speak, but Grymn cut him short.

'If you're through getting reacquainted, Tegrus, we were discussing matters of import,' the Lord-Castellant growled. Tegrus glanced at Grymn, a retort on his lips, but kept his mouth shut. Grymn had a sharp tongue, but he had led the Hallowed Knights safely through the innumerable terrors of Rotwater Blight. Tegrus remembered Grymn's quiet words of reassurance as the drone of the Dirgehorn ate away at their courage and sanity. The Lord-Castellant had been a rock, immoveable and unstoppable.

Grymn met his gaze and nodded tersely. Tegrus stepped back. Grymn looked at Gardus. 'You spoke of the Hidden Vale, Lord-Celestant...' he urged.

Tegrus blinked. The Hidden Vale... no wonder Grymn was short-tempered. Other Stormcasts had been dispatched to bring Sigmar's offer of alliance to Alarielle, the Radiant Queen and Mistress of Ghyran, but they had all failed to discover her hiding place. Some had hoped that the appearance of the sylvaneth warglades in the final moments of the battle for the Gates of Dawn had signalled some awareness on her part, but others, like Tegrus, had suspected that the treekin had acted on their own initiative. He glanced around, seeking out the mysterious creatures that had escorted Gardus back to them, and was not surprised to find them already gone. The sylvaneth went where they willed, and no man or beast could stop them.

If Gardus had somehow found a way to the Hidden Vale,

they could bring Sigmar's words to Alarielle. They might even be able to encourage her to rouse herself to fight alongside the Stormcasts in defence of the Jade Kingdoms.

Tegrus turned his attentions back to the words of his Lord-Celestant. Gardus' face had a haunted look, and he was silent for several moments, as if trying to marshal his thoughts. Then, slowly, he began to speak.

'We must first find the Oak of Ages Past,' Gardus said, speaking carefully, as might one who was trying to convey something he only barely understood. 'Celestial driftwood, cast through the void of time, which came to rest in the misty swamps of this realm. A stream of immaculate water, cleaner than any in the Mortal Realms, gushes forth from its ancient trunk. It is a river, bestowing life-giving energy to every part of this realm.' His voice faded, and he stood silent, as if lost in thought.

'Gardus,' Grymn said, harshly. Tegrus glared at the Lord-Castellant and put his hand on Gardus' shoulder. There was no telling what horrors the Steel Soul had experienced in his sojourn through Nurgle's garden. Gardus looked at the Prosecutor-Prime and nodded his thanks. He cleared his throat and continued his tale.

'While I was... elsewhere, I learned that this river – the River Vitalis – has become corrupted. Waters that once carried life now carry only the seeds of death.'

'A plague?' Grymn asked. They had seen similar pestilences far too often since arriving in the Realm of Life. Nurgle's influence had corrupted the very air itself.

'A daemon,' Gardus said. 'A Great Unclean One, like the beast I... fought at the Gates of Dawn.' He shook his head.

'The servants of Nurgle call it Pupa Grotesse, but that is not its true name.' He spoke with an iron certainty. 'I *know* its name. And we must break its hold over the watercourse, if we are to have any hope of finding the Hidden Vale and its mistress.'

He lifted his head. 'We must fight our way to the mouth of the River Vitalis, and destroy the daemon that festers at its heart.' He looked around, catching the eyes of every man present.

Tegrus raised his hammer. 'If you so command, Steel Soul, then that is what we shall do.' Grymn had led them well, and he was the reason they had survived to reach this point, but Gardus was their true leader.

Grymn grunted and shook his head. 'Lead on, then, Steel Soul. Lead on.'

CHAPTER SEVEN

Ambush on the fen road

'Oh, my boils and scabs,' Morbidex Twiceborn said as he cut a coiling forest spite out of the air with his scythe. 'Look at them all, marching in lockstep, so pretty in their shiny armour. What do you think, Tripletongue? Think they'd taste of starlight, my pet?' he asked the burly pox-maggoth he rode. Tripletongue roared and stamped in reply.

The arrayed ranks of Stormcast Eternals – or so they were said to call themselves – marched towards Morbidex's forces through the field of high cairnstones, driving forward in a stoic rhythm. The nurglings that made up his army, for their part, either hadn't noticed the newcomers or else didn't care. They were too busy fighting the horde of forest spites.

And it was such a wonderful ambush as well. Took me weeks to get the little fellows to understand what that word meant, Morbidex thought as he snatched a glittering spite out of the air and stuffed it in his mouth. But the spites had ruined it when they'd provoked the nurglings from concealment and put paid to all of Morbidex's hard effort and planning.

Brightly hued and peculiar, the diminutive arboreal spirits had forms ranging from horned serpents to enormous dragonflies that glowed with an inner light, and they fought savagely against the fat-bellied nurglings. They slashed, clawed and bit at one another in the mire along the wide sprawl of moss-covered cairnstones that served as Rotwater Blight's only true road, making a loud mess of things.

The forest spites might have had the upper hand despite being outnumbered if Morbidex had not joined the fray. Granted, his attack had been made more out of boredom and annoyance than any concern for his nurglings. The fat little daemons could take care of themselves, and they regarded war as play.

And who am I to ruin their fun, eh? Morbidex thought, as he drove his knees into the sides of Tripletongue's skull, turning the beast towards the newcomers. *Besides which, we've accomplished what we set out to do… Our foes' eyes are on us, even as Grandfather wanted…*

'Hup, Tripletongue,' Morbidex said. 'Up my beauty, up and at them!'

The eyeless maggoth gave vent to a burbling warble as it knuckled towards the approaching invaders, scattering spites and nurglings alike. *Lightning-men, Torglug calls 'em,* Morbidex thought, as he hunched forward in his saddle and swung his scythe back. *Fools, is what I think.* 'Think they can just roll over Nurgle's own children, don't they? Let's show them what we think of such foolishness,' the maggoth-rider roared, as he swung his scythe out in a savage blow towards the vanguard of the newcomers. One of the silver-armoured Stormcasts was torn from his feet by the force of the blow and sent flying. Tripletongue struck out with simian fists, battering others flat, or else rending them crown to gullet.

The nurglings followed, swarming over the warriors. Morbidex bellowed encouragement to his little friends, and smiled in pride every time a Stormcast went down, blanketed by squirming, bloated little bodies. 'Good! Keep it up, my little friends – Grandfather smiles on us all,' he shouted. I bet old Bloab and the Daemonspew wish they were here, he thought. His fellow maggoth lords were as much lovers of a good brawl as Morbidex himself; one reason among many that he found them such good company.

But the best company were his diminutive followers – the nurglings who had been his closest companions since the day he'd climbed Pox Peak, looking for a way into the Grandfather's garden. Aye, that was a good day – the best day, he thought, smiling widely. Since his slimy rebirth he had become more powerful than ever. 'And sitting atop you, my beastly beauty, I'm unbeatable,' he said, patting Tripletongue's head. The maggoth gave a gurgle of pleasure at the gesture. Morbidex laughed and swung his scythe out, catching a Stormcast in the back and wrenching the armoured warrior into the air with ease.

He eyed his struggling prey for a moment before slinging him over his shoulder. Take a lot of killing, these fellows, he thought, as Tripletongue smashed into another phalanx. These ones were the colour of overripe fruit, rather than gold or silver, but they fought just as hard. How many of you are there? And how many flavours do you come in, he thought, as he saw a host of winged warriors hurtle towards him.

Tripletongue was surrounded, but Morbidex wasn't unduly concerned. Getting their attention had been the whole point of his little display. The Stormcasts had been making a nuisance of themselves since they'd shattered the Dirgehorn and killed old Gluhak.

In the days since the Dirgehorn had fallen silent, the silver-armoured invaders had clashed again and again with Grandfather's children – from running battles with the skaven to the siege of jolly Slaugoth's Rotfane, even as Torglug had predicted. They'd erased the avian defenders of the Vulturine Geysers, and sent Gutrot Spume's Drowned Men into flight at the battle of Canker Cascade. Slaugoth and Spume were fit to be tied. Their stock with the Glottkin had fallen sharply in the aftermath of their defeats and new favourites had been chosen. So this matter had fallen to him. Good old reliable Morbidex. He'd been tasked with pulling the Stormcasts into the swamp, and keeping them distracted long enough for...

Ha! he thought, as the festering swamp on the other side of the Stormcast column began to boil. That's it... keep looking at me, my fancy friends. Eyes on ol' Morbidex. Pay no attention to the fellows rising out of the mud.

Rising from the muck, brackish water sluicing from their twisted frames, came the tallymen of Nurgle. The plaguebearers uttered a monotonous drone, counting the diseases abroad in the swamp as they strode towards their unsuspecting enemies. In their lead was an old friend – the creature known as Wrech Gab'larr, Herald of Nurgle. He glared at the Stormcasts with malign intent, and whipped one warty hand forward.

Plaguebearers loped past him to slam their plagueswords into the backs of the Stormcast Eternals. Wrech's expression became one of befuddlement when the silver armour remained unmarked where a blow wasn't immediately fatal. Stormcasts who didn't immediately discorporate in a blur of azure energy whirled with a fierce precision to lay their attackers low. Wrech bellowed in frustration as his carefully prepared afflictions failed to take root.

I could have told you that wouldn't work, Morbidex thought, as he ducked a blow from one of the winged Stormcasts. These warriors, wherever they were from, were singularly resistant to the plagues and diseases born in Grandfather's laboratories and gardens. The stuff of them burned too hot for sickness to take hold, Morbidex suspected. Wrech roared and hacked a gap in the Stormcast lines. He and his plaguebearers stormed into the midst of the enemy, determined to bury their blades in Stormcast flesh.

'Ha! That's the way, Wrech,' Morbidex shouted. 'That's the way to do it, O Herald of Fresh Woes… Smash these shiny upstarts.' He hefted his scythe and lashed out at one of the winged warriors, who swooped around him like so many stinging insects. He cut the Stormcast from the sky, and cursed as the warrior dissolved into azure light. 'I hate it when they do that,' he snarled.

'Not as much as we do, I'd wager, brute,' a voice tolled. Morbidex twisted in his saddle, searching for the voice's owner. His eyes widened as he caught sight of the winged shape diving towards him on wings of crackling flame.

'Oh buboes,' Morbidex said, moments before the warrior swooped past him. The Stormcast lashed out with a hammer as he hurtled past and caught Morbidex in the face with a thunderous boom. The force of the blow catapulted the Twiceborn from his saddle. He hit the marshy ground with a splash. Every bone in his face felt as if it had been splintered, and he groaned as he rolled over. Tripletongue shrieked and reared up, pawing blindly at the swarm of winged killers. Without Morbidex's guidance, the beast was reacting on instinct.

Morbidex pushed himself awkwardly to his feet. He'd lost his scythe in the fall and he stumbled back as the warrior who'd struck him landed nearby. Lightning crackled across the Stormcast's limbs. Eyes the colour of the unclouded sky stared at Morbidex from behind the too perfect features of a silver mask. He held two hammers, the heads of which were wreathed in energy. Morbidex flexed his thick fingers.

'Well... come on then, silver-back,' he gurgled, setting his feet. 'You caught me by surprise once, but you'll not do so twice, or my name isn't Morbidex Twiceborn...'

The warrior shot forward, quicker than Morbidex's eyes could follow. One hammer crashed into his chest, and a blow from the second snapped his head to the side. Morbidex fell onto his back, wheezing for breath.

'Ow. Fine. Fine. Best... best two out of three,' he groaned, as he rolled onto his belly. He shook his head, trying to clear it. The Stormcast dived forward again, intent on finishing the job. Morbidex twisted aside, and clamped a hand down on the back of the warrior's crested helm. With a roar, he cut short the Stormcast's flight, and flung him down. Morbidex stomped down, but his opponent rolled aside. One wing snapped out, and the crackling feathers gave Morbidex's belly a searing kiss. He staggered back, hands clamped to his burned and ruptured gut.

The Stormcast pushed himself to his feet. Morbidex grinned at him.

'Didn't like that, did you? Faster than I look, aren't I?' he chortled. He looked down at his wound, and gingerly took his hands away. Bloated entrails pressed against the blackened flesh, and he gave a grunt of consternation. 'I'm going to twist your head off for that one, friend.'

The Stormcast sprang forward, and his hammers snapped out. Morbidex caught one on his palm, but the second smashed into his shoulder. He roared and slugged his foe, denting his silvery helm. A wing flared out and blinded Morbidex. He clawed at his eyes, cursing virulently. Hammer-blows rained down, striking his head, shoulders, arms and back.

Morbidex sank to one knee, ears ringing. He'd never been hit so hard, or so fast. The Stormcast was fast, faster than any creature that Morbidex had ever had the pleasure of fighting. But speed wasn't the sole route to victory. Morbidex dug his hand into the muck as he bent forward, and, with a wild howl, hurled a gobbet of mud into the Stormcast's face. The warrior avoided the improvised missile, as Morbidex had known he would, and stepped within reach of his opponent.

The maggoth lord gave a shout and lunged, arms spread wide. The Stormcast pivoted, hammers raised, but this time Morbidex was ready. He caught the warrior's wrists and prevented the blows from landing. The two strained against one another, their feet sliding back and forth through the muck. Morbidex grinned down at his opponent. 'I've introduced myself, it's only polite you do the same,' he said.

'My name is Tegrus, monster. Treasure it – it's the last name you'll ever hear,' the Stormcast growled.

Morbidex laughed. He was still laughing when Tegrus abruptly fell backwards and pulled the maggoth lord off his feet. He bellowed in shock as Tegrus' boots slammed into his wounded belly. Morbidex rolled onto his back, but too slowly. Tegrus dropped towards him, hammers raised, and the maggoth lord squeezed his eyes shut, waiting for the impact.

However, rather than the pain he'd been expecting, he felt a wash of hot, foul air and heard a familiar guttural roar. He cracked an eye open, and saw Tegrus flying backwards. A shadow fell over him, and he looked up, a smile spreading across his wide, green face.

'Ah, Tripletongue my beauty, just in time,' he rumbled, as the maggoth bent towards him, its teeth clicking in concern. It snuffled worriedly at him as he got to his feet, and he patted its scaly skull. 'Who's a sweet brute, eh?' Morbidex said, as he hauled himself back into the saddle.

As Tripletongue rose to its full height, Morbidex took in the battlefield at a glance. What he saw wasn't good. Wrech's ambush had gone sour and the Stormcasts were counter-attacking, led by a figure who blazed with holy light. Morbidex shaded his eyes and peered at the figure. That's the one old Bolathrax was after, he thought, doubtfully. As he watched, nurgling swarms were crushed underfoot, hammers fell, horned heads burst and Nurgle's tallymen reeled.

Wrech bellowed a command and the remaining plague-bearers belly-flopped into the swamp, digging into the muck and disappearing from sight.

'Well, that tears it,' Morbidex murmured as he sat up in his saddle. He slapped Tripletongue on the head. 'Time to go, my lad.' The maggoth rumbled assent and turned, smashing a tree out of its path as it dived deeper into the swamp, moving as quickly as its thick legs could carry him.

No sense remaining to fight all on his lonesome. Grandfather didn't favour fools, despite his sentimentality. He hunched forward in his saddle, urging his mount to greater speed. Have to fall back, get to the Gelid Gush and make a final stand, Morbidex thought. That was where they were going. It was the only place of value in the immediate vicinity.

He twitched his head abruptly, trying to dislodge the flies that were gathering about his face. Wait – flies? His eyes widened as the flies suddenly rose from his flesh, and swirled about in a cloud, coalescing into a familiar face.

'*Going somewhere, Twiceborn?*' Ethrac Glott asked, in a voice made from the droning of a hundred flies. '*I could have sworn we asked you to handle these invaders…*'

'Our ambush was ambushed,' Morbidex said, unapologetically. 'Forest spites got the nurglings all riled up. The Stormcasts interrupted a very satisfying drubbing, if you want my opinion.'

'*Did I ask for it?*'

'Well… no.'

'*Then what makes you think I would?*'

'A sense of unbridled optimism,' Morbidex said. He glanced over his shoulder, but saw nothing. No pursuit appeared to be forthcoming. 'What now, Glott?'

'*Bloab Rotspawned and Orghotts Daemonspew are making for the Gelid Gush. Join them, Twiceborn…*' Ethrac hissed. '*It is time for Grandfather Nurgle's children to go to war.*'

CHAPTER EIGHT

The ruins of Arborea

Lord-Celestant Gardus pushed through the veil of vines, and gazed at the faded glory of the fallen city of Arborea. The treetop city was a thing of flowing curves and soft angles, of great stones held aloft by the thick branches and boles of an immense elder tree, perhaps grown from a seed of the Oak of Ages Past itself. The latter was visible in the distance, its broken shape jutting across the pale green sky. He could just make out the pale swathe of foulness that was their destination on the horizon.

He repressed a shudder as he stared at that foulness.

Help us, Garradan… help us, the ghosts murmured in the back of his head. They had been whispering to him since he had reeled out of that mad garden and back into the Mortal Realms, aflame with white fire. They had clung to him, like the tatters of his warcloak, as he had waded into the fray between the sylvaneth and the skaven in the Glade of Horned Growths. He had instinctively sought out his foes, and ruined any who sought to bar his path, seeing not ratkin but the barbarians who had murdered the man he had been, in another time, another place.

Help us... Garradan, help us...

'Quiet.' He squeezed his eyes shut, forcing the voices back into the cage of his memories. When they had at last fallen silent he strode forward, following the scampering forms of the forest spites the Stormcasts had rescued from Nurgle's followers a few days before. The colourful spirits swirled about him for a moment, clicking and murmuring in their strange tongue, before they faded, like reflections on water. Where they went, he could not say, and did not like to guess.

'Thank you,' he called out. The spites had led their Stormcast allies to Arborea by secret paths only they knew, and Gardus was grateful to them. It had been the first time in many days that the Stormcasts had been able to travel without fear of attack or ambush, and such a respite had been much needed, though it would be brief. Even Sigmar's chosen warriors required rest, and Rotwater Blight had more dangers than just those that came armed with swords and axes. The servants of the Ruinous Powers were many and varied, and the Hallowed Knights and their allies had fought for every patch of ground between Profane Tor and here.

He looked about in wonder. What stories were in these stones, he wondered, tracing the faded features of a vine-shrouded statue as he looked around the vast plaza he had wandered into. What folk had built this city? What had happened to them? Where were they now?

He closed his eyes, suddenly recalling the guttural laughter of the daemon Bolathrax and the nightmare pursuit through the Garden of Nurgle. He knew what happened to the people of Arborea as surely as he knew what had happened to his own folk, before Sigmar had claimed him.

Garradan... help us...

Weathered stone and withered vine crumbled beneath his fingers. Gardus opened his eyes and took his hand away from the statue.

'No more,' he said hoarsely. 'Never again.'

'Gardus,' a harsh voice said from behind him. He turned, and saw Lord-Castellant Grymn stalking towards him, his gryph-hound padding at his side, his lantern glowing with a soft, warming light. 'Are you ill?'

Gardus smiled thinly. 'You sound almost concerned.'

'I would not have asked if I wasn't,' Grymn said. 'You have... been through much.'

Gardus said nothing for a moment as he marshalled his thoughts. He wanted to tell Grymn what he had seen in Nurgle's grim garden. Even now, safely returned to the Mortal Realms, he could not cleanse himself of the stink of that place. It ate away at him, mind, body and soul. His armour was clean, but sometimes he could not help but see filth, a slow, creeping mould, insidious and inexorable. Idly, he scraped at his chest. 'I am fine, Lorrus.'

As they had traversed Rotwater Blight, Gardus had sent his Prosecutors winging ahead to scout out the lay of the land. They had brought back word of the great, hollow trunk of the Oak of Ages Past, rising up from the horizon, and Arborea smouldering in its shadow.

Too, Tegrus had spied a number of strange, floating islands, their snow-capped peaks crowned by ugly green clouds.

Gardus shook his head.

'Tegrus,' he called out to one of the winged shapes flying through the upper reaches of the city above. 'Is this the place?'

'This is the city I saw, my lord,' Tegrus said as he dropped to the ground. His wings blazed once, stirring dust and pollen, and then folded behind his back. 'We sit in the very shadow of the Oak of Ages Past.' He extended his hammer to the northeast. 'And there, the river's source. We're close, Gardus.'

Lord-Castellant Grymn grunted. 'It seems those forest spites did not play us false.'

'Why would they?' Gardus asked. 'It is in their best interests to aid us.' He looked at Grymn. 'Or do you still not trust them, Lorrus?'

'I trust nothing in this realm,' Grymn said, one eyebrow raised. 'Nor should you, Gardus. We are strangers here, however much blood we've shed. The sylvaneth are allies of moment, nothing more. Who knows what goes through the heads of creatures like that?'

'I know,' Gardus said, softly. 'They could have killed me, Lorrus. Instead, they brought me back. They told me of this city, and the islands in the sky. We are their best hope for awakening Alarielle to the danger she is in. The talons of the Plague God seek her heart, and they close about her, even now. We must get to her first, to put ourselves between her and her enemies. That is why we are here, my friend.'

'Yes, to take control of the realmgates in Sigmar's name,' Grymn said. 'Why must we...' He fell silent and turned away.

Gardus called after him, but the Lord-Castellant walked away, bellowing orders to a phalanx of nearby Liberators.

'As pleasant as ever,' Tegrus murmured.

'He is worried. We are all worried. It has been a hard path to walk, and we have shed much blood in the name of something I saw in a mad realm,' Gardus said. They had done much good along the way. Or so he hoped. They had torn down the vile redoubts of Nurgle's champions, and slain many a corrupted warrior on their trek across the Blight. But they had not been able to continue to follow the river. To tarry too long in the vicinity of such a corrupted body of water was dangerous, even to Stormcast Eternals. They'd had to find a safer way to the river's source – and a quicker one. When the forest spites had offered to lead them by hidden paths to Arborea, Gardus had quickly accepted, despite Grymn's misgivings.

He looked up at the trunk of the immense elder tree which stretched far above the city, piercing the very clouds themselves. 'Are they up there, then?' he asked Tegrus. 'The floating islands you saw?'

'Aye, far above,' Tegrus said. 'It'll be quite the climb for those of you without wings.'

Gardus laughed. 'We've climbed worse... Remember the Star-Heights of Azyr? At least this time we won't have enemies hurling fire and spears down on us as we climb.'

'As far as we know,' Tegrus said. He looked up. 'I will take my Prosecutors and make sure your route is a safe one. Do not doubt yourself, Steel Soul. We believe in you. All of us.' Then, without waiting for a reply, he leapt into the air and was gone, speeding towards the dark clouds above. Gardus watched Tegrus go until he lost sight of him. He turned, as someone placed a hand on his shoulder.

'Morbus,' he said, recognizing the chill of the other Stormcast's presence.

'Grymn is worried,' the Lord-Relictor intoned.

'As are you, I expect,' Gardus said.

'No,' Morbus said. 'I do not worry, Gardus. I merely observe.'

'Maybe he's right to be worried,' Gardus said, looking up at the tree.

Morbus laughed softly. 'Grymn is stone. He is sigmarite – hard and unyielding. He will break before he bends, and calls it strength. But you...'

'Bend,' Gardus supplied.

Morbus nodded. 'Yes. You bend. You adapt, you persevere. That is why Sigmar chose you as his sword, Gardus. You do what must be done, rather than what you have been ordered to do.'

'So would Grymn, if he had seen–' Gardus began.

Morbus cut him off with a sharp gesture. 'Grymn would never have come out of Nurgle's garden alive. He would have fought, and died.' The Lord-Relictor hesitated. 'Nonetheless, sometimes he is right. I have... seen things, Gardus. I have seen death and damnation, and I would not see it come to pass.'

'Whose death?' Gardus asked, mouth suddenly dry. 'Whose damnation?'

Morbus was silent. Gardus looked away. He shook himself. Only the faithful, he thought.

'We must climb, Morbus,' he said. 'We have a way to go, and little time.' He looked at the Lord-Relictor. 'Gather the others – my fellow Lord-Celestants included. We must reach the sky-islands floating above.'

'And then what?' Morbus said.

Gardus hesitated. Then, 'I will know when I get up there.'

He clenched his fists. He could sense Morbus' concern. Before the other Stormcast could speak, he continued on, his words coming in a rush. 'I am being driven by something I cannot define, Morbus. A vague certainty compels me – fragments of knowledge, stolen as I fled through ruined worlds, snatches of things seen at a remove of centuries – the whispers of the sylvaneth, as they bore me to safety.' He shook his head. 'They, and perhaps even Ghyran itself, want Alarielle found, Lord-Relictor. They want her to know, to see what has become of the world she has shrunk from. Once she *sees*… she will *fight*. Ghyran will fight. The Jade Kingdoms will rise. And all of this will not have been for nothing.' He looked at Morbus. 'But we must find her first.'

Morbus was silent for a moment. Then he nodded.

'We must climb,' he said.

CHAPTER NINE

The floating islands

Lorrus Grymn slammed the edge of his halberd into the bark of the titanic tree. Tallon chirped from his perch. The gryph-hound lay across the Lord-Castellant's chest, held fast by hope and a sling made from Grymn's cloak.

'Easy boy, almost there,' Grymn muttered as Tallon's beak rubbed against the underside of his war-helm. The animal was worried, as he should be. Though they had the heads of eagles, gryph-hounds lacked the bird's wings, or ease with heights. 'Almost… there, my friend.' He dug his fingers into the ridges of the bark, and tore his halberd free. 'Almost there.'

This is the sheerest folly, he thought, as he paused for breath. He chanced a look back at the way he'd come. Below him, figures in silver, amethyst and gold swarmed up the trunk of the vast tree like insects. Further below them, the crumbled city of Arborea was but a series of pale indentations in the all-pervasive mist. It had taken them hours to climb to the uppermost boughs of the great tree, moving so slowly that Grymn feared the war for the Jade Kingdoms would be over before they reached the top.

One missed step, one loosed hold, would be fatal. Already several Stormcasts had perished, falling to their deaths far below as the great tree swayed and shifted on its roots. He twisted his head upwards. Gardus clung to the topmost bough of the tree, staring out over the horizon, as if lost in thought.

He'd hoped Gardus' return meant that things would proceed as Sigmar had decreed. Instead, they had travelled halfway across Rotwater Blight to fight battles they were not prepared for, all in the name of a vision that Gardus had experienced while lost in a daemon-realm. Grymn shook his head.

When Morbus had first told him of his dreams, he'd wanted to act, to save Gardus from the fate that awaited him. Gardus was a brother Stormcast, chosen by Sigmar and worthy of Grymn's concern. But this venture seemed doomed to failure. Others had searched for the Radiant Queen, but had found no sign of her. If Sigmar's own hunters had turned up no sign of their quarry, who could hope to find her?

'Only the faithful.'

Grymn looked up. Gardus' voice was soft, but it carried far. It was no parade ground bellow, but rather the quiet rumble of a dracoth. Gardus was not looking at him. Instead, the Lord-Celestant tensed and then, before Grymn could stop him, he flung himself into the mist that obscured the air around them. Grymn hesitated. He'd known this was coming. It was the only way to reach the floating islands that Tegrus said were hovering somewhere out there. He heard a scrape of metal and saw Lord-Relictor Morbus do the same, reliquary staff in hand. He watched the other Stormcasts vanish, and gritted his teeth. What sort of madman flings himself blindly into the void? he thought, angrily.

Tallon chirruped, and Grymn looked down at the gryph-hound. He smiled thinly. 'Yes, I know… only the faithful.' Then, wrapping one arm protectively about the animal, he shoved himself away from the trunk of the leviathan tree, and plummeted into the swirling mist. A second of weightlessness stretched out before ending abruptly in a soft landing on the loam of the floating isle. He felt rocks and roots crumble beneath his weight, and Tallon gave a startled screech as Grymn began to slide down an incline of spongy vegetation.

He twisted about, and saw, through the thinning mist, a jagged precipice. Grymn cursed and tried to hook his halberd into something solid, but to no avail. His stomach lurched.

'Gardus!' he shouted, and his slide was brought to an abrupt halt as an iron grip caught hold of the haft of his halberd. Grymn looked up into the eyes of the Lord-Celestant. Gardus, hammer hooked in the loam of the island, dragged Grymn back up with his free hand.

'Have no fear, Lorrus. I will not let you fall,' Gardus said.

Grymn said nothing as he caught hold of a thick net of roots and began to push himself up towards his fellow Stormcast. Morbus appeared above him and reached out a hand. Grymn took the Lord-Relictor's aid gladly, and soon found himself kneeling on relatively solid ground. He looked about, heart thudding in his chest. More Stormcasts appeared, dropping through the mist to fall onto the island's mossy scree. From the look of it, almost all of their warriors had made it. He could see Zephacleas and Ultrades and their men as well.

'Tegrus wasn't playing the fool after all,' he said, fighting to keep all sign of the fear he'd felt out of his voice.

'No, he wasn't,' Gardus said. He spread his arms. 'Behold – the lost island of Talbion!'

Grymn looked at Morbus, who nodded tersely. Grymn rose to his feet and let Tallon out of his sling.

'Well, now what, Lord-Celestant?' he said. 'We're here… wherever here is.'

'Talbion,' Gardus repeated.

How did he know its name? Grymn wondered. Obviously, he'd learned it wherever he'd learned of its existence, but it was nonetheless disconcerting – Gardus knew things no other Stormcast did.

'It might as well be the Brimstone Peninsula for all that that name means to me, Gardus. My question stands… what now?' Grymn asked.

Overhead, the grey-green fog clouds that plagued the floating isles rumbled angrily and an unclean rain began to fall. Grymn grunted in disgust as the oily water pelted his armour and the mist seemed to condense about them, like the coils of an agitated serpent.

Zephacleas and Ultrades trotted towards them. The Lord-Celestant of the Astral Templars swiped at the mist. 'Nothing like a good climb. Don't care for this mist, though. Smells like those beasts we fought at the Vulturine Geysers.'

'It is the work of the Ruinous Powers,' Ultrades said.

'This island, much like the realm of Ghyran itself, is a prisoner of Nurgle,' Gardus said. 'This cursed pox-mist is holding the island in place. We must somehow disperse it, and in doing so, free the island and then Ghyran itself.' He looked at the Lord-Relictor and gestured with his hammer. 'Morbus, call down the lightning.'

Morbus inclined his head and lifted his reliquary. He began to chant, his hollow tones rising above the patter of the rain. Azure lightning began to crackle within the depths of the reliquary, and it spread to the mist, flashing through it. It grew in strength, until it was blinding in its ferocity. The mist and smog writhed in the grip of the energy, like a serpent in the claws of a bird of prey. Morbus' voice rose in pitch, his harsh tones lashing out with the savagery of the storm itself. Grymn could feel the power of the Lord-Relictor as it thrummed through the air and waged war on the very elements themselves.

Morbus rarely stirred himself to such heights, but when he did, it was a sight to behold. Grymn watched in awe as the mist began to burn away, seared to nothing by the fury of Morbus' storm. He felt the ground beneath his feet shudder, as if in gratitude. Grymn looked up, and met Gardus' solemn gaze.

'Do you feel it, Lorrus? The island quakes, grateful to its bedrock. This is the realm of Ghyran, and even the stones themselves bristle with the stuff of life,' he said.

The rain, once filthy, became as clean and pure as the summer storms of Azyr itself. Gardus lifted his arms and tilted his head back.

'We have freed you, great island! Now bear us east, to the river's mouth!' Gardus' voice echoed from the low peaks of the floating island.

Silence stretched out for several long moments. Not a single soul in the gathered Stormhosts dared speak. Then, with a rumble, the island began to shudder beneath their feet. Grymn looked about and saw the clouds in the sky moving. No, not the clouds... the island itself. The airborne mountain had begun to slide eastward through the pale emerald skies of Ghyran.

Grymn shook his head, incredulous. 'How?' he asked.

Gardus said nothing for a moment. Grymn wondered if the Lord-Celestant was as surprised as he was. Then Gardus lifted his hammer and roared, 'Who will be victorious?'

'Only the faithful!'

'Only the faithful!'

CHAPTER TEN

The bursting of the world pimple

'Well… there's something you don't see every day,' Morbidex Twiceborn said, looking up at the island as it hove to through the clouds far above. Its shadow stretched across the heartlands of Rotwater Blight. Tripletongue grunted, and Morbidex patted the maggoth's head.

Morbidex and his fellow maggoth lords had been stationed here to prevent the Stormcasts from advancing on the source of the Gelid Gush, as well as the roots of the Oak of Ages Past. Torglug, Spume and the others were positioned at the other various crossings and headwaters; every conceivable route to Pupa Grotesse and his bathwaters was guarded by the Grandfather's own, on the orders of the Glottkin.

Morbidex glanced over his shoulder, back towards the distant shape of the Great Unclean One. Pupa Grotesse was larger than any other examples of his kind that Morbidex had ever had the pleasure of knowing. He was a mountain of jolly filth, though even he was made to look small next to the immense roots of the Oak of Ages Past.

'Ever seen the like, Bloab?' he called out to his fellow maggoth lord. Bloab Rotspawned shook his hooded head, causing the swarm of insects that accompanied him everywhere to flutter about in agitation. He was a bulky lump whose flesh, where it was not hidden by his black armour, was covered in insect bites and raised pustules, and his tattered robes were stained with strange ichor and covered in squirming maggots.

'A new one on me, Morbidex,' Bloab droned. 'Even Bilespurter izz in awe, eh?' He scratched the mottled flesh of his maggoth. Bilespurter gave a warbling snort in reply. Bloab turned towards Orghotts Daemonspew, the third of the maggoth riders present at the edge of the Gelid Gush, where the world pimples bulged obscenely. 'What zzay you, Orghotts?'

'What is there to say, companions-mine? 'tis an island, and she floats,' Orghotts rumbled, through malformed lips. His maggoth shifted impatiently, and he gave its scaly skull a thump with the flat of one of the two large Rotaxes he carried. 'Be still, Whippermaw. Thy hunger will soon be sated.' He sat back in his saddle, his armour creaking. 'I do wonder at it, aye.' He stroked the great horn of daemon-bone that sprouted from the side of his face, jaw to crown. 'Think it be our enemies, Twiceborn?'

'The Glotts certainly must, otherwise Ghurk wouldn't be ambling towards us with all the grace of an avalanche,' Morbidex said, pointing towards the massive shape of Ghurk Glott, knuckling his way across the mire towards them, his siblings perched securely on his immense shoulders. Ghurk splashed

through the shallow waters with an excited bellow, shoulder-
ing aside a mossy cairn in his haste.

'What ho, Glottkin? Come to deliver us victory?' Morbidex shouted, cupping his hands around his mouth. 'Do the
silver-skins draw close? Is it to be battle at last? Tripletongue
is hungry.'

'Not here, not yet,' Otto Glott replied loudly. 'Not if Ethrac
is right.'

'Of course I'm right, brother-mine. The evidence hangs
above us. They're not stopping here,' Ethrac said, as Ghurk
loped past them, scattering maggoths and nurglings alike in
his haste. 'They bypassed Torglug's forces, at river's crossing,
and Slaugoth's host as well.' The sorcerer pointed towards
the island, sliding through the sky above. 'Somehow, they
freed one of the cursed sky-mountains of Talbion from the
Grandfather's pox-clouds and convinced it to float towards
the source-waters of the Gelid Gush.'

Morbidex and his companions turned their maggoths about
and set the beasts into motion in Ghurk's wake. The maggoths had to gallop to keep up with the biggest Glott sibling.
Morbidex leaned forward in his saddle. 'Where are the others? What should we do?'

'We're already doing it,' Ethrac snapped. He stamped on
Ghurk's head. 'Keep an even keel, brother. I'm engaged in
delicate sorceries here.'

Ethrac had a brazier standing before him, attached to
Ghurk's harness. It smoked and spat as he chanted over its
open flame, wringing his hands in an ornate fashion. The
smoke tensed like a thing alive as Ethrac's voice rose in pitch,
and before Morbidex's astonished eyes it split like the petals

of a gaseous flower, and a horde of insectile daemons, ridden by plaguebearers, spilled upwards into existence. They were without number, and far too large to have truly emerged from the brazier's open mouth. The plague drones rose in a buzzing cloud, gossamer wings throbbing with an irregular rhythm.

'Go, my pretties,' Ethrac wailed, thrusting a finger towards the distant form of the flying mountain. 'Rain down pox and peril, and make them rue the day they ever tested Grandfather's patience!' At his command, the twisting cloud of daemons tumbled upwards like a swarm of outsized hornets and swept across the sky towards the island. Morbidex gave a cheer.

'Ha! Look at them go,' he roared. He leaned over Tripletongue's head and said, 'Would that you had wings, Tripletongue, and we could join them.' He straightened and looked at Ethrac, who had slumped back into Otto's arms, exhausted by his magics. It was no easy thing to call forth the Grandfather's aerial guard so far from a realmgate or other pestilential portal. The very air of Ghyran resisted such magics – even now, with Grandfather's claws hooked deep in the soil. 'What now? As much confidence as I have in your sorcery, I don't think the plague drones can bring that rock down by themselves.'

'Be at ease, Twiceborn. The Glotts have a plan, yes we do,' Otto said. He extended his scythe towards one of the great boils of earth and mud rising from the face of Rotwater Blight. 'We'll see how well that island stays afloat with geysers of Grandfather's own pus dappling its belly.'

Well, Morbidex thought, grinning in pleasure. Can't say I haven't thought of doing something similar, since I first laid eyes on them. The world pimples were a sign of the Grand-father's interest in the Realm of Life, and a mark of how deep his influence truly went. The blessed muck and filth of the garden had spread to Ghyran, fertilizing the weak land and giving it some pomp and girth. The world pimples had formed soon after Pupa Grotesse had wedged his bulk into the river, bursting out of the ripe soil and spreading across the Blight. Every few decades, one of the Pimples would burst, unable to contain the pressure building up within it, filling the air with the familiar scents of Nurgle's garden.

Ghurk and the maggoths loped towards the largest of the world pimples, followed by Morbidex's nurglings, who could sense a good time when one was in the offing. Morbidex extended his scythe down past Tripletongue's knees so that the quickest of his tiny charges could catch hold of the blade and swing themselves up onto the maggoth's flanks.

Despite the speed of the great beasts, it still took some time to reach their destination. Morbidex sat back and let the rhythm of Tripletongue's barrelling gait put him at ease. Bloab did much the same, the fat sorcerer sitting, head bowed, looking for all the world as if he were asleep. Orghotts, how-ever, incited Whippermaw to greater and greater speeds, rapping the maggoth's flanks with the flat of his axes. Never any patience, that one, Morbidex thought, watching his old ally bellow curses and snatches from ancient songs.

On they rode, across the mires and fens of Rotwater Blight. And above them all, the island crept closer and closer, until its shadow all but swallowed them up. Morbidex could feel the ancient power flowing through the airborne mass of soil and rock; it was unlike anything in the Grandfather's garden, but somehow familiar all the same. It was the power of life unrestrained, life without limit or end, and admirable in its own way. Aye, it'll be a shame to see you gone, but Grandfather bids it, Morbidex thought.

The world would be better when such things knew their place, in any event. Ghyran had yet to be tamed. That was why the Glotts were so determined to find the so-called Radiant Queen. It was Alarielle who was somehow stymieing Nurgle's advances in this realm, Alarielle whose subtle song raised forests to walk and cleansed that which had been fairly befouled. And it was Alarielle whom Nurgle wanted. It was said, by those who would know, that there was a cage of crystalline pus, hardened in the heat of Nurgle's cauldron, somewhere in the garden, waiting for its prisoner. When the Radiant Queen was at last his, these knowledgeable sorts said, Grandfather would cage her, and hang her from his bower, and listen to her beautiful song into eternity.

Who says the gods don't understand romance, Morbidex thought, as he brought Tripletongue to a halt in a cloud of dust. The largest of the world pimples was a truly mountainous boil of dripping earth, topped by a cloudy bubble of beautiful vileness. It was magnificent.

'Too bad,' Morbidex murmured.

'What was that, Twiceborn?' Otto asked, peering down at him. The oldest of the Glotts was a bulky warrior, as big as Morbidex, and his lumpen frame was fair to bursting with the favour of Nurgle. He carried a scythe, like Morbidex, though his was wreathed with even more baleful enchantments.

'I said it's a shame,' Morbidex said, reclining in his saddle. He scratched the chin of a nurgling. 'Think of how big it might get...'

'We all must make sacrifices to keep pests out of the garden,' Otto said. He smacked Ghurk on the head with the butt of his scythe. 'Hup, Ghurk. Give it a squeeze.'

Ghurk made a sound of assent and reached out with his giant tentacle. The tendril slithered about the cusp of the world pimple and contracted with a sound like grinding rocks.

'Hurry, Ghurk,' Otto said, as he hunched forward. 'Hurry! They are almost past us!'

Morbidex looked up, and saw the island pass overhead. Soil and rocks fell from its vast belly, to smash into the mire below. Water exploded upwards as a chunk of rock hammered down nearby, and Tripletongue gave a bleat of surprise. Morbidex leaned forward and dug his fingers into the maggoth's hide.

'Easy, you fearful brute, it's just a bit of soil, think nothing of it,' he grated, even as he cocked an eye towards the hovering landmass.

'Mayhap we should seek safer ground,' Orghotts said, looking around warily. More stones fell, plopping into the water with ground-shaking finality. Bodies fell with them too, some clad in silver, others dripping with Nurgle's blessings. Ethrac's daemons had met the enemy, and the air was rent by the sounds of battle as winged Stormcasts clashed with plague drones. Morbidex watched, momentarily distracted by the aerial war. He'd never seen the like, at least not in the Mortal Realms. Where the Grandfather's garden abutted the killing fields of Khorne or the colorful palaces of Tzeentch's realm, such conflicts were commonplace. But those things were but grand duels, exaggerated and only mockingly serious.

This, however, was true war, and part of him longed to be up there amidst it. He glanced around and saw that his fellow maggoth lords were as rapt as he was, watching the sky-borne battle. Then Ghurk roared, and with a sound like splitting rock, the world pimple ruptured.

CHAPTER ELEVEN

Battle in the sky

'Only the faithful,' Tegrus shouted as he folded his wings and arrowed towards the plague drone. Hammer crashed against plaguesword as he swept past. Prosecutors from three Stormhosts had launched themselves aloft to engage the daemon-flyers, as the latter swarmed the island, seeking to attack those who stood upon it.

As he swooped through the air, back towards his quarry, Tegrus could see the grey-green reaches of Rotwater Blight spreading out far below him. There too was the shattered husk of the Oak of Ages Past, larger than a range of foothills and rising up as if to catch hold of the sky. From its end flowed a ribbon of pure crystal water, turning midstream to a flow of putrid slop. There, squatting amidst that filth, was the being they had come to find, the Great Unclean One that Gardus had spoken of.

You were right, Steel Soul, he thought, as he rolled through the air.

One of his hammers snapped out to catch a plaguebearer in the head. His blow sent the daemon tumbling from its buzzing mount. The fly contorted with malign urgency, its hairy legs crashing against Tegrus' armour as it sought to crush him. The acrid stench of it washed over him, choking him. With a strangled shout, he drove his hammers into its pulsing thorax, rupturing the shiny carapace and covering himself in a pungent tide of squirming maggots. The fly plummeted from the air, following its rider to the ground far below. Tegrus grimaced and pressed his hammer to his chest, burning away the creatures that clung to the sigmarite.

He looked around, taking in the aerial battle going on around him. When the daemons had appeared, every Prosecutor capable of flight had thrown themselves into the air. Tegrus himself had been eager for the fray. It had been too long since the battle at the cairns. His quarry, the bloated beast-rider calling himself Morbidex, had escaped Sigmar's justice, fleeing deeper into the swamp. Though Tegrus had pursued him, his foe had escaped. The thought of the beast-rider's gurning face still sent a pulse of anger through him. Such a creature, steeped as it was in the stuff of Chaos, could not be allowed to live, but Gardus had commanded him to leave it be, fearing, perhaps, that his Prosecutor-Prime was being led into an ambush.

In his heart, he knew the Lord-Celestant was right. Nonetheless, he was frustrated. And when the plague drones had shown up, he had seen them as an opportunity to work out some of those frustrations. So he fought, waging war in the manner to which he had become accustomed. It had taken some getting used to, in those early days after he'd been raised up to the ranks of the Stormcasts, reforged from the simple hunter he had been and made into one of Sigmar's avenging warriors. Rarely did he think of those bygone days. He knew some of his fellow Stormcasts dreamed of their old lives, or were tormented by memories they did not recognize. But for him, the past was the past; it was as banished as the daemon whose head he'd just split.

More plague drones hummed towards him, swooping and diving. Tegrus turned and gave a flap of his wings, pushing himself back towards the island. He led his pursuers low over the ranks of the Stormcasts, and the bows of the Judicators sang.

Tegrus heard a dim rumble from somewhere far below. He swooped out over the rim of the island and his eyes widened as he saw the geyser of boiling pus rising from the mire below. Alarmed, he turned, wings flapping, knowing even as he flew that he would not be able to warn the others in time. He didn't know what it was, but it was nothing good. The pus splashed against the underside of the island with a roar, causing the great mountain to quake down to its roots. It pitched to the side, like a vessel caught in the grip of a storm, and where the pus struck, it clung, a greenish vapour issuing forth in great, blistering gouts.

The island fought to stay aloft, sagging and rising, but Tegrus could see that it was doomed to fail. Whatever magic, life-force or animating spirit kept it afloat, it was still weak from the vile rains that Lord-Relictor Morbus' magic had dispatched. The jet of burning pus was eating away at its roots and hollows, carving great wounds in its belly and sides. The mountain began to shudder. Tegrus flew over the heads of Gardus and the others, shouting, 'It's coming apart. If you value your lives – hold on!'

Stormcasts leapt to obey, anchoring themselves the best they could as the shuddering grew in strength, until whole sections of the rocky slopes gave way and slid down, tumbling into the void below. Several Stormcasts were caught by the falling rocks and carried to their deaths. Others raised their shields, or called out Sigmar's name, as if by his hand they might gain the strength to survive the next few moments.

'Steady,' Gardus roared. The Lord-Celestant stabbed his sword into the ground to anchor himself, and the others did the same. Even so, dozens of Stormcasts were thrown from their perches, or ripped upwards by the force of the island's descent. Tegrus and the Prosecutors not still engaged in battle with the plague drones soared upwards, fighting the storm, trying to save any that they could. Their wings crackled as they forced themselves up against the drag of the island's passage. Their wings had been forged by Sigmar himself, each feather a scintilla of the God-King's holy lightning, and they flashed brightly as they beat. Tegrus narrowed his eyes, fighting to see through the wind and the vast contrail of foul steam spilling from the wounded island.

A glint of silver caught his eye and he bent towards it, rolling through the air. His wings tore through the cloud of steam and he saw a number of Liberators falling upwards. As Tegrus neared them, one came apart in a flash of blue light, returning to Sigmaron to be reforged. Tegrus put on speed, trying to reach the other two before they met a similar fate.

Tegrus caught one of the Liberators by the hand even as the second hurtled out of reach, disappearing into the clouds. There was a flash of blue. I'm sorry, brother, he thought as he banked and turned back towards the island. Other Prosecutors sailed upwards, continuing in their efforts. 'Hold fast, brother,' he said to the Stormcast whose wrist he held. 'I will get you down in one piece, if I'm able.'

The Liberator's reply was lost in the howl of the wind. Tegrus aimed himself towards the island, hoping that it would hold together long enough to land more or less safely. The mountain drifted lower and lower, losing pieces of itself all the while, as the acidic pus ate away at it from roots to crags. A dull groan, as of a living thing in agony, rose from it as it sank towards the shallows of the River Vitalis.

Tegrus rose upwards as the island struck the ground with a thunderous roar. Entire mobs of plague daemons were crushed beneath it as it fell, and more were similarly obliterated as the island collapsed in on itself. A tsunami of infected water surged back along the course of the river, escaping the banks and washing over the massive shape of the Great Unclean One squatting at the river's heart. Tegrus stared in horror at the monstrosity. The creature was far larger than the beast that had attacked them in the Ghyrtract Fen, as if swollen by the stolen vitality of the river. The greater daemon roared in outrage as the dust thrown up by the island's fall began to clear, and yanked a rusted flail from the water.

Pupa Grotesse forced himself to his feet with a second, rolling bellow and slashed out with the flail, smashing at the river. Turgid, brown-frothed waves smacked into the remains of the island, washing over it and clearing the dust and steam.

Tegrus dropped from the air, depositing his burden. The Liberator looked at him.

'Olanus,' he said, raising the hammer he'd somehow managed to retain in salute.

'Tegrus,' Tegrus said, returning the warrior's salute. He looked around. He saw no other Stormcasts – he couldn't even see his Prosecutors, thanks to the haze thrown up by the island's descent. Talbion crumbled behind them, dying if not already dead. Tegrus felt something that might have been sadness as he watched the mass of rock and earth split and dissolve in the flowing waters of the river. There had been something – some spirit, some soul – in it that was, while not human, still a life to be mourned.

We will not see your like again, he thought, as he turned back to face the distant shape of the Great Unclean One.

It was enormous, almost a mountain in its own right, if a mountain could walk. Where its shadow fell, the water frothed and was made foul, and its motion set the river to churning. 'That is the beast Gardus spoke of,' Olanus said.

'Aye, it is,' Tegrus replied. He said it calmly, masking the worry he felt. Perhaps the others were simply trapped – he had seen no telltale flash of azure, signalling the demise of his fellows. Either way, they were not in evidence.

Tegrus made ready to thrust himself into the air once more. If he could get above the beast, he might be able to distract it long enough for Olanus to get in close. He turned to say as much to his fellow Stormcast, when Olanus suddenly gave a grunt of pain and stumbled.

Tegrus spun, and saw a plaguebearer rising from the water behind the Liberator. Some of the daemons had survived the island's fall, after all. This one had found a gap in Olanus' armour, and it wrenched its sword free with a ghastly grin as blue light erupted from the eye and mouth slits of the dying Liberator's helm. Tegrus moved to strike the beast down, but a splash from behind alerted him to his own danger. More of the daemons burst from the foetid waters and launched themselves at him, rusty blades drawing sparks from his hammers as he interposed them. More plaguebearers rose around him, erupting from the water like aggressive flotsam.

He fought desperately, trying to hold them at bay. His wings snapped out, swift as sword-strikes, their crackling feathers burning open loathsome guts as his hammers shattered diseased blades and plague-ridden bones alike, but there were too many of them. Rotting hands caught his limbs and he was yanked off-balance. He fell onto his back in the water, frantically parrying the weapons that sought his belly and head. Plaguebearers flung themselves on him, weighing him down, scrabbling at his armour, seeking to pry open the gaps so that their fellows could finish him off. Tegrus screamed in futile rage as his forearms were pinned beneath the water and a flabby, peeling foot crashed onto his chest, holding him down.

The plaguebearer that stood on him raised its sword in two hands for a killing thrust. It leered down at him, single eye burning with malign pleasure as it considered his plight. Tegrus thrashed, but was unable to tear himself free.

Suddenly, his would-be killer's skull burst like an overripe fruit. A sword flashed, lopping off limbs and chopping through heads, and then Tegrus was free. He looked up as Gardus sheathed his sword and extended his free hand.

'Up, Tegrus... I need you in the sky, Prosecutor.'

'Gladly, Lord-Celestant. I confess, I am not at my best on the ground,' Tegrus said, as Gardus pulled him to his feet.

Gardus nodded.

'So I noticed.' He stepped back and raised his hammer. Beyond him, Tegrus saw silver-clad shapes emerge from the murk thrown up by the death-throes of the island. Grymn, Morbus and others, including Astral Templars and Guardians of the Firmament, strode through the swirling waters, weapons in hand. Gardus, hammer held over his head, shouted, 'Who will be triumphant?'

'Only the faithful,' came the reply. Tegrus added his voice to the rest, glorying in the thought of the battle to come. Gardus was with them. They had survived every horror the enemy could throw at them, and now they stood on the cusp of victory.

Pupa Grotesse roared in fury, and slammed his flail down again and again. Every time the weapon crashed down, the water erupted in flopping, splashing shapes – slug-like monstrosities, with gnashing teeth and flailing limbs, which bounded through the river towards the Stormcasts with unseemly speed. Gardus faced the oncoming horde, and drew his runeblade with his free hand.

'Who stands with me?' he called.

'Only the faithful,' Tegrus and the others responded, their voices rising into a communal roar as they clashed weapons and struck shields in a fierce display.

'Only the faithful,' Gardus shouted.

And then the enemy was upon them, and there was no more time for words.

CHAPTER TWELVE

The naming of the beast

'Forward – for Sigmar, for Ghyran, and the Celestial Realm,' Gardus called out. He crushed the skull of one of the beasts of Nurgle as it tried to flatten him beneath its weight. The great beasts had crashed into the Stormcasts' vanguard like eager children, shrugging off stab wounds and hammer blows with gurgling aplomb. They bellied and crushed their way through the ranks of the Hallowed Knights, warbling as they surged through the water. They had been joined by plaguebearers, who rose from the befouled river and launched themselves at the distracted Stormcasts. But it was the beasts of Nurgle who were the true danger here, large and tough as they were.

Only the Retributors had proven capable of felling the creatures, and with each swing of their hammers they had reduced the daemons to gobbets of wet ash. Zephacleas led the Retributors of all three Stormhosts forward, his armour dappled with gore as he fought his way to the front. Gardus' fellow

Lord-Celestant was a man of few words, but possessed an almost limitless capacity for violence, and was in his own way almost as eager for battle as the beasts he fought.

In contrast to the savagery of Zephacleas and his amethyst-armoured warriors, Ultrades and his Guardians of the Firmament were of a more stolid philosophy. They fought with a stoicism second only to that of the Hallowed Knights themselves, their circular phalanxes grinding forwards like millstones to crush the unruly mobs of daemons between them. Shields slammed forward to trap plaguebearers and yelping beasts, as Prosecutors dove down to smash them flat with all the precision of the arrows fired from the bows of the Judicators advancing behind the Liberators.

He saw a Liberator driven beneath the water by a flailing creature. Before he could reach the unfortunate warrior's side, blue light exploded upwards from the water, signalling another hero's soul sent back to Sigmar's forges. He killed the daemon as it turned towards him, and then whirled, bisecting a plaguebearer as it leapt into the air, sword raised over its head.

Too many of them, Gardus thought. Everywhere he looked, daemons leapt and capered. It was like the Ghyrtract Fen all over again, only this time, there was no realmgate to close. He looked at the Great Unclean One. It was no Bolathrax. Though such creatures bore a resemblance to one another, they were as much individuals as any Stormcast. He'd learned that much in his time in Nurgle's garden, and more besides.

It had been Bolathrax who had first spoken the name of Pupa Grotesse, as he pursued Gardus. The daemon had bellowed of the canker afflicting the Oak of Ages Past, of the champions arrayed against the Stormcasts, of the Rotfane, the Profane Tor, and the Gelid Gush, and more than that. Bolathrax had been overly loquacious, in the way of those who think words alone can break a spirit.

But Gardus' spirit was not broken. He would do what no other champion of Sigmar had been able to do and bring the God-King's words to the Radiant Queen, thus removing the mark that Nurgle's garden had left on his soul. And maybe he would silence the ghosts which yet clung to him in doing so.

Garradan... help us...

'Only the faithful,' he croaked. He could see their faces everywhere, rising from the sludge in the spray of daemonic bile. Victims of plagues long past: men, women and children he had not been able to save. Nurgle had been his enemy for longer than he had ever suspected. The ghosts crowded around him, clutching at him, begging him for aid that he could not give. Anger lent him new strength.

'Only the faithful,' he snarled, shattering a daemon blade and chopping into its wielder's chest.

A second blade glanced from his shoulderplate and he spun. Gardus bashed the plaguebearer from its feet with a swipe of his hammer. Before it could even attempt to rise, a halberd flashed, removing its head from its shoulders. Grymn tore his weapon free of the daemon's remains as it sank below the swirling waters and said, 'The big one is our true foe.'

'Agreed, Lorrus,' Gardus said. 'But there's an army between him and us.' He crossed his weapons and caught a descending plaguesword at their crux. The plaguebearer groaned and Gardus kicked it in its bulging belly, knocking it backwards. As it fell, Grymn's gryph-hound shot forward and leapt upon it, savaging it mercilessly. He ignored the daemon's squeals and turned back to Grymn. 'We'll have to carve ourselves a–'

'A path? It seems Ultrades beat us to it,' Grymn said, gesturing with his halberd. 'Look!'

Gardus did, and felt his heart stutter in his chest, as his fellow Lord-Celestant led a wedge of Stormcasts through a gap in the enemy ranks, straight towards the greater daemon. Their charge slowed as they reached the thick slop emanating from the daemon's flabby haunches, where filth and water had mingled to form a tarry barrier. Ultrades tore his men a path and a phalanx of Liberators lurched forward, shields raised.

Pupa Grotesse glared down at the interlopers and bellowed in rage. A boulder-like fist descended from on high and Stormcasts were crushed, their bloody forms swiftly discorporating. The massive flail whirled and whole retinues were hurled back like broken dolls. Only Ultrades and his Decimators made it past these obstacles, but their blows rebounded harmlessly from the Great Unclean One's elephantine hide. Pupa Grotesse roared in fury and swiped out one long arm to send shattered bodies flying. Many vanished in explosions of blue light, while others sank without a trace in the noxious waters.

Ultrades himself was nearly felled, driven to one knee in the water by a blow from Pupa Grotesse's flail. He strained against the weight of the weapon, even as he was driven deeper and deeper into the filthy waters. Ultrades was strong – all Stormcasts were – but even he was no match for such a creature. Nonetheless, he was keeping the beast occupied, which meant they had a chance, however slim. We have to move quickly, Gardus thought, and looked at Grymn. 'Hold here, rally our brothers, keep them away from that beast.' He turned. 'Morbus – to me!'

A burst of lightning danced across the water, frying a plague-beast in mid-bound. Lord-Relictor Morbus stepped through the swirling cloud of ashes.

'I am here, Lord-Celestant. Proceed, and I shall follow,' he rasped. Gardus nodded sharply, and began to bludgeon his way towards the greater daemon.

He lashed out with sword and hammer as he moved. Both weapons crackled with white fire as he slew plaguebearer and beast of Nurgle alike when they dared interpose themselves. Morbus followed close behind, lightning snarling from his reliquary to streak across the waters towards their foe. The crackling bolt slammed home, and the Great Unclean One reeled with an agonized roar. Smoke boiled from his gaping pores as he stretched out his long arm towards Morbus, who drew the beast's attention away from his Lord-Celestant with a second bolt of lightning, as accurately aimed as the first. Sigmar bless you, Morbus – as ever, you know what I require before I ask, Gardus thought, as he charged beneath the sweep of the daemon's flail. The daemon turned away from Ultrades, who sank back into the water, exhausted.

Morbus lashed out with his hammer, shattering one of the creature's fingers. Pupa Grotesse roared out unintelligible curses and, ignoring his wounded digit, plucked Morbus from the water. He raised the struggling Lord-Relictor up and examined him, as Morbus struggled futilely in his grip. He said something in a rumbling, glottal voice that was too deep to be understood by human ears, and lifted Morbus higher. The Great Unclean One's grotesque jaw distended, gaping wider than seemed entirely possible, even for such a massive being.

Gardus put on a burst of speed and ran up a stump of rotten driftwood. As he moved, he summoned a word from the pits of his memory – no, not a word, rather, *a name*. A name spoken by Bolathrax, in his heedless gloating. The true name of the being that called itself Pupa Grotesse – and to a daemon, its true name might as well be a blade aimed at its black heart. Gardus leapt, sword raised, and screamed the name, spitting the deranged syllables as if they were bolts from a crossbow. The name quavered on the stinking air, and the Great Unclean One turned, eyes wide, Morbus all but forgotten.

Gardus brought his sword down, chopping through the daemon's thick wrist, freeing the Lord-Relictor in a geyser of foulness. The daemon shrieked and reeled, clutching at his wounded limb. Stormcast and daemon-hand crashed into the water, and Morbus swiftly bulled his way free of the spasmodically twitching hand.

'Morbus – now!' Gardus cried as he landed.

Morbus rose, reliquary in both hands, and began to chant. He called out to the tempest, and the tempest answered. Crackling bolts split the skies, swathing Grotesse in sacred lightning. Gardus watched as bolt after bolt struck the staggering monstrosity, even as the daemons around him turned away, eyes seared by the light of Sigmar's wrath. Pupa Grotesse's flesh began to smoulder and turn black. Steaming cracks appeared in his body, and the daemon abruptly stiffened, mouth wide in a scream that never came.

There was a deafening bang, and the daemon exploded like a sack of rotting offal left too long in the hot sun. The effect was immediate. The filth and sludge that marked the waters began to clear, turning to ash and crumbling away beneath newly crystalline waters. The clean waters ate at the remaining daemons like acid, dissolving them even as they fought, or tried to flee.

Gardus dipped his hand into the waters as they surged around him, and felt his weaknesses and hurts fade away.

'It is like the rivers of home,' Ultrades said in wonder, as Morbus helped him to his feet. He looked at Gardus. 'Did you know that this would happen?'

'I had hoped,' Gardus said. He watched as the last of the daemons were dispatched, and turned, staring out over the river. In the sound of its waters, he thought he could hear a woman's voice, singing an unfamiliar song. Hesitantly, he placed his palms over the water, trying to feel something, anything that might tell him that he wasn't simply hearing things. As he peered down, he thought he could see something in the reflection on the water. He looked up as a shadow passed over it. 'Tegrus, can you see anything?' he called out as the Prosecutor-Prime swooped overhead.

'Aye, though it might simply be a trick of the light,' Tegrus called down, as he circled around. 'There is an emerald light, where the river's bed should be.'

Gardus looked at Morbus. 'Morbus, do you–'

'He feels it,' Grymn said, splashing towards them, accompanied by his gryph-hound and Zephacleas. 'We all do, Gardus. Every one of us.'

The Lord-Castellant looked at him warily. 'What is it? Who is she? Who is singing?'

Gardus shook his head. 'You know as well as I, Lorrus. She

117

is the one we have come to find.' He motioned to the vast shape of the Oak of Ages Past, and the clear, shining waters that now spilled from the cleft in its trunk. 'There is a reason the enemy had no more luck finding her than we did. She was hiding beneath their very noses, in a place they thought already conquered. She is here,' he said, voice rising. 'The gate to Athelwyrd is here. We have found the Hidden Vale.'

CHAPTER THIRTEEN

Nurgle's deluge

Torglug shook his head, trying to clear the flies from his ears, as the skaven grey seer chattered obsequiously up at the Glott-kin. The creature had summoned them to the banks of the Gelid Gush. At Torglug's suggestion, the ratkin had been placed on the invaders' trail, and had pursued the enemy across Rotwater Blight. Their skulking spies had scurried in the wake of every battle, keeping track of the foe's movements. And now, at last, it seemed the time had come to run their quarry to ground. 'Storm-things pass into the river,' the grey seer chittered, gesticulating towards the water. 'The water… it is the portal!'

As it spoke, there came a sound like a hundred rats gnawing a hundred stones, and the verminlord Vermalanx dropped into reality. The rat-daemon shrieked at his charge, snapping long fangs in obvious agitation. The grey seer shied away from this display, and Torglug wondered what contest was being waged between master and servant. The rats aped men in that way more than any other, always seeking the advantage even over their own kind. The rat-daemon was clearly enraged, and Torglug suspected that the grey seer had been ordered to report the whereabouts of Athelwyrd to Vermalanx first.

Whatever the reason for it, the verminlord's anger was like the sweetest bile to Torglug, and he extended his axe between the rat-daemon and his servant.

'You are ceasing this unseemly display, vermin,' he rasped. 'We are being allies in this endeavour, and we will be needing every one of us to take the Hidden Vale and its mistress.'

'If this treacherous rat isn't simply lying,' Vermalanx hissed, glaring at the cowering grey seer. 'If this place is indeed beneath the river.'

'It would make a certain sense,' Otto Glott said, twirling his scythe. Idly he swatted at the flies that clustered about the crusted wounds in his belly. 'Why else would they come here, into the very heart of Grandfather's blight?' He looked at Torglug and inclined his head. 'A good plan, this, letting the rats skulk and spy.'

'I am pleased you are satisfied, Master Glott,' Torglug rumbled. He shook his head and looked at the now-pristine river, sparkling in the setting sun. 'It is under us the whole time,' he murmured, leaning on his axe. 'We are running around, and here it is. How she must be laughing.' He looked aside, at the portly shape of the sorcerer, Slaugoth, who stood nearby, wrapped in his ragged cloak, leaning on his boil-covered staff. 'Why did we not look here, jolly one? Why was it the rats who are finding it first?'

'We assumed nothing would survive in such close proximity

to Pupa Grotesse, that's why,' Gutrot Spume interjected before the sorcerer could reply, his tentacles coiling and clenching about the haft of his axe. The champion stood on the other side of Slaugoth, glaring at the river as if it had offended him. 'More fool us, I'd say.'

'Quiet,' Torglug snapped, irritated by Spume's presence. The other champion had grown increasingly infuriating since the fall of Profane Tor. Spume seemed to regard the continued assaults of the lightning-men as a personal affront, rather than as the danger it truly was. But Torglug knew better... The Stormcasts were anything but weak to get as far as they had. They had humbled Spume, Slaugoth and the maggoth lords alike, and crushed every obstacle that the Grandfather had placed in their path. Normal men they were not.

There were vast things afoot, in the spaces between moments. Torglug could feel them, deep in his blighted marrow. The Grandfather stirred uneasily on his throne, and the world shuddered, as if slowly coming awake after a long sleep. He looked up at the sky, peering at the greenish clouds, wondering what force lurked above, watching. What power had sent them, these Stormcasts? And why now? He looked at the Glotts, considering.

They were not worthy, those three. Ghurk, perhaps, but Otto and Ethrac were fools, and lazy ones at that. Industry was a dirty word to them. They knew nothing of effort, and their only loyalty was to one another. It was not they who had poisoned the lifewells, or conquered the tribes of the Ghyranic highlands. It was not the Glotts who had tamed the ogors of the Graven Peaks or decimated the sacred groves of Thyrr. Yet they reaped the Grandfather's rewards while better men were left to sit and simmer, forgotten. Torglug's grip on his axe tightened, and he wondered what might happen in the hours to come.

'Deep in thought, Woodsman,' Slaugoth murmured, startling him. The sorcerer peered at him, yellow eyes narrowed in speculation, as if he could read Torglug's thoughts. 'What are you thinking, Despised One?'

'Nothing of import,' Torglug said.

'They say that you were once a man of this realm, Ironhood,' Slaugoth pressed. 'I myself come from more distant climes, though I find the air here quite congenial.' He smiled widely. 'They say that the Grandfather himself tutored you in the ways of pox and plague while you rotted in a pit. It must have been something to see, especially for a barbarian from the wilds of Ghyran,' the sorcerer said slyly.

'The Grandfather is blessing me,' Torglug said. He looked at Slaugoth. 'Why are you asking?' He leaned closer to the sorcerer. 'Are you thinking Torglug is worried?'

'Not worried. Plotting, perhaps, as we all are, in our own ways,' Slaugoth said. He smiled, as if amused. 'We all had our designs on the glory to be had from this moment, all save that fat fool, Morbidex. We all wished to stand here alone, beneath Grandfather's benign gaze, to claim the maggoth's share of the credit. And instead...'

'The Glotts,' Spume growled. 'The Brothers Three.' He shook his head, and the kraken mouth in his side snapped angrily. 'Sneaks and rogues, so they are. No better than the skaven.' Spume grunted and looked at Torglug. 'We're for it now, Woodsman. We're under their maggoty thumbs and I'll be barnacled if they don't claim this was all part of some blasted plan.'

'Grandfather will be knowing the truth,' Torglug said confidently. He lifted his axe and held it parallel to the ground. 'Now what are we to do?' he called out, to the Glotts.

'Simplicity itself, Woodsman,' Otto said, planting his scythe. 'We go for a swim.' He looked at his brother, Ethrac. 'Ethrac, oh second-favoured sibling. That river is too pure by half. Summon Grandfather's Deluge so we can flood this place for good.'

'A meritorious idea, brother from my mother's womb,' Ethrac said. 'Gates can be forced open as well as unlocked. Slaugoth! Attend me, O portly one.' Ethrac snapped his fingers at Slaugoth, whose head bobbed in agreement.

'Commendable thought, Master Glott. I most heartily agree,' the sorcerer murmured, scratching his chins. 'We could fill that entire vale with noisome fluid, and thus claim it forever in the name of Grandfather's infinite putrescence.' He made a pudgy fist. 'Serve those silver-skinned pests right for the drubbing they gave me. They tore down my sludge-walled keep without so much as a by your leave, and washed away my lovely, filthy rains with their god-blasted tempest. Aye, let us wake the Deluge, and drown 'em all.'

'More than that, I think,' Ethrac said. 'Oh, we'll flood it good, but we'll take its mistress captive, and haul her in chains of fungus and mouldy bone to Grandfather. The Radiant Queen has hidden from us for far too long, my friends… She will hide no longer. Tonight, Alarielle is ours, and she will be in a cage in the Grandfather's garden, and Ghyran ours, by the first rays of morning.' He clapped his hands together in satisfaction.

'Oh yes, yes, yes and yes again,' Otto roared. 'Ha! Yes, that'll do – Ghurk, give the signal. Loud as you like, my lad. Call 'em all, every drone and nurgling, every maggoth and beast. Bring them all here, double-quick. We're going in.'

Torglug winced as Ghurk rose to his full height and threw back his misshapen head to unleash a deafening howl. The grey seer cowered, hairy hand-paws pressed over its ears. Spume stuffed tentacles in his rotted ear canals. Slaugoth hunkered down and turned away, body clenched against the sound. The howl stretched up and out, riding the breeze across the vast wilderness of Rotwater Blight.

And in the middle distance, as the echoes of the howl faded, war horns answered Ghurk's call by the score.

CHAPTER FOURTEEN

Secrets of Athelwyrd

Grymn pushed himself to his feet with his halberd, Tallon by his side, chirruping nervously. They were atop a lichen-clad slope of rock. Above their heads stretched the undulating shape of the River Vitalis, strange glimmerings of light playing across its underside. Other Stormcasts were rising to their feet around him, shaking off the effects of the transition to this hidden bower.

'Beautiful, isn't it?' Gardus said, sitting nearby, his hammer across his knees. He was gazing out over the slope, across the vale which stretched out beneath them as far as the eye could see. It was breathtaking, Grymn had to admit. Alarielle's Hidden Vale was so large that it had its own mountain ranges, stretching off into cloudy distances. Each of these was draped in evergreen forests and hung with glittering waterfalls so pure that they hurt the eye to even look upon them. 'All of Ghyran, I am told, once looked as this does,' Gardus continued, softly. He extended a hand. 'See how the trees glow, Lorrus... have you ever seen the like? They are as bright as the stars themselves.'

Grymn said nothing. Instead, he noted the arboreal citadels that sprouted from the entwined trunks of those distant trees, and silently calculated their size. They must be massive. But who resides there? The thought was not a pleasant one. He was not beguiled by the gossamer floating through the warm air, or the brightly hued fan-tail birds that swooped above through the coloured mist. If this was a paradise, it was not one meant for men. He turned and saw that the closest Stormcasts were, like Gardus, enraptured by the strange beauty spread out before them.

He slammed the butt of his halberd down on the rock, once, twice, three times. Every eye turned towards him. 'On your feet,' he growled. 'Did we come all this way to look at the flowers then? Did we fight our way through forest and swamp so you could gaze at the greenery? Up, up! Up, or I'll have Tallon on you – up,' he roared. 'We still have a queen to find, or did you forget? Up I say.' He turned towards Gardus. 'And you as well, Steel Soul. Up, Lord-Celestant. There is an example to be set,' he said, as he reached out a hand and hauled Gardus to his feet.

'I see something,' Tegrus shouted from above. The Prosecutor-Prime swooped low over them, in a wide circle. 'I see a grove, down the slope... lined with standing stones of some kind. Not like those we saw in the Ghyrtract Fen.'

Gardus looked in the direction that Tegrus indicated, and then said, 'Lead on, O Sainted Eye. That is as good a place as any to meet our hosts, if they are willing.'

Grymn formed the Steel Souls into a marching column. He left the others to their respective Lord-Celestants. Zephacleas' warriors split into bands and ranged out alongside the column of marching Stormcasts, warily watching the trees that covered the lower part of the slope, while Ultrades' retinues followed the Hallowed Knights. Above them, Tegrus and the other Prosecutors drifted lazily through the air, keen eyes seeking any sign of danger.

The Stormhosts wound down the slope and through the trees that separated them from the grove Tegrus had seen. Gardus led the way, Grymn and Morbus close behind. Grymn felt eyes on them the entire way, and every bird, insect and beast fell silent at their approach. The Stormcasts began to grow uneasy, and more than once Grymn was forced to fall out of line and berate a warrior for hesitating in the face of the vast silence that had enveloped them. After the fifth such incident, as he rejoined Gardus and the Lord-Relictor, he said, 'This place… It's waiting for something.'

'It is not a place,' Morbus intoned. 'Not truly. It is Alarielle's will made manifest, and we are intruders here. She is drawing back from our approach like a frightened beast.'

'It is not us she fears,' Gardus said. He stared straight ahead as he moved, as if all of his attentions were fixed on a point beyond the sight of those who travelled with him. Grymn shivered softly, for as Gardus spoke, the trees seemed to rustle in agreement. 'Alarielle is not simply queen of the Realm of Life. She is life itself, inextricable and inseparable. Nurgle's advances upon her realm have wounded her most grievously, in mind and soul.' He shook his head. 'Or so the sylvaneth whispered to me, as they bore me from the Glade of Horned

Growths. Since the Dark Gods invaded this realm, she has become withdrawn and cold, even from her most loyal servants.'

'Has she sealed herself away here, while her realm crumbles in anarchy and destruction?' Grymn asked, incredulous.

'Did Sigmar not seal the Gates of Azyr?' Gardus said softly. 'The Mortal Realms burned, as Azyr prospered. We were each of us plucked from places where we might have done good, might have helped those who counted on us, to be reforged on Sigmar's anvil.' He met Grymn's disbelieving gaze and continued, 'I learned more than true names and hiding places while in Nurgle's garden, Lorrus. The Ruinous Powers weave lies with truth.' He looked away, and half-raised his hand, as if to clutch at his head. He looked up, abruptly, and said, 'We are here.'

Grymn saw the grove. It was lined with spiral-etched menhirs, and sunlight marked its centre. Gardus stared at it, as if uncertain of what to do next. Grymn looked at him. 'What is it?'

Gardus didn't meet his gaze. 'Something is wrong,' he said.

Grymn looked at Morbus, who shook his head. 'Well, if it is a trap, one of us had best spring it so that we might move on,' Grymn said. He started forward, lantern raised and halberd over his shoulder.

Tallon made to follow him, but he shooed the gryph-hound back. 'No, my friend,' he said. 'Stay – guard.' He indicated Gardus. Tallon whined softly, but did as the Lord-Castellant bade.

Grymn looked at Gardus. 'Not going to stop me?'

'Could I?' Gardus said.

Grymn laughed. 'Sigmar made you the sword and me the

shield – and it is the shield's task to ward blows,' he said and turned back to the glade. Without hesitation, he stepped between two menhirs. He strode towards the centre of the glade. When he reached it, he turned in a slow circle, peering at the marks on the stones. 'Warriors of the sylvaneth,' he called, 'we are here.'

A soft slithering sound filled the air. He froze, listening. A heartbeat later a thicket of iron-thorns shot up from the soft earth to ensnare him, tearing armour and flesh alike. Grymn bellowed in pain as he was hurled to the ground in a bloody heap.

Outside of the ring of stones, sylvaneth dryads burst from the trees with eerie shrieks to fall upon the Stormcast Eternals. Warriors died in blazes of blue light, and Grymn cursed as he tried to pull himself to his feet. A talon of bark and thorn tore through his midsection, and he found himself wrenched into the air. He clutched at the talon with blood-slick fingers, fighting to free himself despite the agony. He turned his head, and saw a lithe figure of vines and wood untwine itself from about the trunk of an elder oak. With a hiss, the creature tore its hand free of him, and let him fall to the ground. It stepped towards him, as he tried to crawl reach for his fallen halberd. He heard Tallon screeching in rage, and men screaming.

Through blurring vision, he saw Gardus racing towards him, and heard the Lord-Celestant shouting. He saw the creature that had stabbed him unleash strangling vines upon Tegrus and his Prosecutors as they swooped to the attack. Pain thrummed through him, and his limbs felt like lead. His hand flopped to the blood-soaked soil, a mere fingerbreadth from his halberd. He fought to reach out, to grab it, to no avail.

A trap, he thought blearily.

And then Lorrus Grymn knew no more.

CHAPTER FIFTEEN

The coming of the Glottkin

'Shields!' Gardus roared. 'Use your shields. No blades. These are not our enemies.' He charged towards the creature that had wounded Grymn, bulling aside the shrieking dryads that tried to intercept him. Grymn's gryph-hound loped at his side. Why is this happening? he thought. The being crouched over Grymn was the Lady of Vines. He recognized the branch-wraith from the Glade of Horned Growths; it was she who had saved him from his wounds, and whispered answers to his questions. It was she who had seen to his return to his Stormhost.

'Why are you doing this?' he called out.

Behind him, he heard the sound of his Stormcasts striving to defend themselves from the sylvaneth pouring out of the forest on all sides. As the men died and the sky was filled with blue light, he bolted into the ring of menhirs.

The branchwraith shrieked and lashed out at Tegrus and his

Prosecutors as they dived at her, trying to draw her away from the limp form of the Lord-Castellant. As Gardus drew close, she spun and lashed out at him with a thorny tendril. Tallon leapt, catching hold of the vine in his beak before it could reach Gardus. The gryph-hound held on, even as the branch-wraith swung him through the air, trying to dislodge him.

Gardus caught another vine as it slashed at him, and wrapped it around his forearm. 'Lady, heed me,' he cried, trying to catch the creature's attention. 'Why are you doing this? How have we offended you? Why has it come to this?'

The creature's blazing green eyes met his, and the Lady of Vines stretched out a gnarled hand and pointed, trembling with rage, towards the other side of the vale. Gardus turned, his heart sinking, as he heard the blare of grotesque horns and the thud of war drums. 'No,' he whispered. 'Oh no...'

Pouring down the opposite valley wall was a wave of feculent fluid, and knee-deep in it were horde upon horde of Chaos worshippers, of every size and description. It was as if every follower of Nurgle in Ghyran had come to this place in answer to some powerful call – there were goat-headed beast-men, scurrying skaven and fat-bellied daemons, and at their head a lumpen giant, upon whose shoulders sat two gesticulating champions of the plague god. As Gardus watched in growing horror, the vanguard of the plague-legion smashed headlong into the dryads spilling from the trees.

'We led them here,' Gardus said hollowly. It was the only way the lost and the damned could have found their way to this place. He turned back to the Lady of Vines, but no words came to his lips as he looked up into the grief-twisted features of the branchwraith.

'Yes, son of Azyr.'

Gardus turned as all about the menhir glade the trees shook down to their roots. As one, the dryads sank to their knees and the air grew still and heavy. Every loose leaf, twig, and branch in the glade was caught up in a whirlwind that carried them towards the trees and as they moved, Gardus thought he saw a shape coalescing within them. Not human, not quite, but something else… something older, and at once as vast as the Hidden Vale and as small as the flowers that sprouted in its wake. As the whirlwind struck them and dissipated, the trees twisted towards one another, entwining their branches together, weaving twig and leaf to form a female face – a face Gardus recognized, though he had never seen it before, save in murals and bas-reliefs.

'Alarielle,' he whispered.

Burning jade eyes met his own, and a voice as powerful as a summer storm, as piercing as the whisper of a thousand winds, spoke.

'You have led the enemy to my sanctuary, Gardus of Azyr. Whatever your reasons, I have awakened from my dreams of more pleasant times. Athelwyrd is invaded. This day the armies of Azyr and Ghyran must fight together, or we will surely die apart,' the Radiant Queen said, her words carried by creaking branches and rustling leaves. 'Whatever I once desired, now only sad necessity remains – fight, my children. Fight, sons of the storm. *Fight…*'

Her voice rose to a keening wail, shaking the menhirs and causing Gardus to clutch at his ears. As the trees returned to their previous positions and the echoes of her voice faded, a wash of emerald light flooded the glade.

Grymn groaned as the Lady of Vines stepped back. Gardus looked down and saw, to his amazement, that the other man's wounds had been healed. Grymn looked up at him.

'I'm not dead,' he said, as he grabbed his halberd and levered himself up. The Lady of Vines strode past them, stalking towards the battle, her thorny tendrils lashing in fury.

'Not yet,' Gardus said. 'But the day is not yet done.' He gestured to the Nurgle army. More had arrived in the moments since Alarielle's words. As the deluge of filth spilled into the Hidden Vale, the dire fug that followed the plague-worshippers swept along the valley floor, corrupting vast swathes of lush vegetation. Pox-afflicted skaven scurried through the dying undergrowth, the smoking censers they whirled above their cowled heads only adding to the foulness in the air. When dryads moved to bar their path, they were smashed to smoking flinders.

As he and Grymn headed to join their men, Gardus heard Morbus chanting. The Lord-Relictor's voice rose up, and the cloudscape of Athelwyrd seemed to respond as he invoked the energies of the tempest. The gathering storm fought against the noxious plague-clouds, and each ebbed and swelled in turn. The boom of thunder echoed down the valley, shaking the combatants to their bones and causing the great trees that covered the slopes to tremble down to their very roots.

'Gather as many men as you can. Form a shieldwall around the glade,' Gardus said, as he backhanded a squealing skaven with his hammer. 'You must be the rock that this foul sea cannot wear down.'

'What about you?' Grymn said, chopping down on a plague-bearer. He spun his weapon in a circle, cutting down a second daemon.

'I intend to take the battle to the enemy,' Gardus said. He drove his sword through a snarling beastman's gut. More of the goat-headed creatures charged towards him as the sickly rainclouds overhead thickened and fat, black raindrops began to fall. Gardus swung his hammer in a wide arc, splintering bones and crushing skulls. He heard Grymn bellowing orders behind him, and he smiled grimly. Stand fast, my friend. Be the shield, and I shall be the sword. He moved forward at a trot, dispatching any creature that sought to bar his path.

Across the vale, warriors clashed. Wooden-clawed dryads slaughtered skaven and beastmen alike as looming treelords strode into battle with earthshaking strides. Hallowed Knights, Astral Templars and Guardians of the Firmament fought back to back against the innumerable hordes surrounding them. Gardus smashed the skull of a plaguebearer and caught sight of Zephacleas standing over the body of a fallen treelord, defending the sylvaneth against its attackers. He saw Ultrades and his paladins fighting their way towards Morbus, who drew lightning down from the boiling skies and sent it crackling into the massed ranks of plaguebearers which stumbled towards him.

'Only the faithful,' Gardus shouted, forcing his voice to carry over the clangour of battle. His men responded in kind, and Gardus fought all the harder. He would not fail. 'Only the faithful,' he cried again, crushing cyclopean heads with every swing of his hammer. White flames crackled across his weapons and armour as he stormed through the bloody melee, gathering his warriors about him. 'Fight, brothers! Fight in Sigmar's name! Fight–'

'*Gardus*,' a horribly familiar voice thundered, interrupting him. He whirled, smashing aside an armoured warrior. No, he thought, filled with a sudden loathing.

'Gardus,' the voice called again, and Gardus looked up as something immense rolled down into the valley like a giant boulder, scattering daemons and Stormcasts alike as it hurtled across the field through the driving rain. When it stopped, the shape rose to its full, towering height, a flail made from the skulls of giants whirling about its antlered head.

'I know you are here. Did you think you could escape Bolathrax?' the greater daemon roared, smashing Stormcasts aside. 'Where are you, Gardus? Where are you, Garradan? Face me, unless you plan to flee again.' Bolathrax paused, eyes widening as he caught sight of Gardus. 'Ah, there you are,' he burbled and started towards the Lord-Celestant, flail whirling and plaguesword drawn.

Gardus stared at the Great Unclean One. He snapped out of it a moment before the greater daemon struck the ground perilously close to him. He was knocked sprawling by the impact. Gardus rolled aside as the weapon slammed down again. 'Stop squirming,' Bolathrax gurgled as he waddled in pursuit. 'You led the Grandfather's legions here, and I'm obliged to make your death quick.'

Gardus flung himself aside. He crashed into a fallen oak, and hauled himself over it. Between the rain and the confusion of battle, the daemon lost sight of him, and he had a moment to catch his breath. Quickly he took stock of the battle. He saw with some relief that Grymn had managed to organize a shieldwall, and that Morbus and the others were fighting their way towards it.

Hold fast, brothers, he thought. We might still be able to preserve this place…

Bolathrax's flail crashed down, shattering the oak. The force of the blow sent Gardus sliding through the muck.

'Found you,' Bolathrax roared gleefully.

Gardus rolled to his feet, and lunged. Hammer and blade both found their mark and bounced off the daemon's rubbery flesh. Bolathrax laughed and thrust his blade down. The Stormcast stepped aside, and the great sword slammed into the muck. He spun, set his foot onto the flat of the rusty sword and ran up its length. Bolathrax gaped as the Lord-Celestant leapt towards him. The daemon jerked his head back, but too late, and Gardus' sword pierced the creature's bulging eye.

Bolathrax shrieked and swiped his flail about his head blindly. Gardus was caught by the pox-hardened skulls and sent flying. He smashed into a standing stone and flopped into the muck, weapons lost, body a mass of pain. As he tried to push himself up, one of Bolathrax's splayed feet came down on his back. Gardus cried out, as his spine cracked and a tidal wave of agony washed through him. The skull flail came down a moment later, and one of his legs was reduced to a red ruin, pulverised by the blow.

'No more running, Garradan,' Bolathrax grunted, as he looked down at Gardus. 'Pain is but a door to experience, as the Grandfather says. It does wonders for the soul. Just ask Torglug the Despised. We made a man of him. I wonder what we shall make of you, when you have suffered enough, eh?' The Great Unclean One reached down and snatched Gardus up by his remaining ankle. Gardus couldn't breathe. He clutched weakly at the air, reaching for weapons that were not there.

The ghosts had gathered beneath him, and were staring up with mournful gazes. They did not speak, but they did not need to. Gardus coughed, and felt his shattered ribs dig into the soft places within him.

'I shall put you somewhere safe, until you are ready to be reborn,' Bolathrax chortled, as he reached down and lifted his belly folds wide, exposing the swirling vortex within him. 'What do you say to that, eh?'

Gardus stared at the vortex – a black maw of horror, as deep and as dark as the spaces between the stars. His mouth was dry, but he forced the words out regardless.

'Only the faithful,' he croaked. Bolathrax began to laugh.

Gardus closed his eyes.

CHAPTER SIXTEEN

The Sainted Eye

Tegrus hurtled through the smog-choked air, his hammers catching a bullgor across the skull with a thunderous crack. The beastman toppled over as Tegrus swooped past on wings of light. He rolled through the air, aiming himself towards the beastmen skidding down the scree of the valley wall. The creatures were charging towards the forest of glowing trees from which the arboreal citadels rose, axes raised.

'Lord-Castellant,' he cried, searching for Grymn. 'We must…' He trailed off as he saw the shieldwall of the Hallowed Knights momentarily buckle beneath the weight of the enemy, before it stiffened once more. He saw the Lord-Castellant amidst his brethren, exhorting them to greater effort as plaguebearers swarmed them. There would be no help from that quarter. Up to me, then, he thought.

Tegrus folded his arms to his sides and sped across the valley, leaving dust and deafened foes in his wake. His retinue of Prosecutors followed, though none were able to match his speed. But even he was too slow. Sap sprayed like blood as the bestigors and bullgors hacked away at the ancient forest. Tegrus dropped into their midst a moment later, crushing a bestigor's head as he landed. He whirled, catching another in its mouth, silencing it mid-roar.

He saw one of his Prosecutors pulled from the air by a bullgor and broken over the monster's knee. Another was brought low by a bestigor axe, and hacked to pieces as he writhed in the muck.

'No!' Tegrus snarled, as he brought his hammers down on another beastman, smashing the squalling creature to the ground. He saw a horde of skaven clad in rotting robes scuttling between the legs of the larger beastmen. They too began to hack and slash at the ancient trees.

'Keep them back,' he cried, before he realised that he was alone. The last of his warriors had fallen, throttled by a bullgor. The creature joined the Stormcast it had killed a moment later as Tegrus sent his hammer ploughing into its bestial skull.

More and more of the creatures pelted past him, heading for the trees. It was like trying to fight the tide. For every one he killed, it seemed two more slipped through. As he drove his hammer into the gut of a bestigor, crushing the creature's ribs, he heard an ethereal screech. It sawed through his skull, causing his teeth to twitch in his jaw and his head to ache. All around him, beastmen stumbled, clutching at their heads. Whatever he'd felt, they had felt it worse. He reacted swiftly, lashing out with his hammers, shattering kneecaps and spines. He flung himself into the air as a light grew amidst the carnage. Beastmen staggered away as the light blossomed into the shape of a woman. No, Tegrus realised; not a woman.

Alarielle, the Radiant Queen herself had at last joined the battle. She was a thing of light and mist, of leaves and splintered wood, her shape at once that of a woman and something greater and more terrible. She was air and water, fire and earth. She was the summer rain, and the rage of the hurricane. And she was angry.

A bullgor rushed towards her, bellowing, and a hand, limned in emerald light, snapped out to catch the creature by its throat. Alarielle lifted the beastman and snapped its neck with merciless ease, cowing the enemy around her. Skaven and bestigor alike began to edge away, their terror of the Radiant Queen obvious. She dropped the twitching body of the bullgor to the ground, where it immediately began to convulse. Green buds burst from the corpse, twisting up towards Alarielle's hand. She threaded her fingers through the coiling shoots and came away with a handful of glittering seeds.

Without a word, she took the seeds in her hands and cast them away. In a single heartbeat, a hundred new green shoots burst from the ground. As they rose, they swelled and thickened, growing swiftly, becoming massive. The great bulbs on the end of each split with a sound like water slapping metal to reveal a cavernous maw. As one, the great plants snapped up their prey – skaven and beastman alike – and broke their bones to powder.

As he swooped past the twisting plants, Tegrus saw a strange shape lope suddenly from the depths of the smog that clung to the ground. A verminlord. The monstrous rat-daemon plucked a shrieking grey seer from the ground as it sprinted through the ranks of the ratmen. Tegrus flew after it, hoping that he would be in time to prevent whatever malign scheme the daemon had in mind. Whatever else happened, he would not allow the Radiant Queen to come to harm.

The verminlord sprang from the fallen body of a bullgor to one of the half-toppled trees, and dropped the grey seer to the ground beneath it. It hissed and snarled at the cowering skaven in the language of their vile kind and pointed one of its cruel blades towards the oblivious Radiant Queen as she tore a herd of bullgor to shreds with crackling magics. The grey seer pushed itself upright and hesitantly extended a shaking paw towards Alarielle. The air around it pulsed wetly, and a terrible light flickered in its eyes as it began a stuttering incantation.

Tegrus sped forward, faster than he'd ever flown. His wings blazed with all the fury of the storm, and his body ached with the force of his dive. Sigmar guide my flight, he thought as he plummeted towards the grey seer.

The creature's fur stood on end, and its eyes glowed green as its outstretched claw started to tremble violently. Black smoke rose from the skaven's pores as if it were being consumed by whatever energies it was summoning forth. Tegrus twisted through the air as a beam of unclean light shot from the skaven's claw towards the Radiant Queen.

'Only the faithful,' Tegrus murmured, and swooped into the path of the beam, hammers crossed. The energies tore at him as they splashed across his armour, causing the god-forged sigmarite to bubble and melt. The light from his wings grew brighter and brighter as he plunged on through the beam. His hammers blackened and began to crumble in his hands, but he did not stop, or veer away. It was too late for that now. It was too late for anything except taking his foe down into death with him.

Tegrus screamed as he streaked towards the grey seer. He could feel his body warping and changing within his armour. Bones cracked and reshaped themselves into new and horrible forms as his flesh burned. But still he hurtled on and even as his hammers dissolved into nothing, he struck the grey seer full on.

The rat-thing exploded into swirling ash and streamers of green fire, its final, forlorn squeal cut short by the impact. Tegrus hit the ground a moment later, wreathed in smoke, his body contorted in agony as it continued its forced metamorphosis. His wings flickered and grew dull as new flesh squeezed out between the seams of his ruptured armour. Feathers of lightning were replaced by useless pinions of leather and bone, which flapped limply. His body shuddered as his spine split and grew, and his lungs shrank in his chest, forcing him to fight for every breath. His newly shaped bones had been shattered by his landing, and he could only thrash in pain as something monstrous approached him, tail lashing in anger.

'Fool-fool,' the monstrous verminlord hissed, glaring down at him. 'You dare pit yourself against the will of Vermalanx, man-thing?' The creature raised one of the heavy, curved blades it carried. Before it could strike, however, a tendril of emerald energy struck it full in the chest. The rat-daemon reared back and screeched in pain. A moment later it was plucked into the air. Through pain-dimmed eyes, Tegrus saw Alarielle stride forward, cloaked in ash and feathers, her inhuman visage sorrowful.

'Who is the fool here, little mouse?' Alarielle said, her voice causing the air to throb. The verminlord howled as it fought to break free of her magics, but to no avail. Alarielle reached up and flicked a silver acorn into the rat-daemon's slavering maw. Instantly, green shoots burst through the creature's form in great profusion. The daemon screamed in agony as the shoots flourished into branches and then boughs, before it was ripped apart in a stink of sulphurous musk. Tegrus coughed and tried to speak, but only managed a strangled screech. He reached up to her, with a hand that was more claw than anything else, and she nodded in understanding.

'Be at peace,' the Radiant Queen said, as her aura became blinding. 'Sleep now, and forevermore, son of Sigmar.' The light grew until it enveloped Tegrus, and he felt a moment of pain and then...

Nothing.

CHAPTER SEVENTEEN

The drowning of the vale

'No,' Grymn snarled, as he watched the Great Unclean One pluck Gardus from the mud. 'No, not again.' He glanced at Morbus, and the Lord-Relictor looked away. Lightning snarled from his reliquary over and over, hammering into the daemons that pressed them. This is what you saw, Grymn realised. They had been wrong, before. This, then, had been Gardus' doom, and they might as well have escorted him to it.

He turned back to Gardus, and saw the greater daemon pry open its belly to reveal a nightmare maw within its flesh. The creature made as if to drop the limp form of the Lord-Celestant into the black abyss of his gut, and Grymn knew then what he must do. He dropped his halberd and spun to snatch a nearby Judicator's thunderbolt crossbow from his hands. He whirled back and took aim.

Damn you, Gardus, he thought, we shall not lose you a second time – not like this. He fired. The bolt sizzled gold through the rain, and struck true. Gardus thrashed as the bolt tore through the back of his neck. There was a blaze of blue light, and the greater daemon howled as azure flames wreathed his paw. Gardus vanished, lost to the Hallowed Knights once more. But not forever. Grymn, heartsick with guilt, shoved the crossbow back into its owner's hands, and glared at Morbus.

'It had to be done,' he snapped. 'It was the only way to save him.'

'We will join him soon enough,' Morbus rasped, as he set his reliquary and gestured with his hammer. The Great Unclean One had turned towards them, smoke rising from his form, as if sensing that they had had some part in the disappearance of his prey. As he lurched towards them, his followers redoubled their efforts to break the hastily formed shieldwall. Beasts and ratkin hurled themselves at the Liberators. The Stormcasts were holding them back, but only barely.

'Maybe so,' Grymn said. 'But I'll not do so in shame.' Tegrus was nowhere to be seen, and what few Prosecutors were in sight were locked in battle with the plague drones that buzzed through the rain-choked air above. Zephacleas and Ultrades had formed their own shieldwalls, and were being pressed as hard as the Hallowed Knights. The rain was falling faster and harder with every passing moment, and the foul waters lapped at their shins. But they would stand firm, whatever fate awaited them.

'Who will be redeemed?' Grymn cried, raising his halberd high.

'Only the faithful,' the nearby Hallowed Knights replied.

'Who will stand until the world cracks open?'

'*Only the faithful!*'

'Who will honour the Steel Soul, and fight in his name?'

'*Only the faithful!*' came the reply.

Grymn lifted his halberd.

'Make ready to charge,' he shouted. 'We shall meet them head on, and show them how Stormcasts fight.' No more the shield. Now, I will be the sword, until we meet again in the Gladitorium, Gardus, he thought. At his next word, weapons were raised and shields lowered. But before he could utter the command to charge, the enemy abruptly began to fall back.

A green light spread over the Stormcasts, rising from the ring of menhirs behind them. An ethereal screech suddenly echoed across the vale, causing even the Great Unclean One to pause in consternation. Grymn turned, and saw a glowing manifestation stalk through the ranks of the Hallowed Knights.

'Alarielle,' Morbus said. 'The Radiant Queen has come at last.'

'Why now?' Grymn hissed. 'Why not before, when Gardus...' He trailed off as Alarielle's eyes met his, and he looked away, unable to bear the torment he saw there. She was not mad, not quite, but there was nothing human, nothing mortal in that gaze.

Men stepped aside as Alarielle moved past them with an eerie grace, her robes whipping about her as if she were the eye of a storm. Leaves and shattered branches swirled about her, and her long, golden hair flowed in her wake as she stepped across the glistening surface of the water. Impossibly thin, and as pale as ice, she resembled nothing so much as a marble statue gifted with life, and her eyes blazed with a power far beyond anything Grymn had ever witnessed.

'What is she?' he whispered.

'Life,' Morbus said. 'In all of its fury and power.'

Alarielle pursued the retreating forces of the Nurgle worshippers with slow, stately steps. Where the end of her staff fell, the water turned cool and clear, and ravaged vegetation sprouted green and lush once more. Any daemon so foolish enough as to move towards her, rather than away, was reduced to swirling ash in the blink of an eye.

'This place is not yours,' she said, gazing at the Great Unclean One. Her voice rang out, as clear as a bell, as loud as thunder. Daemons quailed back, and the sylvaneth began to shriek and howl. 'I ceded my realm to you, but I shall not cede this place.'

'What you will or will not cede is of no concern to me, my lady,' Bolathrax said, leering at her. 'Nurgle's deluge falls, and this place will soon not be fit for such delicate flowers as those you call children. The sky roils with magics, and this place will fall to Grandfather. All will drown in his sacred slurry.'

'No,' Alarielle said. She looked around, and Grymn followed her gaze. Athelwyrd was flooding inch by inch. Soon, they would have no choice but to return the way they had come. Otherwise, this hidden bower would become their tomb. 'No,' Alarielle said again, but more softly. Her face contorted suddenly, and she threw back her head in a scream of denial so intense that sylvaneth and daemons both writhed in agony from its reverberations. Stormcasts clapped their hands to their ears as the dolorous sound washed over them.

Before the echoes of that cry had faded, Alarielle gestured sharply and a thick net of iron-thorns erupted from the waters to entwine the Great Unclean One.

'I know you of old, Bolathrax,' Alarielle said. 'Long have I desired to take what I am owed from your rotting flesh.'

Bolathrax struggled against the vines, but for every dozen he tore from him, two dozen more replaced them. Alarielle began to chant, her voice rising and falling like the wind, and the cage of briars constricted about the greater daemon. The thorns dug into his flesh, lacerating him. Bolathrax's roars became screams and then squeals as he came apart at the joints and collapsed into a gory ooze. His cries caused those daemons nearby to shudder, and many joined him in dissolution, falling apart even as they tried to flee the destruction of their leader. The briar vines rose from Bolathrax's remains like angry serpents, and struck out in all directions. As the Stormcasts watched, those daemons that had not already come apart died in droves, torn asunder by Alarielle's anger.

Though the leader of the daemonhost had been slain, his lieutenants still remained, as zealous as their opponents. Grymn fought on, and his warriors followed his example. Everywhere in the vale, where the Stormcast Eternals fought, the enemy died in hordes.

It was not enough, in the end.

The rain still fell, and it soon became evident to even the most stubborn amongst the Stormcasts that Athelwyrd was doomed. The storm hammered down as malign and benevolent magics crashed against one another in the sky above the battle. The pox-rain fell, harder and faster, inexorably claiming the vale.

'We will drown if this continues,' Zephacleas roared, fighting to be heard over the storm as he and his warriors joined the Hallowed Knights. 'None but a servant of Nurgle can survive in this place now.'

'We must move,' Grymn said aloud, as he booted a struggling plaguebearer from the blade of his halberd. They would need to get to higher ground to escape back into the mortal lands of Ghyran. 'We'll have to fight our way back. Where is Ultrades?'

Zephacleas pointed with his sword, to where the Guardians of the Firmament had formed up in a shieldwall around a retreating grove of dryads. The bark of the treekin was cracking and burning beneath the plague-rain. Grymn shook his head.

'Help him,' he said. 'We must fall back.'

'Fall back to where, Lord-Castellant?' Zephacleas asked, filthy water running down the contours of his battered war-helm. 'Where is there for us to go?'

'The only place we can,' Grymn said. He extended his halberd towards the shimmering expanse of the River Vitalis above. 'Up. Gather your warriors. Fall back to the River Vitalis.' He paused. 'The Hidden Vale is lost.'

EPILOGUE

Only war

In the end, the Hidden Vale was hidden once more.

On the banks of the River Vitalis, Grymn stared into the depths of the water, seeking any sign of it, but all he discerned was a faint scar of murk, running along the river's bottom. The forces of Nurgle had not followed the Stormcasts and the sylvaneth as they retreated, first to the upper reaches of the valley, and then back through the breached portal, to the dubious safety of Rotwater Blight.

Then, why should they have? he thought grimly. They had what they wanted, he suspected. The Hidden Vale was gone, and Alarielle was cast adrift into a world that was no longer hers. Her power, while great, would not be enough to win back her realm. I wonder if she realises that, he thought, as he gazed surreptitiously at the Radiant Queen, where she stood nearby.

Alarielle's screams of denial still rang in his head. They had echoed across the near-infinite kingdoms of Ghyran, he suspected, so loud had they been. She had wept and raged as they retreated, her cries of anguish so intense that daemons had shivered into incoherent fragments at the sound and Stormcasts had fallen, skulls burst. And while she was now silent, he could still feel the heat of her rage.

'Where is he?' she asked, suddenly, in a voice like the croaking of a murder of crows. 'Where is the one who led my enemies to me?'

Grymn stiffened. 'He is… gone. He fell in battle, defending your realm.'

'Defending a realm he endangered,' she snarled, and the fury in her voice shook him to his core. 'My kingdom… my people… All gone, all lost,' she keened. Dryads hissed and shrieked mournfully as they clustered about her. She looked at Grymn, and he stepped back. Her eyes burned like twin suns, and he knew that she could kill him as easily as she had healed him before. Life in all its fury and power, he thought, recalling Morbus' words.

'My lady, they are gone, as are our brethren. But we still live,' he said. He set his halberd. 'And while we live, so too does Ghyran. While we stand, your realm shall not fall. So I swear. We shall fight. We shall win. Your kingdom will be free.'

'Free,' she breathed. Surrounded by her dryads and branchwraiths, her tall form blazing with a strange light, Alarielle turned towards the Hallowed Knights. Her shimmering gaze flickering across their ranks as she studied them. Grymn hesitated, uncertain, then stepped forward. 'But for now, my lady, you and your folk must come with us. We have cost you your haven. The least we can do is see you to safety.'

'Safety,' Alarielle intoned. Her voice echoed in his very marrow, and he trembled slightly to hear such despair. 'There is no safety now,' Alarielle said, 'no safe haven or sanctum left in all the Jade Kingdoms.' The Radiant Queen smiled sadly.

'Only war remains.'

THE ELDRITCH FORTRESS

Guy Haley

PROLOGUE

Many centuries ago...

The heavens writhed with flames of blue and pink. In every corner of the Hanging Valleys of Anvrok smoke rose. Only Elixia, the Sculpted City, held firm, but it could not do so for much longer. A circle of unmarred sky hung over the Great Monument as the city's already lurid lightning flickered hungrily around this single, pure space.

In the shadow of the Great Monument stood the House of the Aldermen. It was here that Celemnis, Swordmaiden of the Argent Sisterhood, had come.

She entered the central chamber, a space forbidden to everyone but the council, at a swift stride, accompanied by a handful of her men. All the guard were at the walls and the council had fled; Celemnis was not denied.

Within the council chamber an uneasy peace held sway.

The clamour of war breaking the city's defences was distant. Above the ring of arms and roars of beasts was a dreadful keening. Odd and terrible were the sounds of Chaos as it forced itself upon the realms of Order, but this too was muted in the chamber.

From the courtyard garden outside the chamber a blackbird sang as if there were nothing amiss with the world. Celemnis could almost convince herself that the breeze wafting the window drapes was born of the summer, and not the burning of her home.

'Celemnis!' Forge Leader Jethelir waved at her from a curtained doorway. 'He's in here.'

Celemnis crossed the room. Her whole life she had walked quickly; there was always more to do. Why waste one's time in ambling? And now time had nearly run out and she could walk no faster.

The High Alderman was sitting behind a desk in one of the many clerks' cubicles of bronze and marble. He had taken refuge there, seeking some last pocket of sanity. His long beard brushed over thin sheets of tin as he read and reread the glyphs impressed into them. His fine clothes were dirty and his eyes red-rimmed with smoke and tears.

'Ah, Celemnis,' he said. 'Do come in.'

Celemnis rested her fists on the desk and leaned over him.

'Now will you return the hammer?' she said.

The High Alderman glanced out of the window. He frowned as if he had noticed it were about to rain. 'The hammer?'

'Ghal Maraz. The Great Shatterer. Sigmar's weapon. Now will you return it to him?'

'We have had this conversation many times, my dear,' he said. The High Alderman rolled up the tin scroll. 'There is no one to return it to. The only way Sigmar would have parted from his hammer is if he were dead.'

'The oracles told us he was tricked into casting it away,' she said.

'The oracles went mad not long after the gods abandoned the realms. Why do you trust books written a century ago?'

Celemnis thrust her arm out behind her, pointing in the direction of the battle. 'Because the oracles prophesied this, Alderman. Let us offer up prayer and unlock the shrine. Let him know where it is!'

The Alderman radiated defeat; he had no more of himself left to give to this world.

'And why should we? If the oracles were correct and Sigmar himself cast it away, why should we strive to return it to him? He left us. His hammer was drawn here by fate. Who are we to question fate?'

'Everyone should question fate when it dances to Tzeentch's tune,' said Celemnis. 'The armies of Chaos are breaking through the walls! The hammer cannot protect us, not anymore. We should never have kept it.'

'Oh, my dear, dear Celemnis,' said the High Alderman. His usual vitality had been stripped away by sorrow; now he looked his age, and worn out by it. 'It is all rather academic.' He took one of her callused hands gently in his own. 'I am sorry. Perhaps you were right all along. Perhaps–'

The rattle of armoured men interrupted him. Celemnis ran from the room to witness a band of Chaos warriors thundering into the main hall. Each one was a head taller than a mortal man, far heavier and clad in ornate blue plate armour. They reeked of dark power.

Celemnis' last few men attacked immediately. Their arms were strong from years in her smithies, and they carried her silver blades. The swords' keen edges bit deeply, felling three of the warriors, sell-souls who had betrayed their own kind for a touch of power. But these men were mighty beyond her workers' skill in war, and her swords were not enough. Within seconds the blood of her followers ran red on the marble floor.

Her hand flew to the hilt of her own weapon. The Chaos warriors surrounded her, swords levelled at her throat. Their leader's face was drunk on triumph.

'Now now, my lady,' he said. 'Stay your hand. We will not harm you.'

A delicate cough sounded behind the warriors, and they parted. There in the doorway stood a thin man, entirely bald. He was clad in robes covered in arcane sigils and wore a great deal of jewellery. His skin shone with scented oil. But the richness of his garb hid a sickness; a second glance showed his slenderness to be cadaverous and his skin grey beneath its copper tan. Behind his make-up his eyes were pouched and sunken, and there was something of the vulture to him. His smile was reptilian.

'Celemnis of the Swords, the maiden who makes blades of such legendary strength and sharpness.' He approached her, his eyes gleaming. 'Here we are again.'

'Ephryx of Denvrok,' she said. 'I should have realised that your hand was behind this.'

He dipped his head modestly. 'I have worked a long time to undo this city's defences. It was not easy. I am humbled that you see through my artifice and recognise me as the mind behind Elixia's downfall.' He held out his hand. 'Are you not impressed? I have more to show. I agree circumstances could be better, but my offer still stands.'

'I would not have you when you were merely a sorcerer. Now you are a slave to darkness. Never.' She spat full in his face. Swords came closer to her neck.

Ephryx's outstretched hand clenched. He withdrew it and waved his men back.

'You are the daughter of a Ninemage, and should have greater respect for wielders of magic.' He wiped her spittle away with a silken handkerchief. 'Have you not heard, my dear? It is the season for treachery. The war against Chaos is lost. Only those who side with the victors have any hope of survival.'

'Better to die with a clean soul than to sell it for baubles,' she said. 'You do not act from expediency. You chose your side a long time ago.'

'Ah, if only it were so simple,' he said. He beckoned forward a group of nine lesser sorcerers waiting by the bronze doors. They stepped nervously around the pooled blood of Celemnis' men.

Ephryx waved another hand. A cruel-faced Chaos lord went into the cubicle where the High Alderman sat, his sword drawn. A moment later he came out, and his sword dripped red. The Alderman died as he had lived his last days: meekly, and without protest.

Ephryx smiled thinly. 'We go to the vault. I must be sure that the treasure of Elixia is what it is purported to be.'

Celemnis was roughly disarmed and forced along with Ephryx and his acolytes through the gardens of the House of the Aldermen. The gates had fallen and the enemy ran riot through the streets of the city; a chorus of screams rose and fell in shrill waves. The smell of burning was overpowering, but in the garden peace lingered and the blackbird still sang its song.

They went through the portals of the monument. The building was deserted, and they descended its wide steps unchallenged. At the bottom was the vault, sealed with doors of black volcanic glass locked by wheels of silver. Upon the doors, Sigmar's legend had been carved by the duardin. Tiny figures in long strips told of Sigmar's life and his deeds in the realms.

Ephryx stood in thought for a moment, then indicated one of his acolytes with a finger and a smile. 'You,' he said.

'Can I bear it, master?' asked the acolyte hesitantly. 'Will I die?'

'That rather depends on you,' said Ephryx. 'If you can, then I will have no more to teach you. If you die, well...' His smile broadened. 'I could say the same thing.'

The acolyte nodded nervously. 'Very well, master, I am ready.'

Two of Ephryx's biggest warriors took station either side of the obsidian doors and grasped the wheel-lock handles. All but Celemnis and the acolyte averted their eyes.

'Begin!' said Ephryx. The Chaos warriors spun the wheels and heaved backwards. The doors parted and a line of brilliant light burst across them all.

The acolyte looked into the vault and made a noise of deep pain.

'Is it there? Is it the Great Shatterer?' asked Ephryx.

The man gasped out a reply. 'Yes. Yes! I see a hammer, radiant with power. Oh, master, let me look away!'

'I must be sure – describe it further. My favour will be yours. This is your final test!'

'I see a comet with two tails upon the head, and the face of a great cat circles the haft. A spike is upon the… A spike… Ah, oh, it burns! It burns, ah, ah…'

Ephryx's acolyte screamed and flames jetted from his mouth and his eyes. He flung out his arms and fell to his knees. His robes caught fire and his skin blackened from the inside out. He fell to the ground and rolled around, aflame. Within moments he was consumed utterly, leaving a pile of grey ash.

Ephryx held up a handkerchief to his nose and ordered his servants to sweep the mess away. 'Close the gates!'

His warriors obeyed. The doors shut with a dull bang, sealing the light from view. Ephryx smiled again at Celemnis. 'Well. I have in my possession one item I desire. What say you now to my offer? Be mine and rule at my side. Worlds could be your toys, such things I have learned! I will share them with you.'

'I have seen what your favour brings,' Celemnis said. 'I will have none of it.'

'You will submit yourself to me.'

'If you are so powerful, make me,' she said.

Ephryx bared his teeth. For a moment it looked like he would try to enslave her with his magic. One hand clenched and the other raised up, poised to release his arts. For a minute he stared at her, and she stared defiantly back. He let out an explosive sigh, and his hands sank back to his sides.

'No. You will submit willingly, or you will die. You have fifty nights. Take her away.'

* * *

And so for fifty days and nights Celemnis was kept prisoner, and at every sinking of the sun she was brought before the sorcerer. Every night Ephryx would ask, 'Do you submit?' Every night she would spit upon the ground, or stare over his head, or look at the floor, or weep. But always she said no. 'I will never be yours, Ephryx of Denvrok.'

For the first twenty days she was given every luxury, and was kept in a tall tower that had sprung fully formed from the wreck of the city. There was no way in or out, and she could never recall how she was taken to Ephryx. There was a single window of enchanted crystal, and through this she was permitted to look at the horror inflicted upon her home.

The days went by. Outside, the racket of industry set up. Slaves were driven into the city from all corners of the Hanging Valleys of Anvrok. Whipped and weeping, they were made to tear down the centre of Elixia.

The Great Monument was the first to be demolished.

Perfumed baths, fine food and wine, and exquisite clothes were all provided to her by unseen hands, while outside the remaining populace was enslaved. She could not eat at first, so dismayed was she, but hunger drove her to it. Every mouthful felt like a betrayal.

The clothes she ripped and destroyed every day, until after the first ten days she awoke every morning to find herself dressed in them while she slept – hideous, filmy things that stripped her of modesty.

Perhaps Ephryx was a fool and did not realise his actions only strengthened her resolve. Or perhaps he knew full well that she would never give in to him and tormented her out of spite.

'No,' she said to him every night. 'Never.' And so she was taken away again.

Ephryx's patience wore thin. For the next twenty days she was confined to a cold cell. Foul food and stagnant water was all she was given. This she forced herself to eat, for she was still hopeful of opportunity and would not let her strength dwindle. None came. Awful screams broke her sleep.

The enchanted window came with her, magically set into the dripping metal of her cell wall, and her view of the world remained. Through it she saw Ephryx's armies of slaves labouring in the Shattered City, melting its grand arches of steel and adamant and recasting them as giant plates bedecked with grimacing faces and spikes.

Over Ghal Maraz, they raised a cairn of lead, and then around that a stone keep. The foundations of a giant tower were being laid to encase the keep when she was moved again.

For the next ten days she was subjected to physical torments. Nothing that might mar her body permanently, for her beauty Ephryx coveted above all other things save the hammer, but excruciating nonetheless.

Still she would not yield.

'I can make it stop. I will make it stop. Be mine, join with me and rule this land,' said Ephryx on the final night. 'Help me, guide me. Chaos does not have to be excess. We can coax beauty from the world.' He had become more wan than before, and on his forehead were the buds of horns. A mark of favour from his dark master.

Celemnis burned with fever. Her red hair was matted, her body filthy. Every muscle ached.

'No,' she said, her voice made little more than a croak by

thirst. 'There is no beauty to be had from evil. Even if I were to sell my soul to Tzeentch, if I were to embrace his madness myself, then still I would not submit myself to you, Ephryx. I will never be yours.'

Ephryx snarled.

'Poor Ephryx,' she said. 'The whole of the realm might fall under your spell, but I will not.'

Ephryx's face hardened. 'So be it.'

He performed a series of conjurer's gestures, and a large crucible appeared. Above it was a cage shaped to hold the human body. Silent torturers stood either side, their heads horned, faces hooded. A jet of warpflame hissed from thin air to warm the crucible, and the iron of it glowed as prettily as roses. From the crucible's gaping mouth came the unmistakable smell of molten silver.

'By your own favoured metal will you be killed,' said Ephryx. 'I shall boil you in it, and coat your corpse in it, and make of you a statue. You shall stand where all other statues have been cast down. There you shall watch for all time the city you so loved. Your beauty will be mine to enjoy, and my victory your torment. Now, you have one last chance. Join with me, and rule forever, or die in agony and suffer for an eternity.'

At that point Celemnis' resolve wavered. She looked upon the end Ephryx had devised for her with mute horror. The sorcerer leaned forward in his golden throne, keenly anticipating her surrender.

She stood tall, and shook her head.

He threw himself back in his throne pettishly.

'Very well! Executioners!'

They came for her and strapped her into the cage, and hung it out over the bubbling metal.

'Ephryx!' she said.

He looked sidelong at her.

'Victory is fleeting. The day will come when I shall return, and I will play my part in your downfall. This I swear.'

'Impossible,' he said.

She laughed. 'Magic blows strongly in this age of Chaos. Your lord unwittingly makes wizards of us all! This is your doom and mine, Ephryx. Ask your master.'

'I would have made you a queen,' he said bitterly. He jerked his hand down. The cage dropped.

Ephryx found Celemnis' screams were not to his taste, and he was glad when they were over.

Celemnis' death did not pass unremarked. In Sigmaron, in Azyr, upon the half-finished tails of the Sigmarabulum which embraced the world fragment of Mallus, the Bell of Lamentation tolled. The God-King Sigmar looked up from his labours. Mallus quivered, pulsed, and pulled in on itself, diminished by another victory for Chaos. A moan went up from Azyrheim far below.

Sigmar looked to the shrunken world fragment, half visible through the tracery of his great endeavour. Soon the tendrils of iron and steel would reach for each other, close all gaps, and hide the secrets of his plans until they ripened to fruition.

On the other side of sealed gates, the denizens of a dozen hells beat their fists upon doors that would not open. The tolling of the bell focused Sigmar's thoughts on all those trapped outside Azyr, those who must suffer the age of Chaos while he completed his work.

He returned his attention to his forge, and his tears fizzled on hot metal as he took up his tools again.

CHAPTER ONE

The Age of Sigmar

Now...

Vandus Hammerhand crouched in a world of light. He was alone, naked, bereft of comrades. Was he dead? Had the measure of godly power bestowed upon him been taken away? Was he Vendell Blackfist once more?

The glow dimmed. Vandus straightened. He had returned to Azyr, and stood within a quenching chamber. His sight took a moment to return; the light had been dazzling and the chamber was now dark. First he saw stars shining through an aperture at the apex of the dome, then he held up his arm and the starlight glinted from muscles larger and more powerful than those of any mortal man. His physique was still that of a Stormcast Eternal, and his skin was unmarked by the forge burns of his former life. He had not met death, not this time. Relief rose in him, and he felt ashamed that he had feared his power gone. Power was what the followers of the Four craved, not the Stormcasts. For the warriors of Sigmar, there should only be vengeance.

He thought back to Aqshy, to his plea to the skies as he had stood within the arch of the Gate of Wrath. Sigmar had struck him down as he had requested, but rather than destroy his bodily form it appeared that the God-King had taken him up to Azyr, just as he had centuries before. He only hoped that Korghos Khul's realmgate had been destroyed by the storm bolt that had effected his escape, and that the battle for the Brimstone Peninsula had not been lost for his sake.

Light of a different sort grew. Shining shapes resolved around Vandus, burnished plates of golden armour that orbited him in stately dance. Vandus reached for them with a thought. Lightning leapt out from his skin to the armour plates, pulling them sharply into place until he was clad in the raiment of a Lord-Celestant once more.

A twinge affected him. Strange thoughts intruded upon his dressing. He felt there was a hollow space in his mind, as if in returning home he had chanced upon an unknown door and opened it to find an empty room pregnant with disquiet.

Vandus shook the sensation off, and called upon his war-mask. The visor, shaped into the impassive face of a judgmental god, slid into place. Vandus extended his hand and the hammer Heldensen crackled into being from nothing and clapped into his grip. The Lord-Celestant raised his other hand and grasped at the night sky, pulling down his cloak of star-silk from the heavens.

Outside, a trumpet note sounded, high and sweet: a

summons. Sigmar called for him. The doors of the quenching chamber peeled themselves back. Vandus stepped outside into a long, curved corridor where many identical doors were set. Magical lamps burned with unchanging light in alcoves all the way along. Like everything else in Sigmaron and the Sigmarabulum, the corridor was beautiful.

Vandus was met by Knight-Heraldor Laudus Skythunder and Lord-Castellant Andricus Stoneheart, his friends and fellow officers, lords of the Hammers of Sigmar and its primary Warrior Chamber, the Hammerhands.

Laudus hung back, his silver horn tucked under one arm. Stoneheart was of a more demonstrative character, and he grabbed at Vandus' upper arms and peered at him in wonder. His helmet was open. The battle armour topped with Andricus' cheerful face instead of the blank war-mask of the Stormcasts made for an incongruous sight.

'You're alive then, lad?' said Andricus. He unexpectedly embraced the Lord-Celestant. 'Good to see you, Hammerhand. We feared you lost.'

'Sigmar promises us an eternity, Andricus. I was taken from the battle whole and unharmed.'

Andricus stepped back. 'Of course he does, of course. But we did not know for certain if you would survive the energies of the gate. You were snatched from the very jaws of the Realm of Chaos! And there have been...' He shook his head, then forced a smile back onto his heavy features.

'What?' asked Vandus. 'Why do you look at me so strangely? It is I, Vandus who was Vendell! The Hammerhand! Come, my friends, what did you fear?'

Andricus and Laudus shared a look. 'Now's not the time,'

said Andricus. 'There's much to discuss. We have been summoned again.'

'How did you come to be here? You were not struck down?'

'We were fortunate to avoid the agonies of death, my Lord-Celestant,' said Laudus. He was altogether more aloof than the Lord-Castellant. Where Andricus spoke of his life as a peasant, Laudus had been noble born. They sometimes bickered over whose existence was the more honest. What was not in doubt was that they had both been heroes.

'We returned to Azyr via the realmgate.'

'The battle is won?'

'Yes, son,' said Andricus. He had been an old man when taken; to this he insisted he owed his cheerfulness. 'We've all been invested with the power of the storm, but my joy doesn't come from that,' he was fond of saying. 'I'm happy to see clearly, to get up from my bed without the crack of aching joints.' When had he heard this, Laudus had pulled a face. 'You'll never understand how it is to be old now, my lads. And be thankful for it!'

Certain habits of speech and manner persisted from Andricus' prior existence: his custom of speaking to all as if they were years younger than he, for one. Vandus was half-convinced Andricus did it simply to annoy Laudus.

'Korghos Khul's armies have been driven back from the peninsula,' said Andricus. 'His pyramid is cast down and his gate closed forever. More Stormhosts arrive every day. Our territory in Aqshy grows.'

'I must have been absent for days.'

'A week, my lord,' said Laudus.

'A week?'

'Sigmar's arts are mysterious,' said Laudus.

'None of us here know how long we were senseless when we were first gathered,' said Andricus. 'Why should it be any different this time?'

'I must get back! Khul awaits me. I have failed to slay him twice, I will not fail a third time.'

'You'll have to put your own vengeance out of your mind,' said Andricus. 'We've a greater task at hand.'

'We have been summoned to the palace. A new campaign awaits,' said Laudus. 'The palace is all abuzz. Sigmar is eager for something – none have ever seen him so roused.'

'All the Hammers of Sigmar are here?'

'All, my Lord-Celestant,' said Laudus. 'Those who fell are reforged. We are ready for war again.'

They left the quenching chambers and came through obscure ways to the exposed surface of the Sigmarabulum. Once more it churned with industry. The quiet before their assault on Aqshy had been but a pause, and now the magics and machineries there worked hard again, healing and remaking those warriors who had fallen. Sigmar's wizard-artisans and their helpers hurried about. They paid no attention to the demigods striding among them – such sights were unremarkable in this city of wonders.

The Sigmarabulum gave off a nervous energy that had a man frantic to be about his work, and it stank of hot metal and magical discharge. However, its odd animus could not blot out the wider world around it.

To their right loomed the sphere of Mallus, the world remnant. It had swollen in the wake of the Stormhosts' first victories. The metal was glutted with magic, and the surface glinted with an iridescent sheen. To their left the heavens of Azyr opened. Nowhere in any realm was there a night sky more beautiful; it blazed with stars of all colours and sizes, jewels set upon sumptuous cloths woven from nebulae. Rising through it was the Celestial Stair, a slash of bright metal climbing impossibly high, its top anchored beneath the High Star Sigendil. A handful of Azyr's many moons arced gracefully along their heavenly tracks, while the lands of the Celestial Realm slumbered below. Rivers glinted in lazy loops of beaten steel, and towns and villages were picked out by yellow dots of lamplight. Forests were seas of purplish black in the moonlight, and farmland an orderly miniature landscape wrought in silver.

Vandus looked down on the land, and part of him yearned to enjoy its peace. He never could – that much had been made clear to him – but he could protect it so that others might live and grow old there. He did not resent his duty.

'This way,' said Laudus. They approached a trio of small realmgates set off to the side of the main roadway in the shadow of a giant foundry, glinting with soft blue light. The Stormcasts walked through this shimmer and emerged into a different place. Cool night scents hit them and crickets chirred in the dark.

They were far above the forges and factories, upon the dark moon Dharroth. The Sigmarabulum was forged in the shape of Sigmar's twin-tailed comet, two arms reaching to embrace Mallus. This black satellite formed the head of the comet, and it was here that Sigmaron, the palace of the Heldenhammer, was situated. Vandus, Laudus and Andricus emerged into the grounds on the path they called the High Road. Sigmar's palace soared above them, as wide and sprawling as any city, its many domes and spires gleaming by the light of the moons.

They made their way through the magnificent halls and vaults of the palace. Even the meanest chamber was monumental beyond anything Vandus could recall from his old life. Every stone was perfect, every decoration of the finest craftsmanship.

They took paths followed only by others of their kind, corridors they must take as ritual prescribed. Down they went, past the Forbidden Vaults, their heads resolutely turned away. Their oaths demanded they never look upon the vaults' doors.

So it was that his companions did not immediately see Vandus stumble.

The strange sensation he had experienced in the quenching chambers returned redoubled. Vandus went down to his knees, clutching at his head. His mind burst aflame with visions.

He saw golden figures climbing endlessly up a glacier of precious metal, battles upon bridges that spanned an ocean of bubbling silver, and innumerable, wicked eyes glinting through a hole in the sky. He saw a two-headed winged shadow silhouetted before a portal of terrible power, and a tide of daemons. Holes ripped in the world's fabric split the vision, clawed hands and needle-toothed snouts pushing through until nothing remained. Light burned them away, and he saw the sigil of the twin-tailed comet upon a hammer that shone brighter than any sun.

'My lord!'

The hammer.

'Vandus!'

Ghal Maraz.

Vandus came to his senses with Laudus Skythunder clutching his shoulders.

'Vandus? Are you well? What is happening?' Laudus was saying.

Andricus spoke quietly in reply. 'It is the same as with the others. The reforged…'

'Silence, Lord-Castellant. Vandus has not passed the gates of death. I will hear no more of your morbid talk!'

'Vandus?' said Andricus.

Recovering himself, the Lord-Celestant looked to his fellows. Concern radiated from them both. 'I'm fine,' he said hoarsely. He got unsteadily to his feet, pushing Andricus' hand away when he tried to help him. Once up, he marched on as steadily as he could, leaving the others to follow.

Lord-Castellant sentries slammed their halberds against their chests as the three Stormcasts entered the throne room through doors fifty feet high. Within were the command echelons from a dozen Stormhosts, arranged in rows according to their rank and order either side of a carpet, a night-blue road that led from the doors to the celestial throne. Upon this, the God-King Sigmar sat tall in his majesty. The ceiling retreated up and away. Hundreds of feet overhead, carved panels shone, and it was as if the assembled host basked in the light of many suns.

Sigmar smiled broadly as Vandus approached. Andricus was right, something had occurred. Sigmar's manner betrayed his excitement.

'Vandus, my favoured son,' said the God-King. 'I am gladdened that you are here with me again.'

Vandus bowed his head. He dearly wanted to kneel, to show his pleasure at being in the presence of his lord, but the God-King had no time for sycophancy.

Before the throne was another Lord-Celestant, clad in the turquoise livery of the Celestial Vindicators Stormhost, and he was kneeling.

'Thostos has discovered something,' said Sigmar. 'All of you have performed well, my sons. I bring you here to share with you Thostos Bladestorm's discovery and to set for you another task of great import.'

The god turned his radiant eyes upon the kneeling Thostos, who had made no movement or sound.

'Stand, Thostos Bladestorm!' commanded Sigmar.

Thostos slowly lifted his head and looked around him. He appeared confused.

'We shall kneel no more,' said Sigmar. He gestured, encouraging Thostos to rise.

The Lord-Celestant of the Bladestorm got unsteadily to his feet.

'You are reforged,' said Sigmar. 'Now tell me of Chamon.'

Thostos paused before he began. When he spoke, it was falteringly. His voice sounded hollow behind his impassive war-mask. 'There was... There was a fortress of magic. We breached its walls, only to die in a burst of unlight that was fought by a greater light.'

Sigmar leaned forward. 'Speak to me of this greater light.'

'Golden,' said Thostos with difficulty. 'Not the energy of Chaos. Violent, but pure.'

Sigmar tensed, a man who had undone the final fetters on his passions. Vandus realised then that the wait for the war through the Long Calm had been harder on the God-King than it had been on any of the Stormcasts.

'I remember it well,' Sigmar said. 'Lord Vandus!'

Vandus stepped up to Thostos' side.

'Prepare your warriors,' commanded Sigmar. 'That light is mine.' He sank back into his throne and gripped the metal gryphons on the arms. 'We have found Ghal Maraz.'

Sigmar swept his piercing gaze across the assembled officers. 'This knowledge has been bought at great cost. Many of the Celestial Vindicators were slain and returned to the Reforging chambers, victims of evil magic.' He looked to Thostos again. 'Centuries ago, I was deceived into casting Ghal Maraz from me at the Battle of Burning Skies by Tzeentch. He has since conspired to hide its whereabouts from me, but long have I suspected that Ghal Maraz rested in the mountains of the Hanging Valleys of Anvrok.

'I am sorry, Thostos, that I did not reveal to you my suspicions. I am certain you and your comrades wondered why I would send my most vengeful warriors to seek out old allies when their hammers thirsted for war, not words. I needed your fury there, in case the hammer was uncovered and needed to be snatched quickly. Here in Azyr my actions are secret, but out there in the realms they are not. I could not risk rumour of my intuition coming to the ears of the Changer of the Ways. Now you know.'

Thostos said nothing. Vandus looked sidelong at him.

Sigmar stood. 'Warriors! Stormcasts! This is your quest! Go to Anvrok in Chamon and assail this fortress of which Thostos speaks. Destroy it and return what is rightfully mine to my hand! I had not dared hope Ghal Maraz could be recovered so early in our struggle. With it, we might begin our war in earnest!'

A rousing acclamation roared from the Stormcasts. 'Sigmar! Ghal Maraz for Sigmar! Sigmar!'

'Vandus and Thostos shall lead you,' continued Sigmar, his godly voice cutting through the shouts of his men. 'Hammers of Sigmar! Anvils of the Heldenhammer! Celestial Vindicators! Lions of Sigmar! Twelve Stormhosts shall I send. We shall crush the servants of Chaos within Anvrok. The hammer shall be ours. Nothing will prevent our victory!'

CHAPTER TWO

Kairos Fateweaver

In a place outside of time, Kairos Fateweaver peered intently into the Flame that Consumes the Now, its strange lights reflected in his four eyes. Both his faces frowned.

'This troubles me, this fixation on the present and not the past,' said one head to the other.

'Or the future. But needs must. I must bear the agony of the instant. Watch our petty friend, as he postures in front of his minions.'

In the fire, an image rippled of Ephryx, Ninth Disciple of the Ninth Tower. He stood atop the walls of his broken fortress, addressing a crowd of lords and knights: the nobility of Chamon.

'So many schemes, so many ambitions,' said the left head. 'So many little heads to hold them in.'

'None of those schemers can match Ephryx's plans. They would tear him limb from limb if they knew what he intended.

Their mistake is to think his ambitions are as limited as theirs. Their horizons are not broad enough.'

'There! His scheme I say – I talk like him. It is *my* scheme.'

'When I look into the past, I see his hand more in evidence than mine,' rejoined the other head.

'And when I look into the future, I see my victory and not his.'

'Much must be done to make fate bend to my will. The sorcerer does not deserve another chance. He had nearly enough magic to complete the translocation, but frittered too much away to save his pointless mortal life.'

One shoulder shrugged. 'It was Tzeentch's plan.'

'Of course.'

'Of course, of course, but I must take an active hand,' said the right head.

'Ephryx is vulnerable,' said the left.

'His magic must be replenished.'

'How to accomplish that?'

'Time. The dearest coin of all. He must have more of it.'

Kairos leaned forward to the flames, keen to listen to what the doomed sorcerer had to say to his allies.

'War has come to Chamon!' shouted Ephryx. His voice echoed from walls of steel and copper, from bastions of brass and bronze. He had dressed himself in his finest occult robes and his horns gleamed with fresh lacquer. It was an effort to maintain his appearance of power – a necessary fiction.

A week ago, the Eldritch Fortress had been a gleaming example of Ephryx's ingenuity. But his perfect kingdom, so long laboured over, was much damaged. A gaping hole had opened in the curtain wall, gouged out by the wild magic of Ephryx's mutalith during its fatal fight with the turquoise storm warrior. Many of the skulls that had adorned every inch of the outside walls, transmuted to copper to store magic, had been burned away by lightning or smashed to pieces by hammer and sword. Too much of Ephryx's hoarded power had been spent driving off Sigmar's warriors.

There were several minor breaches elsewhere. None were quite so devastating as that in the wall of the huge, central tower. A long crack ran up from the base, showing the domed keep inside. This too had suffered damage, and the cairn of lead within had been shivered from its foundations. A wild glory shone out through the ragged gaps, brighter than the sickly sun. There was no more hiding for Ephryx's artefact. Its painful light was plain for all to see.

Ephryx was sure that the hammer's location was no longer secret. They would be coming for it, and soon. On the other side of the breach, Ephryx's tall tower cast a thick black shadow, as precise as a sundial's. It provided a measure of relief from the blazing light, and so there gathered all the might of the Hanging Valleys of Anvrok. Lord Maerac of Manticorea had emptied his kingdom of dukes and barons. They sat sullenly upon their manticores, or lounged against their mounts' flanks. Even Mutac the Silent had come down from the remote island. The sorcerer had once fancied himself a rival to Ephryx, until Ephryx had called upon Tzeentch to curse him for his impertinence. Mutac had gone about cowled ever since. Ephryx alone knew what lurked under Mutac's hood in place of a face – nine fleshy towers, capped with nine eyes; an unsubtle reminder of who was the supreme mage of the Hanging Valleys of Anvrok.

That Mutac had come down suggested he thought Ephryx's time was done. Ephryx looked out from his broken walls seeking allies, but instead saw two dozen scheming rivals that weighed and measured him as if he were a bullock ready for slaughter.

'Friends,' he began. 'Allies!' There were no such things under the gaze of the Great Changer, unless they were of convenience. Ephryx gave a silent prayer that the lords of the Hanging Valleys of Anvrok would find him convenient for a little while longer. 'We must defend ourselves!'

'You mean we must defend you!' shouted Baron Kergoth of Ungivar. Scattered laughter came from the nobles. A manticore growled and rolled upon its side. Scratch my belly or I shall eat you, the expression on its face suggested.

Ephryx licked his lips. There were a lot of Maerac's men below. They all had manticores. In the Shattered City, ten thousand campfires burned. There, the bondsmen of Maerac's followers waited. For a fleeting instant the sorcerer worried he may have miscalculated.

'Defend this tower, and you defend your own kingdoms,' said Ephryx.

'Rubbish!' shouted a minor count, far beneath Ephryx's disdain and as thin as he was unimportant.

Maerac sneered. 'Look at him. He has some scheme. I do not think he lies directly to us, although he will be lying about something. Tell us, Ephryx, the Ninth Disciple of the Ninth Tower, what have you hidden in this fortress? Why is it so imperative that we defend you, when we should look to our own in the face of this threat?'

Ephryx's warped face split in an apologetic smile. He pressed his hands together. 'The artefact is none other than Ghal Maraz! The hammer of Sigmar Heldenhammer himself.'

The nobles went quiet. They looked askance at one another. Now they appraised each other, and not Ephryx alone, each one evaluating his chances of seizing the weapon for himself.

That was more like it.

'You had the Great Shatterer in your possession all this time, sorcerer, and you told no one?'

Ephryx shrugged. 'The people who dwelt in this city before me raised a great monument over it. It was the talk of the realm. You did not know of it. Sigmar did not know of it. I knew of it. Why do you think this is, Maerac?'

Maerac scowled but held his tongue.

'It is because the Great Changer desired me to have it, and removed it from the eyes and memories of other men,' Ephryx said, smiling condescendingly. 'Forgive me that I have not told you, but do you not see? Had this artefact fallen into the wrong hands then these valleys would have a different set of lords. I was entrusted with it. So you see, from me your power flows.'

Maerac stared hard at Ephryx. It was clear he felt Ephryx's hands to be the wrong ones.

'Protect me and you are doing not my will, but Great Lord Tzeentch's will.' Ephryx pointed a long finger upwards. 'Tzeentch demands its safety.'

'Why has he not claimed it for himself? He has had ample opportunity!' shouted the Baron of the Floating Marches.

'The Twisted God is untrustworthy. Perhaps he desires it to fall into Sigmar's hand,' yelled the Yellow Duke, a pompous little fat man with an over-fed mount. He fancied himself a wizard, and Ephryx loathed him. He did, however, have a point; second-guessing Tzeentch was impossible. Any plan was plausible.

'Whatever our god's plans, they are unknowable to us. We need to focus on certainties, my friends. If Sigmar's hand closes about the haft of Ghal Maraz, then it will be used against all of you! Our land plays host to the Silverway, the duardin roadway between all realms. If he intends to storm each of the eight realms, the Silverway will be of great importance to him. How long do you think your fiefdoms will stand? The servants of the man-god must be halted before these walls, or your days of power are numbered.'

Murmurs of assent rippled over the gathering. Better still.

'We tried for the Silverway last week and they cast us back. Even now they fortify it against us,' said Kergoth.

'There are more of them coming every day via the Bright Tor Gate. It is reopened and in their hands,' said the Indigo Quester. 'They rebuild the forts there, and have taken the road from the valley.'

'Do you see? By your own words have you made prophecy!' shouted Ephryx.

'This fortress is breached and it will not stand long. I say we look to our own,' said another. 'This fool's day is done.'

'We will fight and die for nothing. Every day the numbers of the Stormcasts grow by the thousand. They do not attack, they prepare! How many will there be?' said the Yellow Duke. He had a buttery, jeering voice.

Ephryx raised his hands to quell the rising debate. 'Fear not, I have a plan. One that will save this fortress, and bring Tzeentch's boon to us all!'

Furious shouting erupted, mostly in his favour.

If only they knew what I intend, thought Ephryx, and it was all he could do to stop himself from laughing.

Kairos waved the image away irritably. Ephryx's plan had some merit, but that was chiefly because it was Kairos' plan. The eyes of one head slid shut as he peered into the future. What he saw there made him shake his head.

'What do I see?' asked his past-seeing head, which had no faculty of foresight.

The other head whispered, its eyes still closed. 'Ephryx will succeed in removing himself, but his persecutors will not rest. More time is needed. More time! The pursuit cannot be halted, but it can be delayed.'

'I must be rid of Ephryx.'

'I shall.'

'Favours must be called in.'

'I shall remind those that owe them of their debt,' soothed the other head.

Kairos opened his eyes. The warpflame flickered. The image of Ephryx whirled away and became a view of a desolate fane.

'My guest will be here soon,' said the past-seeing head.

In the old temple, a glowing green blade slid through the air, as if cutting through the painted backdrop of a stage set. A pink hand curled around one lip of the cut and pulled it wider. A twitching, rodentine nose poked its way through.

It snuffled at the air, then withdrew. 'I saw him set out two days past. He will be here…'

'…now,' said the future-seeing head.

A ratlike figure, nearly man-high, wriggled through the slit in space. It scurried from wall to wall, pausing at the corner to sniff at the air. The creature was half flesh, half machine. One leg was steel prosthetic and one arm had been replaced by a flare-mouthed weapon of brass, but these crude embellishments did not appear to slow it. Satisfied it was alone, it reached within its jerkin and produced a set of chalks. With a quick, trembling hand it began to draw an arcane circle of surprising artfulness around the altar in the middle of the shrine. Kairos watched as the ratman calmed and became absorbed in its work.

'This is no true champion of Chaos.'

'No. An opportunist. A sneak thief. Like all skaven.'

'Still, time is of the essence when one is buying time.'

'It will have to suffice.' The head looked to its counterpart. 'Must I wait until his circle is complete?'

'Why wait on convention?' said the other head.

Kairos waved his hand. A column of vibrantly coloured fire erupted from the cracked altar at the centre of the ruined temple. A burst of multi-spectral light shone up from the circle in reply. The skaven was taken by surprise, and emitted an acrid stink. He jumped back, holding his claw up to his sensitive eyes.

'You are looking for me, child of Chaos,' said Kairos' heads in unison. Through the vortex of warpflame, the Oracle of All loomed high over the creature.

'Yes-yes!' the skaven squeaked and shrank back before the apparition. 'How you know?'

Kairos clattered his beaks. 'I know everything. That is why you are here, is it not? To seek my knowledge. I am an oracle.'

'I am *the* oracle,' said the second head.

'Always,' complained the first head, 'they are fools!'

The skaven cringed in on itself, but nodded. 'Yes,' it gasped. 'Shreeglum, warlord of five clans, seeks the Great Oracle! And Shreeglum has found him, summoned him!' The skaven grew bold, impressed by its own success. It held up its chalk and stared at it in wonder, then gobbled it down. It came a little closer, stood a little straighter. 'I come with great treaty-gift! I see things no other sees! I go through the ways between the worlds, to the hall of the god-thing Sigmar.' Shreeglum stroked at its whiskers, its long face calculating. 'What you give me for the clever things I learn there?'

'You come to tell us that Sigmar has found his hammer.'

'How very dull,' said the other head.

A look of consternation gripped Shreeglum. He stooped low, cautious and suspicious. Already he was backing away, preparing to flee.

'How you know-guess?' he said again.

'The same question!' said one head.

'I refer you to the same answer,' said the other.

'Do not flee. I have use for you yet. All is not lost. You must do me a service, and you shall have what you want,' said Kairos.

'A very great service,' said the other head.

The skaven stopped, his nose twitching. He crept forward tentatively, and looked up at the apparition within its column of fire.

'Listen, then,' said Kairos. 'I bid you breach Chamon at

Silverfall in Anvrok, and take battle to the Stormcast Eternals. Do you know where that is?'

'Dead-ruined man town. Much silver. Hot-hot! Yes,' the skaven nodded. 'I know the secret ways.'

'Good. The Stormcast Eternals must fall there. Is that clear?' said the second head.

'Yes-yes,' said the skaven warlord. 'I will do this task for you. And in return…'

'Do not tell me,' said Kairos wearily, 'you wish to usurp your leader's position.' Always it was the same with the Horned Rat's brood, scheming and plotting against each other. Tiresome.

The skaven warlord squealed gleefully. A dribble of warp-fire squirted from his arm-cannon, hissing onto the ritual circle. 'Yes-yes!'

'Very well,' said Kairos, gesturing theatrically. He was getting into the spirit of the occasion. 'Kill the one called Hammerhand and the fates shall align as you wish.'

The skaven paused, nose bobbing up and down as if it would smell the veracity of what Kairos had said.

The daemon leaned forward.

'You may *go*.'

'Yes-yes!' chittered the skaven, scampering into the darkness. 'Biters! Drillfiends! Hurry! Follow the tell-smoke!'

The skaven ran out of the fane. Kairos extinguished the flame and nodded both his heads.

'It will not be enough.'

'I know.'

'I shall call the rest of the Nine,' said both heads together. 'They will be needed.'

Kairos, the place he inhabited and everything within it winked out of existence, leaving an oily trail of magic that faded away into the formless void.

CHAPTER THREE

Return to Chamon

Upon the narrow plain by the great Silver River of Anvrok stood the Bright Tor Gate, an ancient edifice open once more by Sigmar's decree. A camp had sprung up. The ruins about the gate were thick with artisans from the Eternal City, working under the watchful protection of the Lord-Castellants and their warriors, whose keen eyes were ever searching for signs of attack.

Everywhere were the signs of fresh works. Wizard-wrights levitated the tumbled blocks of broken fortifications to stand once more atop one another, their fellows mortaring them into place with molten stone jetting from lances that burned with a magical heat. New life returned to the bones of the dead town. The gate shone with pure energies of untainted magic. Chrono-smiths worked their gentle but potent spells, walking solemnly around and around the gate's town, and their deep, sonorous chants provided a calming counter note to the clamour of construction. Wherever their sandalled feet passed, the land seemed changed, cleansed.

The realm was healing.

Trumpets and warhorns blared. An honour guard formed up along the wide highway leading out of the gate eastwards towards the Shattered City. These men wore the turquoise armour of the Celestial Vindicators, and had left their Warrior Chambers to hold the gate when the first attack on Elixia had been undertaken. They stood tall and proud, eager to welcome their brothers back.

Black clouds raced overhead and lightning blazed. A vanguard of Stormcasts from five Stormhosts was deposited along the cliffs to the north and upon the road ahead of the gate. Liberators and Judicators took up defensive positions. Prosecutors leapt skyward, scanning the lands for enemies. All was expertly done, but done for the sake of procedure. The lands around the gate already belonged to the forces of Azyr.

Trumpets blew again. The Bright Tor Gate throbbed and opened. The field of magic bowed, glowing brightly, swelling forward over the road. Shining motes detached themselves from this luminescence, dimmed, and took on the shapes of marching men. Lord Thostos Bladestorm, as finder of the hammer, emerged first. A swaying forest of standards followed, the icons and banners of the Celestial Vindicators all together. Then the remainder of the Stormhosts came out.

Excepting a few brotherhoods assigned to guard the Silverway and the Bright Tor Gate, the entire host emerged in a long column. Their fellows lining the way cheered and shouted, but their welcome stumbled and quietened when their greetings were not returned.

The singing of the Celestial Vindicators, once renowned for its volume and fervour, had become restrained, though they marched with no less purpose. Thostos passed beyond the gate plaza, through a tumbled gateway that was already covered in scaffolding. Mortal craftsmen stepped back, first in respect but then in fear. Thostos' armour sparked and fizzed with magic. His eyes glowed a dull blue, not bright enough to outshine daylight, but when he walked in shadow one could see them glimmer coldly. Many of the warriors who walked behind him showed similar signs of change. There was a silence and a certain dreaminess in their bearing. As more and more of those who had fallen and been reforged marched forth, the shouts of their brothers lining the route died altogether.

The grim rearguard of the Celestial Vindicators came out from the gate. A gap opened up. More trumpets sounded, and the gate's light swelled again, and the Hammers of Sigmar came forth. The Hammerhands were at the fore, Lord-Celestant Vandus Hammerhand upon the dracoth Calanax leading them.

Amid Vandus' own ranks were many who had fallen, and this was giving the Lord-Celestant cause for concern.

Vandus had summoned his Lord-Relictor, Ionus Cryptborn, to march at his side. They spoke quietly. Overly cautious perhaps, for the trudge of thousands of feet covered all but the loudest clarions and warsongs.

'Thostos has changed,' said Vandus to Ionus. 'He speaks only a little, and what he says is distant. I feel that I must strive constantly for his attention. His eyes burn with blue fire. The air crackles around him and all who approach him feel the heat of his rage. And he is not alone.'

'Small wonder,' replied Ionus, 'for here in the Bright Tor Mountains, Thostos died. Under these same peaks, he will be avenged.'

'I spoke with him on the way to the muster chamber. I asked him if he had been changed, if we were truly eternal as Lord Sigmar promised.'

'And what did he reply?'

'He said "yes". To which of the two questions, I cannot fathom. Then he strode away from me.'

Calanax rumbled. Vandus absently scratched at the celestial beast's neck.

'I see,' said Ionus.

'Ionus, I call you to me for counsel. You wield the magics of the storm.'

'At my lord Sigmar's command.'

'You came from death, so they say.'

'I have two masters. You know that, friend of old.'

'Then please, as my friend and adviser, tell me what has occurred? We are promised eternity to bring war upon the minions of the Four, but I did not expect it to take this course. I see it in others too, many of my own. Andricus and Laudus are reluctant to discuss it with me.'

'It is simple, Lord-Celestant. Your warriors have died and returned. Their alteration is inevitable.'

The Lord-Relictor carried a heavy reliquary: the bones of a hero from the Age of Myth in an open casket upon a staff. The casket was surmounted by a starburst of gold, and many other fittings of metal besides. It was heavy, but Ionus carried it as if it were nothing, and easily kept pace with Calanax's swaying stride.

'How is this inevitable?'

'Death is a constant. It wraps everything, binding all fate as tight as a funeral shroud. One day, all this will die. Sigmar will die, you and I will die, the Four will die. We are eternal, yes, but even eternity is not without end. When all else is dead, then death will be the last to die. Sigmar defies death with his magic, plucking us from the underworlds and reforging our mortal form. Death is jealous. When our warriors skirt the borders of that dark country, a part of them is stolen away.'

'None can defy Sigmar,' said Vandus.

'Death can, Vandus. Death only seeks to take its due. Sigmar is the thief in this affair, not death,' said Ionus. 'And so death snatches at our spirits, and we return to this life a little diminished as we pass him by. The shortfall has to be made up somehow.'

'With what?'

Ionus shrugged. 'Sigmar is the lord of the storm – I serve him but I am of death's realm. You ask me of death, and are right to do so, for I guard the souls of our comrades. But to know the secrets of the storm, one must ask the lord of storms. And I do not think he will give up his knowledge.'

Vandus blew out a breath.

'There is something else on your mind, Hammerhand?'

'Yes, there is more. I have been troubled by sights of things to come. Visions. I am unsure of them. Are they part of the God-King's gift, or have I too been changed?'

'You have not died. You remain as you were.'

'Nevertheless, I was stolen from under death's nose, and I

was exposed to the fell energies of the Gate of Wrath. The unlight of Chaos touched me, Ionus. Have I become impure?'

'Your visions are nothing to be afraid of. Or they might be. How will you know unless you act upon them? This is an age of wonder. Should your visions lead you falsely, pay them no heed and we shall discuss them further. We are fortunate in being able to suffer the worst lapses in judgement yet live to learn from them.'

'Are you not afraid of what might happen to us when we die and return?'

'Death cannot change me, because I already belong to death. Why would death try to take what it already owns? And if I should fall and become as Thostos after my remaking, then what of it? It will be only for a while. Death is a transition. To change is not only the purview of Chaos, but a necessary part of Order also.'

The road from the Bright Tor Gate turned towards the cliffs and began to climb. The gorge of the Silver River dropped away to their right. Behind them, the bizarre sight of the celestial wyrm Argentine heating the Great Crucible dominated the sky. Beyond the cliffs the mountains stepped up, walling away the sky.

At the brink, where the road crossed the cliff top and joined the main Anvrok highway, were two crumbling towers. Once a toll gate perhaps, they were now piles of windblasted stone. Upon them snapped the banners of the Stormhosts in Anvrok's hot wind. The angle of the road's ascent allowed Vandus to see far up and down the line. He caught sight of Thostos, a lonely figure at the front of a tongue of brilliant blue-green. There was a gap of a hundred feet between Vandus' own position and the last of the Celestial Vindicators. Behind the Hammers of Sigmar came the Lions of Sigmar, and so on, a long stream of warriors that led back to the Bright Tor Gate. The road was a marvel of duardin engineering, and although it had seen no maintenance for centuries there were few holes in its well-paved surface. The buttresses holding back the cliffs had stood the test of time and the roadway remained largely clear of debris.

Vandus thought on what Ionus said for a time, as the wide highway mounted higher and the thin lands of the river's margin dropped away. 'Do you think me a coward for asking on this, Ionus?' he asked. 'I assure you I am not. I pledged myself to Sigmar body and soul, and he has rewarded me well. I only wish to know the full price I am being asked to p–'

Vandus was interrupted by a whooping screech. He looked upwards, towards the top of the cliff, and saw tendrils of dark magic. A titanic rumbling growled across the Vale of Anvrok, building to a deafening cacophony, and a long swathe of the cliff face peeled away and came down. Calanax reared, backing into the Knights-Vexillor following Vandus and Ionus. Thostos' Stormhosts ahead threw themselves into a desperate run as a mountain's worth of ore-rich boulders crashed down upon them. Many could not get clear in time, and were swept away to their deaths or buried alive. Vandus' Hammerhands surged behind him, desperate to get to their buried fellows and pushed by the weight of the column still marching up towards them.

'Back, back! Do not approach!' shouted Vandus.

All heeded the wisdom of their lord and halted. From higher up the mountains a second avalanche rushed from the high peaks, dislodged by the collapse of the cliff face, dumping thousands of tonnes of ice and snow atop the rocks.

'Stop the march!' Vandus raised a hand and a frantic series of trumpet calls rang back down the road. The column came to a stumbling halt.

The noise stopped. Stray boulders bounced only yards from his position. Puffs of storm-magic burst from the landslide, whisked upwards to join the distant thunderheads as trapped men succumbed to their wounds.

Dust sifted through the air. By now it was late afternoon and the sun coloured the metal-rich cloud a pale yellow. For a moment shocked silence reigned, to be shattered by braying laughter drifting down from the mountains above.

'Beastmen,' Lord Vandus shouted. 'At them!'

Calanax roared and his draconic voice carried far back down the road. A score of Lord-Celestants broke from the leading three Stormhosts, their dracoths leaping to the mountainside. Vandus leaned forward as Calanax bounded upwards, his sharp claws and momentum propelling him up the nearly sheer surface. They reached the top of the cliff where the main road ran. There, the Bright Tor Mountains intruded deep into the valley, and five peaks reared their snowy heads high above. The scaled beasts bounded onto the slopes beyond the main road.

The beastmen, a strange copper-skinned breed, occupied a shallow ridge cutting out from the mountain. They were spread some distance along the road, but there was a thick knot of them on a canted ledge, grouped around one that Vandus assumed to be the leader. The beast-chief, a shaman of some sort, was a heavily built mutant, his aura alive with dark power. Vandus headed right for him. To his left and right, beastmen broke and ran, their nimble goat's legs granting them unnatural agility on the steep mountainside. But the dracoths were quicker, as surefooted as mountain lions. Terrified bleating echoed through the peaks as the dracoths ran down their prey and tore them apart.

Vandus burst through the shaman's bodyguard. These were larger and better armoured than the feeble specimens the other Lord-Celestants slew, but Calanax ripped them to pieces with his heavy claws just the same. Crude weapons bounced from Calanax's peytral, and those that hit his body were turned by his thick hide. The dracoth bit down hard on a creature and shook his jaws viciously, casting the broken body aside. Vandus was intent upon the leader. The shaman raised a staff of black oak that burned with unholy power, but Vandus smote the creature on the head, slaying it instantly. The ledge was cleared.

'Back, back to the column!' shouted Vandus. He waved his hammer around as a signal then slid from Calanax's back, bent down to the corpse of the beast-shaman and took his prize.

The Lord-Celestants returned to the column. Vandus rode up to Ionus and cast the head of the beastlord to the ground.

'Swift vengeance,' said Ionus.

'Aye,' said Vandus. 'Yet the damage to the Celestial Vindicators cannot be undone.' He was concerned, and a little afraid. 'Some of these men meet their third deaths today. One wonders what they will become.'

Vandus called to his signallers and his Knights-Heraldor.

'We must hold the march. Get men to the top of the cliffs

and send Prosecutors to the mountain tops. And find me our scouts. I want to know how this ambush was missed.' Vandus surveyed the fan of rubble burying the road. 'Send back to the gate for workers and wizard-wrights. We can go no further before we have cleared the way.' He looked back angrily down the stalled column. 'This will cost us at least a day.'

CHAPTER FOUR

The Shattered City

The clearance of the road took time the Stormcasts could ill afford to lose. Vandus urged his men and the workers on to harder efforts, aware always that the delay suited their enemies perfectly. Once the digging had finished, the column set out again, up onto the great highway of Anvrok, and towards their goal. The Bright Tor Mountains brooded over their march, but even they seemed paltry things to the great tower of the sorcerer. This grew ever loftier as they closed, the great eye of Tzeentch sculpted into the top glaring at them from a great height.

Centuries of desolation had done little to diminish the scale of Elixia, and the men looked upon it with sorrow and awe. The tall walls of the Eldritch Fortress withdrew behind shattered ruins as the Stormhosts marched nearer, leaving only the tower visible. Broken buildings crowded the road with increasing density upon the approach, but the city proper was a jagged silhouette upon a bluff.

Vandus ordered a halt at the foot of these cliffs and called a council of war. The twelve Stormhosts were each sent to a different point of the tumbled walls, while a dozen Warrior Chambers were directed northwards to reinforce the Stormcasts holding the Silverway entrance. This could be seen far away, a dark slot in another tumbledown city clinging to the mountainside.

Bidding his men be wary, Vandus ordered the advance of the Stormhosts. He and Thostos led the way through a melted gateway that must once have been every bit as impressive as those of Azyrheim. As Vandus looked upon Elixia's despoliation a thought troubled his mind over and again – this could so easily have been the fate of Azyr had Sigmar not sealed the realmgates.

Statuary lay broken in the streets, ornate temples and palaces were roofless derelicts, only the dryness of Anvrok saving them from total disintegration. Everywhere Vandus witnessed the touch of Chaos: twisted statues, deformations to the ground, buildings warped into ludicrous monstrosities, terrified faces trapped in stone. Friezes and statues were subtly warped to mocking effect: town dignitaries had the heads of swine, gods the faces of fools. Sorrowful phantoms cried on the wind, and when birds were scared up from their eyries, they clattered skywards on wings of metal, shouting in the voices of men.

The Stormhosts were forced to go retinue by retinue along the streets, for their sheer numbers hampered their manoeuvres. The columns, already split on entering the city, were forced to divide again. Tumbled heaps of scrap further blocked the streets, slowing them to a crawl. The Bladestorm and the

Hammerhand Warrior Chambers went together, always at the fore.

Where the voices of the dead were absent, silence ruled the place, swallowing up the footsteps of the Stormcasts. Thostos burned with a palpable fury, his eyes fixed upon the tower of the sorcerer. Andricus Stoneheart shook his head at Vandus. Both were wary of Thostos' change, and Vandus was tense, anticipating disaster to come.

They reached a wide square, paved with green slabs of copper and bronze. Ruined workshops surrounded the space, with enough of their collapsed arcades still intact to hint at the square's past glories. Upon the wall was a sign in ancient script.

'The Square of Living Blades,' read Vandus.

'Here was the armoury of Celemnis, Maiden of the Blades,' said Ionus. He gestured to an impressive ruin on the west side of the square. 'There she bound threads of her hair into the core of each sword. It is said that they could cut through soul and flesh with equal ease.'

In the centre was a single statue of tarnished silver upon a tall plinth. There was a haunting beauty to the woman it depicted, and an overwhelming sadness.

'That must be her, but she died when the city fell, or so I would have thought. Who raised a statue to her?' Ionus paused, suddenly alert. Vandus held up his fist, halting his men.

'What is it?'

'Death. Pain. Something else…' Ionus' words trailed off. His eyes were drawn to the collapsed arches of the arcade, and a movement there. 'Watch the shadows!' called Cryptborn urgently. His Retributor bodyguard drew in close.

As if Ionus' warning were a signal, hundreds of horned warriors came scrambling from the ruins, screaming incoherently.

'The sorcerer's minions,' said Thostos. 'This time he sends evil men to contest our approach.'

'We shall pass the test, brother,' said Vandus. 'Liberators, forward! Judicators, take the high ground!' he ordered. 'These are irritants, nothing more.'

Thostos made no reply, but lifted his hammer and sword and thundered into the square, sparks fizzling on his armour. Savages leapt from the arcade to fall upon him, but they were hurled back, their blood painting the metal red. Lord Thostos drove on across the square, hacking his way towards the road at the other side. His men streamed from the column and ran after him.

'Thostos, wait!' shouted Vandus.

Within seconds, Thostos Bladestorm had disappeared entirely. Vandus had not the time to go after him. Horns blared, and ambush erupted from all sides.

Throughout the city the vanguards of each Stormhost suddenly found themselves beset. Armoured warrior-chiefs roared, and a horde of bare-chested tribesmen burst from concealment. Vandus' Hammerhands were assailed from both sides of the street. Half a dozen fell as the servants of Chaos got among them.

Vandus smashed down a man who leapt at him from a slender bridge. Calanax blasted another apart with a bolt of lightning from his maw.

'I had anticipated an ambush, not an army. They come as if from nowhere!' said Vandus.

'There is magic behind this,' shouted Ionus. He slammed

his reliquary staff down. White light blazed around him. 'But I have magic of my own.'

The worshippers of Tzeentch recoiled as the men they had cut down got to their feet, ready to fight again. Battle raged everywhere. Thostos' Warrior Chamber in particular was becoming overstretched. They fought without order, their thirst for vengeance overcoming their training. A portion of the enemy in the square broke and fled, and the Celestial Vindicators pursued them. Many were laid low by axes, while others were battered to the ground by a hail of metal chunks cast from on high as they went into the westward streets.

'Hold the line!' called Vandus. 'Halt!'

'You may as well call for a hurricane to halt its fury, son,' said Andricus. 'Their prey is in sight, and the Celestial Vindicators will kill them all, or die in the attempt.'

Vandus took stock of his circumstances. With Lord Thostos missing and his Warrior Chamber over-extended, Vandus' own flank was dangerously exposed. Hundreds more Chaos worshippers came out of the ruins, seeking to cut the line of Celestial Vindicators storming after Thostos in two.

'Stoneheart!' called Vandus, pointing at the pursuers.

'Lord-Celestant,' said the Lord-Castellant. 'Hammerhands, with me!' He ran to meet the foe, three dozen paladins at his side.

Calanax whirled around. More of the Stormcasts were making their way into the city, driving into the rear of the ambush. From north and south, sigmarite warhorns sounded. Vandus' host was at the heart of the attack, but the ambushers were being encircled in turn.

'Into the square!' Vandus urged his men. 'Make formation about the statue!'

With a precision born of long practice, the Hammerhands surged forward, Ionus and his Retributors to the front. They carved out a space around the statue, and the Liberators locked their shields around it. Judicators came running, filling the centre of the Hammerhands' hollow square and loosing their bows as they ran, joining their fire with that coming down from the ruins above. The air hissed with arrows. Prosecutors flew in formation overhead, picking off warriors who showed themselves on the roofs.

'Come out! I call to the architect of the attack!' Vandus bellowed. Calanax bounded around the periphery of the square, the pair of them slaying every man they came across. 'Come out and show your face. I, Vandus Hammerhand, challenge you to single combat!' Mocking laughter echoed across the city, but no one came forward.

'Appeals to martial pride will not work here, Vandus,' shouted Ionus. 'The followers of Tzeentch are far subtler than those of Khorne.'

The roar of battle intensified. The broad road beyond the square rang to the meeting of blades as another Warrior Chamber emerged from the south into the ambush. Both sides fought with skill and ferocity, and soon the gutters ran with blood.

Prosecutors were knocked from the sky with lead-weighted bolas, or caught by leaping savages. Vandus glowered behind his mask. Everywhere, mayhem reigned. Unable to bring their full might to bear, the Stormcast phalanxes were being fragmented.

Ionus held the centre of the square. Vandus sent his own Liberators to intercept a mob of bare-chested axemen forming a battle line to challenge Ionus' position. Knights armoured in blue and yellow thundered out through the tall arches of the ancient Celemnite workshop. At Vandus' command, Judicators broke from the back of the square, firing arrows on the move. To the mouth of each alleyway Vandus sent a retinue of Protectors. They stood no more than five abreast, but their whirling swordstaves set up an impenetrable barrier, and they killed until the alleys were blocked by the dead.

The worst was yet to come. Ionus felt it, a gathering fury rising through the ground.

'Vandus!' he shouted. 'Death calls to death, and this place is rife with it!'

Puddles of molten metal welled up through the paving. From each of these rose a spirit, running upward to make the distorted forms of men and women. The faces of these silver-skinned revenants were masks of fury, and they fell upon any they saw. Ionus cursed, and set his magic to driving them back. The Stormcasts suffered for his distraction.

A shadow passed over Vandus as a manticore swooped low, wings wide. The body was that of a huge hunting cat but the face bore some semblance to a man's, its eyes alight with bestial intelligence. Prosecutors pursued the creature, but it jinked and dived to avoid their lightning blasts. The beast carried a cowled figure with a huge spear. The manticore stooped. Giant paws batted Stormcasts off the ruins and the spear's tip flicked out, impaling heads with each sweep. The manticore soared up, folded its wings, then plummeted down onto the pursuing Prosecutors, smashing two to the ground.

The sky was a-thunder with the passing of Sigmar's warriors.

Vandus counted more than a dozen manticores hurtling down from the tall tower.

Andricus Stoneheart gathered men around him and fought to the west while Ionus wrestled with the silvered shades of the dead in the centre. Vandus rode from point to point, exhorting his warriors to do their best, hoping that the ambush would break before they were overwhelmed. In other streets and courtyards, Warrior Chambers gathered into tight knots of resistance. The Stormcast advance halted, and all the while Vandus' gaze was drawn to the tower. A sense of building power wreathed it. The cowled manticore rider made another pass, shouting arcane words that sent black bolts searing into Vandus' men. He wondered for a moment if he were the sorcerer they were seeking, but Thostos had spoken of a horned man. Then a second voice became interwoven with the sound of the battle, coming and going, instilling the ruins with a throbbing pulse. Vandus guessed that this must be the voice of the sorcerer lord. He searched wildly for its source, but it seemed to come from everywhere.

And then suddenly a haunting song began, drowning out all, beautiful and terrible, a song of sorrow and rage. Silver swords shimmered into being wherever the song swelled. These shot out at speed, slicing into Stormcast and Chaos warrior alike. The blades encountered no resistance from either side's plate, cutting through it as if the warriors were clad in soft robes. Chaos worshippers threw themselves at the swords, hoping to wrest them from the air and take them for themselves. Many died in the attempt, but a handful were successful, and with these blades inflicted sore losses on the Stormcast Eternals.

'Celemnite blades,' said Ionus to his men. 'A legacy of a bygone age.'

A disturbance in the wind drew the Lord-Relictor's attention to the corner of the square. A new puddle of molten silver bubbled from the ground, flowing upwards until it formed a gaunt female figure with hair the colour of copper. Rage twisted her beautiful features as she surveyed the carnage.

She opened her jaws far wider than any human could and her scream tore through the square, lifting a curtain of dust before it. Chaos worshippers and Stormcast Eternals staggered and clutched at their ears and throats. Ionus held his reliquary in front of him, matching his will with the maiden's song. Brilliant light flared around him. There was nothing but the screaming song and the pain and light it brought. The scream stopped as abruptly as it had started. All around Ionus, men were dead. With cracks of thunder the lifeless bodies of his guard flashed up and away. A few lone warriors staggered about, blood leaking from their ears, but all who survived were swiftly impaled by the flying blades.

'This city is not shy of horrors, Vandus,' called out Ionus Cryptborn, but Vandus could not hear, for he was embattled a hundred yards away. 'You cannot fight a curse with blades,' he said under his breath.

The terrifying scream rang out again, slaying more warriors. Ionus found himself alone and he had a clear view to the statue. There was a plaque at the statue's feet he had not seen before. 'She would not yield,' it said. He approached the statue. The face was wracked with sorrow and pain, the same face as upon the silver-skinned banshee. Death magic thrummed strongly from the monument, and he realised then that the epitaph was mocking, and the statue not raised from any respect. Curious, he cracked one arm from its shoulder with his hammer. The statue was hollow, with dry bone trapped within.

Ionus turned across the square to where the banshee wailed. He strode towards her, his reliquary before him.

'Celemnis!' he shouted. 'We fight for the same cause!'

The banshee turned, her face twisting in a curious frown.

'Celemnis! Hear my plea, O Queen of Blades,' said the Lord-Relictor. He went to his knees and bowed his head. Celemnis' skirts pulsed and flowed across the ground towards him, until she floated above him. Within the ghost two magics warred. Ionus sensed dark spells striving to trap her and her own essence fighting back. His respect for the warrior-maiden doubled. 'I beseech you, send your ire against those that earned it.' He took the blade from his reliquary, sliding it from the wired finger-bones holding it fast, and held it out, hilt-first. 'This blade is a gift from Sigmar. Do you see? We fight for Sigmar.'

Celemnis looked at Ionus, and she was the epitome of terrible beauty. Her hair floated in a wide halo around her head. Ionus tensed, expecting his end.

Her hair reached out, taking the sword's hilt. Celemnis looked directly at him, a sad smile on her face.

She screamed again, and the world was upended. A wave of anguish blasted across the square and Ionus leaned into it as a man leans into a gale. At the heart of the shout was the whispered promise of death; sweet, beguiling words. He yearned to give into it, to go back to his other master, away from Sigmar's wars, and to join again with his beloved.

One day he would, he swore.

Not today.

The scream ended. The fighting stopped. Chaos worshippers stood stupidly, weapons dropping from nerveless hands.

As one, every single Chaos warrior in the centre of the city dropped dead. The silver ghosts rose shrieking from the battle, ignoring the Stormcast Eternals. Silver swords hissed after them as they flew onwards to the walls of the Eldritch Fortress.

Vandus was amazed. All of a sudden, his foes were dead.

'Onwards! Onwards!' Vandus bellowed. 'Back into formation! To the Eldritch Fortress!'

The Hammers of Sigmar obeyed without hesitation, forming up into orderly blocks before hurrying forwards. The remaining Celestial Vindicators ignored him completely, running further into the city in search of new foes to slay.

Furious, Vandus vaulted from Calanax and onto a tumbled ruin. He ran up onto the tilted head of a toppled stardrake statue, intending to order Thostos' Warrior Chamber back into the column. But as he drew in his breath to shout, his eyesight clouded, his nostrils filled with phantom scents and his head swam.

'No, not now, not...' A vision seized him with such blinding force it sent him to his knees.

He whirled away to a different place, speeding up over the Anvrok Vale. He came to a dizzying stop, and Lord Vandus saw a waterfall of silver, frozen in time. In the sky beyond it, the silver wyrm Argentine coiled and fought with another dragon mightier still. All the while Vandus' eyes were drawn upwards, towards the top of the falls and the crucible there. He was in the air, with nothing ahead and nothing below.

The vision passed. Vandus shook in its aftermath. Thunder rumbled and it began to rain. Sigmar's lightning clove deep into the city; reinforcements were arriving.

Vandus got back to his feet unsteadily and took stock. The Celestial Vindicators were gone. The area around the square was clear, but the sound of fighting echoed through the streets still. The tower of the sorcerer wavered in a haze of magic. He was running out of time, and made to go back down to the statue and Calanax.

'My lord! The sky! Get down!' shouted his Knight-Vexillor.

The warning came too late. Four manticores rushed at him and his command echelon in the street, claws out. Three struck the Stormcasts; one was smashed into the ground by heavy hammers, but the other two raked a long, clattered furrow in the warriors before shooting skywards again. The fourth was ridden by a huge Chaos lord, and came directly at Vandus. No amount of skill or speed could stop the beast's dive. The Lord-Celestant leapt to the side, but he was still sluggish from his vision and moved too slowly. A heavy blow slammed into his shoulder and a spear transfixed him. He was plucked up and carried away, the ground dropping beneath him. All his weight was upon the spear point. Barbs bit deep into his flesh. Vandus grabbed at it with both hands, fearful his own weight would wrench him into pieces. The iron shaft was slippery with his blood. Gripping it sent agonies sparking down the nerves of his arm.

Let go, part of him said. Take brief pain and be returned by

Sigmar. But then he thought of Thostos and his cold manner since he had returned, and gripped harder.

A cruel face looked down upon him, heavyset and doleful. The lord sneered.

'So you are the Hammerhand. I thought you should be mightier, but here you are speared like a fish.'

'You cannot kill me,' choked out Vandus. Speaking sent further throbs of pain across his upper back.

'We shall see. I am Lord Maerac, and I shall be your death.'

'You are the servant of the sorcerer.'

Maerac laughed. 'Ephryx is a fool if he believes that, and you are a greater fool to say it.'

Vandus gripped the spear. His situation was hopeless. Below him Stormcasts poured through the city, but the battle was far from over. Further in, nearer the shrouded outline of the Eldritch Fortress, there were more servants of Chaos. There the fight continued. Bright lines of Sigmar's warriors duelled on every street with the followers of the Tzeentch while overhead, lightning crackled across a darkening sky.

Maerac scowled at the storm. He twisted the spear and Vandus cried out.

'What is this fascination your god has for dreary weather?' said Maerac. 'Does he think he impresses us with his lightning and his thunder? He is a bigger fool than you! Your attack is faltering, and you face but a portion of the might of this realm. I am only one lord.' Maerac leaned over in his saddle. 'But soon I shall be the only lord. I shall take the hammer. I have been told by the Oracle himself that no mortal army can take Sigmar's weapon. What hope do you have?'

Vandus caught sight of a flash of turquoise at the top of a

bell tower as Maerac banked around it. The lord intended to take him towards the fortress as a prisoner.

'We are no mortal army,' Vandus said.

A blur of blue-green hurtled through the air from the tower. Lightning blazed all around it. The manticore jerked with a heavy impact and Maerac turned in shock to find Thostos standing astride his mount. He dropped his spear, and Vandus made a desperate lunge for the manticore's neck. Pain punished him as he grasped two handfuls of blue mane. The manticore snapped at him, swerving sharply left. The spear dragged at Vandus' shoulder, robbing all the strength from his left arm, and he nearly let go.

Thostos roared. Maerac drew his sword and raised it in a block, but Thostos' hammer shattered it and carried on straight into Maerac's face. The blow was so powerful that it obliterated Maerac's head completely. The corpse spouted blood into the wind and slid sideways in its flying harness. The manticore bucked and twisted, but Thostos would not be shaken loose. The sword in his left hand punched through the manticore's skull and its wings folded, causing it to fall like a stone and smash through the wall of a ruined temple.

Thostos stepped from the dead creature's back. He extended a hand to Vandus, and hauled him to his feet. Then he took up the spear and looked questioningly at Vandus.

Vandus nodded, his teeth gritted against the pain. 'Do it,' he said.

Vandus screamed in agony as Thostos forced the barbs out of his back. He staggered and sank to his knees. One chop of Thostos' runeblade cut the head off the spear and with a ragged groan, Vandus dragged the shaft from his body and dropped it.

'The Stormhosts must see you live,' said Thostos, and there was a trace of emotion to his words that had been absent since his Reforging.

Together they left the temple, battered but alive. Calanax had sought out his lord, drawn to him by their bond. Vandus mounted him with Thostos' aid, and rode to the heart of the Stormcast forces again.

Manticores still swooped and harried the forces. Arrows arced up at them, driving the monsters off, only for them to come back around.

'Maerac is dead!' shouted Vandus, his voice amplified by the divine magic burning in him. 'Lord-Celestant Thostos Bladestorm slew him! Stay and suffer the same fate!'

It was enough. With several of their number dead, their king slain and much fire coming at them from the ground, the beast riders wheeled away and flew back to their scattered domains with all the speed their mounts could muster.

Upon seeing their masters abandon them, the morale of the Chaos army broke. In ever greater masses, the bondsmen of Manticorea fled, the wrath of the Stormcasts following them upon swift wings of light.

The Stormhosts' vanguard plunged on towards the fortress. Vandus and Calanax ran past them all, until they were in front. The sense of magic on the air intensified and the outline of the tower and the fortress walls blurred into obscurity. There came a soft wash of air, and a tremor set the ruins shaking. The ground quaked and the Stormhosts stumbled.

'No!' shouted Vandus. He spurred Calanax into a gallop, gritting his teeth at the jarring pain in his shoulder. Buildings came down around him, ancient crystal shattering and metal tearing with mournful groans. The ground buckled under him, rising up as if turned by a plough. A fresh ridge rose up in the ruins, a wrinkle in the earth that upset the remains of the city, making them lean drunkenly on footings of broken stone.

Calanax surged up the ridge as it stopped growing and the tremors ceased. At the summit, Vandus' worst fears were realised.

The Hammerhands clambered up behind him. Ionus and Andricus arrived at his side. Not a soul amongst them spoke. Before them was a crater, wide and deep.

'It's gone,' said Lord Vandus dully. 'And the hammer with it.'

'So we go after it,' said Ionus Cryptborn. 'We keep going until we find it.'

'But how, if some fell power has claimed it and taken it who knows where?'

Cryptborn shrugged. 'Fear not, Lord Vandus. We will find a way.'

CHAPTER FIVE

Dragonfate dais

The leaders of the Stormhosts gathered atop the crater's crest. Tempers ran hot and bewilderment ruled. No decision had been reached as to what to do next, and as the day grew old none seemed to be forthcoming.

Ionus did not take part in the debate. He found a block of stone to one side and sat upon it, removing his helmet to allow his pale skin to feel the sun and the sweat to dry. He remained there, facing west, as the day's shadows lengthened and the great wyrm shone in the evening, its flames becoming brighter as the sky darkened. When Chamon's sun had slunk past its coils and dipped behind distant Knatrok, a shimmer in the air resolved into a lithe figure.

Ionus stood and bowed, his hand over his heart.

'Celemnis, the Silver Maiden. I give you greetings of the night. We are kin, you and I. United in death.'

She said nothing, but floated forward, the silver of her lower body flowing over the freshly turned rubble of Elixia. She gave Ionus a sad, lingering smile. Her face had lost its ferocious aspect, and Ionus presumed that aside from her skin of metal she looked now much as she had in life: a beautiful, proud face haloed by red hair. She bowed her head and reached out a hand. From it sprouted a long tendril of rippling silver. It steadied itself and became the sword Ionus had gifted her from his reliquary. She took it in both hands and offered it up to him much as he had offered it to her.

Ionus took the returned blade. Its edges glimmered sharp and silver, and he marvelled at the change.

'Your work?'

She smiled again.

'You have done me a great honour, my lady.'

By now, others had noticed what was occurring. The arguments of the war council subsided, and the lords of the hosts turned to watch this strange exchange.

Ionus carefully replaced the hilt of the sword into the clasped hands of the skeleton on his staff. 'Perhaps you could do me another. I would not ask, as you have done so much for us already, but we have come to an impasse. Your efforts are important. If we succeed here, then this city might live again, and you could go to your rest.' He smiled. 'Or you might linger, and remain its guardian.'

She tilted her head to the side, awaiting his request.

'Thank you, my lady. Firstly, tell me – where has the castle fled to?'

She looked upwards at the Great Crucible and pointed.

'I see. And how might we venture there with so great an assemblage?'

She smiled again, and beckoned. Without waiting to see if Ionus followed, she set off west into the city. The Lord-Relictor went after her, tilitng his head to meet Lord Vandus' gaze. Vandus nodded and motioned for his men to follow.

A sepulchral quiet was on the city, and Vandus had no desire to break it in case the maiden's magic be broken also.

'Sound no trumpet and say little,' Vandus said, 'but spread the word. The Silver Maiden shows us the way.'

The Stormhosts gathered themselves rapidly and said nothing as commanded. They had marched for days and fought for much of the morning, but the magic of Sigmar made them strong and unwearying. Sleep they could stave off for days, if need be. And so it was, for Celemnis did not halt to let them rest, but continued westward at a steady, unhurried speed.

They passed back along the Anvrok highway, past the turn to the Bright Tor Gate. There Vandus sent messengers down to the encampment and others to the entrance of the Silverway, and bade them take news of their progress back to Sigmaron.

On for a dozen more miles the Stormcasts proceeded, before Celemnis took them up an unassuming spur of the road into the Bright Tor Mountains. In this part of Anvrok there was no sign of the Stormhosts' recent invasion. They trod secret paths shown to them by Cryptborn's strange ally. Chaos tribes that had yet to face the Stormcast Eternals launched attacks, but they retreated soon enough. Once three had been bested, the army was attacked no more.

Celemnis and Ionus led the way, the others keeping a wary distance. Cryptborn could be seen speaking with the ghost and listening attentively. What they spoke of was his alone to know; he was too far ahead for his words to be heard clearly, and from her they heard nothing at all.

Before the eighth day was out, the Stormhosts emerged from a narrow pass and Vandus stopped in amazement.

'The Argent Falls,' he said.

For the last three days the confines of the mountains had hidden all but hints of the crucible and its strange guardian. Now revealed, Argentine filled the horizon, its coils impossibly vast. The Great Crucible formed a halo around Argentine's upturned head. The roar of the dragonfires that heated the crucible were loud. The mountains there rose up high, but gusting, hot winds blew over them from the drake's fires and molten silver, keeping them warm and free of snow.

The Argent Falls plunged from the edge of the crucible, falling miles through the air in a wide sheet. The surface was silver, but the orange glow of smelting was visible in the folds of the liquid. Where the falls struck the rock of Anvrok, gobbets of precious metal splattered across the mountainside, and a wide area around the river's headwater was covered in globular formations of pure silver. The remains of catcher channels could be seen half-buried in the metal. These ruins of industry were far below the Stormcasts, who looked down onto them from a high road.

Beyond the falls was a little more of the land of Anvrok, then the mountains stopped abruptly and the skyvoids began. The road they were on curled downwards, closer to the falls, before it crossed a bridge over a ravine. Smaller roads led off to the works there, and then the main road rose up again to a township on a crag opposite the army, as ruinous as every other city in Anvrok. At the brink of the cliff the circular platform of a dais rose up on an artfully coiled staircase. Six statues of dragons stood around its circumference.

Vandus was close to Ionus and Celemnis, and heard his Lord-Relictor speak.

'A dragonfate dais?' Ionus said. 'How can that aid us?'

Celemnis pointed a long-nailed finger at the dais and disappeared.

Vandus waited a moment before calling out. 'Has she departed?'

'No. I sense her still,' Ionus replied.

Vandus rode up beside him.

'I am glad. She is a good ally.'

'She is in great pain,' said Ionus matter-of-factly. 'This place must have been fabulously wealthy. I have seen many dragonfate shrines, but never one rendered in solid silver.'

Calanax made a growling purr.

'Calanax approves. This is a fitting honour to the great drakes. Silver is favoured by them.'

Vandus stroked between Calanax's horns. 'And yet, against the barbaric hordes of Chaos, the protection of their old gods availed them little. There is only one god who can stand before the Four, and that god is Sigmar. What would the Silver Maiden have us do, I wonder?'

'Let us consider the question upon the dais,' said Ionus. 'The answer may come to us there more easily, and that is where she pointed.'

'We cannot all go – look at the road. The town is small.'

'We should not go alone. We have suffered several ambushes already. Summon Thostos and let his Warrior Chamber come with ours. He is deeply involved in this affair,' said Ionus.

Vandus nodded. He raised his hand and horns blew. The Hammerhands and the Bladestorms came forward. Together, they went down into the valley and up into the ruined town of Silverfall.

The rumble of the Argent Falls drowned out all other sound. The heat of the silver was intense, and Vandus marvelled that men had lived there at all. Roofless houses and workshops stretched up the mountainside behind the crag for some way, exhibiting that mix of duardin and mannish craftsmanship that was the hallmark of Anvrok's dead civilisation.

They reached the dais. The base of its supporting stair rose from a village square and a low wall edged it, but much of it had fallen away, leaving a dangerous drop to the rocks and silver accretions below.

'Thostos, Ionus, Andricus – come with me onto the dais,' said Vandus.

No sooner had he said the words than a deeper roar undercut the thunder of the Argent Falls: the unnatural grind of machinery. It came from thin air.

'To arms!' he yelled.

'Another bloody ambush,' growled Andricus. 'Judicators! To higher ground. Liberators, shieldwall.'

All around the assembled brotherhoods, slivers of green light split the air. Green-black drills ground through each, ripping wide the fabric of reality before withdrawing.

'Stormfiends!' said a Liberator. 'Skaven!'

His warning was cut short by a hail of bullets. Giant, rat-like monsters shouldered their way out of the tears in the weft of the world. Some bore multi-barrelled guns in the place of fists, and they fired as they came. Dozens of Stormcasts were shredded, falling to their knees before disappearing in blurs of azure lightning. Behind the gun-beasts came more giants, these armed with whirring drills and grinders. They bowed their heads and charged.

'Stand ready!' called Vandus.

'Judicators, loose!' yelled Andricus.

A storm of bolts spat through the air, felling one of the giant rat monsters. It collapsed face first into the dirt with a pitiful grunt, revealing the swollen-headed rat-thing bonded to its back. This twisted ratling mewled horribly until a hammer stroke ended its misery. Liberators charged the stormfiends. Those warriors that were not knocked flying by the swipes of the creatures' arms rained hammer blows upon knees and ankles, hoping to bring the giant beings low. Vandus drove Calanax into the fray, but the stormfiends proved more than a match for the Lord-Celestant and his steed, and they were driven back under the shadow of the dais. The stormfiends grunted in recognition, seeming to single him out, and soon Vandus was surrounded by three of the things.

'Protect the Lord-Celestant!' he heard Andricus shout.

The rest of the battlefield was a blur to Vandus, his attention was focused solely on fending off the hammering blows of the stormfiends. Calanax gutted one and Vandus smashed the shoulder of another, but there were more coming and were it not for the might of Heldensen, he would have been overcome.

Behind the stormfiends came a flood of the lesser ratmen. They leapt from the tears in the world and ran for cover with preternatural speed. Once established there, they opened fire with their rifles, the force of their magical bullets punching through sigmarite and knocking Stormcasts from their feet. The noise of battle rose high enough to challenge the falls: the racket of the skaven's hellish weaponry, the whoosh of slain Stormcasts departing for Azyr, the clang of weapons, the shouts of men, and a frantic chittering at the edge of hearing.

Vandus parried another deadly blow. Calanax was forced closer to the edge of the cliffs.

Then Vandus saw turquoise armour amid the gold of his own men. Thostos roared, and in that war cry was something of the man Vandus had known before. He and his warriors ran full tilt into the stormfiends.

'Vandus! Vandus! We come!' shouted Thostos. He cut a stormfiend's leg free, sending it toppling. Hammers smashed into its head and the grafted rider, bludgeoning both to death.

'Slay the leader!' bellowed Vandus.

The warlord was larger than his servants, more metal than flesh, surrounded by a bodyguard of heavily armoured, black-furred henchmen. Thostos rallied his men about him and began battering his way toward the warlord, while Vandus was fully occupied deflecting the blows of a stormfiend. The next thing Vandus saw was a gout of black-green fire washing over his friend. Thostos' men fell, incinerated within their armour.

'Thostos!' shouted Vandus, and his blow slew a further stormfiend, smashing its ribcage with a blast of energy. He urged Calanax forward but the dracoth was shoved back.

Another blast of fire. What Vandus saw next almost fatally distracted him.

Thostos strode forward, unharmed. The warpfire of the

skaven beast washed over him with no effect, and he slew the creature with a whirl of hammer and sword. Thostos pushed on for the warlord. The stormvermin bodyguard, somewhat tentatively, moved in to engage, but their halberds broke upon the Lord-Castellant's inviolable skin, and Thostos struck them down in seconds. The leader fled, leaping up the stairs in fear. Andricus was close by and went after him.

Vandus was now embattled with only two of the giant rat-men. Calanax clamped his jaw around the leg of one while Vandus battered back the second. With a mighty heave, Calanax sent it toppling from the precipice.

The second fought on. Calanax rounded on it while it was still reeling from Vandus' blow and bit off its head. Still it fought. Whirling blades topped the stumps of its fists and these caught on Heldensen, juddering hard until they pushed the hammer aside. The creature smashed into Vandus' injured shoulder and reopened the wound Maerac had dealt him. He cried in pain, backhanding his hammer into the beast's chest and slaying it finally.

A second wave of stormfiends were emerging from the cracks between the worlds. Two came from a slit nearby, squeak-roaring with idiot rage. A pair of Prosecutors swept over them, blinding them with blasts of their hammers. Vandus and Calanax leapt at them, the impact of their charge sending one of the creatures back into the hole it had come from. Vandus directed Heldensen against the second, obliterating it.

Then green lightning was all about him. A bolt of it sent Calanax to his knees. Vandus urged him to rise, but Calanax was dazed and unresponsive. The Stormcast looked up to see a bizarre, clattering machine bouncing down the ruined streets, spitting more lightning.

'Up, Calanax. Up!' he shouted.

Bright white light speared down. The war machine exploded, raining wood and iron all over the town. A large wheel bounced down the street, and hurtled off the edge of the cliff. From the steps to the dragonfate dais, Ionus nodded at Vandus, the afterglow of his spell lighting his face.

The ratmen were wavering. A strange stench filled the square. As one, they turned and fled, shrieking in terror. They melted into the ruins and vanished.

The noise of battle ceased. There were three isolated crackles of fire, then the roar of the falls reasserted itself. Thostos came to Vandus' side, drenched in blood. He raised his sword.

'Victory.'

'Victory!' Vandus cried, and clanged his hammer against Thostos' blade. He turned to raise a salute to Andricus upon the dais.

Andricus raised his own blade. A final gunshot rang out. Andricus Stoneheart buckled and fell, vanishing in a blur of light a moment before he could hit the street.

Vandus, Ionus and Thostos stood upon the dais. The view over the falls from the shrine was glorious, but Vandus spared it no glance. His jubilation at their victory was ashes in his mouth; Andricus would be sorely missed in the coming fight.

'We cannot call upon the God-King's beneficence again,' protested Vandus. 'The others look to us. We must show strength, not weakness. And how are we to speak to the heavens?'

'Call upon the Great Drake,' rumbled Thostos. 'These statues are raised to him.'

'That was Celemnis' intention,' said Ionus. 'I am sure of it.'

Vandus glanced from one man to the other. His eyes lingered on Thostos' cool blue stare. Would Andricus be that way when he returned? He felt a shiver of unease around Thostos where before there had been only friendship. 'But... I know not how,' said Vandus.

Calanax roared and rumbled as he prowled up the stairs to join the lords atop the dais. The dracoth looked down upon his master, head cocked to one side in question. Vandus nodded hesitantly, unsure if he understood the beast. 'Very well. If you intend to talk with the Great Drake, go ahead. What harm can it do?'

'You must retreat to the edges of the dais,' said Ionus. 'The dracoth intends to speak with his father, the Great Drake Dracothion, the first and greatest of their kind.'

For an hour the dracoth bellowed and roared at the sky. None of the men understood his speech, but the urgency of it was arresting. In ones and twos the Stormcasts ceased combing the ruins for the skaven and came to a halt, all eyes on the dragonfate dais. Upon the other crag where the majority of the army waited, the dracoths of other Lord-Celestants assembled, adding their voices to Calanax's roar one by one.

Darkness fell. The stars were dim against the brightness of the silver wyrm's fires and the town flickered in their perpetual firelight.

Finally, Calanax ceased his petition. The stars grew brighter, and brighter, until they outshone the fires of Argentine. The sky blazed as gloriously as those of Azyr. Stars moved, and the night rippled and resolved itself into a smiling reptilian face as wide as the sky.

'My son!' boomed the Great Drake Dracothion. His voice rumbled from the mountain peaks. He could surely be seen and heard in every country of the Hanging Valleys of Anvrok. His teeth were the glimmer of stars and in his coils galaxies turned. 'How fare the wars of men?'

Calanax roared, his dragon-tongue inscrutable.

'We have a boon to ask of you, mighty one,' called Vandus. He stepped out from between the dragon statues, risking the zodiac beast's scrutiny. 'We must find the Eldritch Fortress that once crested the Shattered City.'

Dracothion's regard pinned him in place. Vandus felt as a mouse must when sighted by a hawk.

'I preferred it when it was Elixia, the Sculpted City,' the drake said. There was a weighty mirth, timeless and savage, behind Dracothion's words.

'Tell us where the fortress is, and Elixia might rise again.'

'A dark place, yet with a heart of light,' said the beast. 'I saw it rise. It bathes within the crucible. Do you seek to reach it? To claim the Hammer of the Stars?'

'We do,' said Vandus.

'Then the sea of silver must cool,' said Dracothion. 'The flames must go out. It has been long since I dared the wyrm Argentine's fires. He was among my most favoured children before pride wormed into him and Tzeentch's promises turned that into a canker. I will go and speak with him, for he is due a father's rebuke. Go swiftly, then, whilst his will is diverted. Farewell, noble Calanax!'

The great dragon disappeared. A cloud of lights streaked

across the sky, shimmering into the west. The assembled Stormcasts watched in awe. The stars halted. Constellations swirled and took on the form of the dragon again. Jaws sketched in stars arrowed towards Argentine, and closed about his throat.

The silver wyrm jerked. Its roar shook the mountains, carried upon an angry wind that made Stormcast banners crack and icons waver. The wyrm's fires were extinguished and flickering twilight was banished. True night fell. The two titans strove against each other in the sky. The underside of the Great Crucible was revealed entirely, the red heat-glow dimming quickly, and the mountains cooling with it.

Slowly the Argent Falls solidified. A thick skin wrinkled over the silver. Great globs appeared, breaking the flow of the metal's silken appearance and rendering it ugly. The orange heat faded away, and the surface became a leaden grey in the fresh-born twilight. Hill-sized lumps of semi-molten silver slammed down, the first splashing apart with the impact, those coming later bouncing messily away and rolling glutinously down the hill, until the lumps that fell free were wholly solid. The river's flow slowed, stiffened and stopped. The falls and river were both arrested, and the whole cooled into a solid, lumpen mass that creaked and pinged with the eerie music of metal.

'Listen!' said Ionus. 'Celemnis returns!'

The Silver Maiden's haunting song filled the mountain valleys. Hundreds of Celemnis' flying swords flew to hang in front of the frozen waterfall.

Celemnis' wordless singing reached a crescendo, and the swords plunged into the metal, making themselves into the rungs of a dangerous ladder.

Overhead, the battle of titans raged on in the sky as Dracothion fought his wayward offspring. The Eternals gaped at the spectacle, for Dracothion had served as Sigmar's mount, and was godly himself.

'We climb, then,' said Thostos. Now battle had gone, his voice had become colourless once more.

'Aye,' said Vandus. 'We climb. All of us.'

CHAPTER SIX

The battle of the crucible

'You seem nervous, sorcerer.'

Ephryx looked up from his scrying bowl. King Vexos Thrond had come into his chamber unannounced again. The man was insufferable.

'You are king of all you survey in the Great Crucible,' said Ephryx. 'But you are not lord of this fortress. Send word you are coming next time – I am engaged in delicate magics that your arrogant interruptions risk.'

Ephryx turned his back on the giant warrior-king, a pointed signal that he should depart. Thrond did not. Ephryx frowned.

'Do you treat all your hosts with such ill manners?' asked Thrond.

'Do you treat all your guests so poorly?' asked Ephryx.

'The beasts of my menagerie are always hungry, Ephryx. Do not insult me.'

Ephryx flapped a dismissive hand. 'Your coterie of monsters

from the rim might be enough to ensure your rule of the crucible, your majesty, but I have the support of Tzeentch himself. Be wary that I do not turn your creatures into statues of tin.'

Thrond snorted and came to Ephryx's side. Thrond was enormous, for he too was favoured by Tzeentch. The sale of his soul had ensured Thrond would rule forever, and the king had become more and more swollen with the energies of Chaos as the years had passed. He had been the lord of the crucible almost as long as Ephryx had ruled Anvrok. The two were long-standing, if wary, allies.

The crucible king bent his horned helm to Ephryx's golden scrying bowl – Ephryx had never seen him without it. Deep in the vision slits, tawny eyes reflected the bowl's picture in miniature: Stormcasts ascending upon a ladder of swords or following the dracoths, who clawed handholds into the metal as they went. 'They are still climbing.'

'As they have been for the last four days,' said Ephryx. In the bowl, the Stormcasts toiled upwards without pause. 'See how they struggle. It is hard work for them. They are created for war.' He laughed. 'Each must weigh as much as three mortal men. They will be weakened when they attain the crucible lip.'

'Yet they near the top. Do they lose many of their number?' Thrond had a reputation for sudden fury. He was frustrated by the demands Tzeentch forced on him, and horrified at the boredom his eternal life brought. A fine jest on Tzeentch's part, but his temper put Ephryx in danger.

'Skyrays dog them, but take only a few. They are guarded by many winged warriors. I have seen others grip the swords too tightly and shear off their own fingers. Those who fall will fall forever through the void. Celemnis is a dubious friend.'

Ephryx smiled unpleasantly. The thought amused him. 'Their force is reduced further by dissension. There was some kind of disagreement before they began.' Ephryx's smile grew wider still. 'Many remained below in my land, and go about other business.' He scowled. The trespassers irritated him, but there was nothing he could do about it from up here.

'How many come?'

'A thousand, I would say,' said Ephryx distractedly. He dearly hoped Thrond would get the point and depart. 'The dragons battle still. Now that is a sight I have never seen.'

Thrond grunted. 'Argentine's distraction at least provides my men with the chance for extra sport. They welcome this unlooked-for solidification of the silver. Ordinarily we must wait for the moon's full waxing before we hunt upon the sea.'

'Do not let them roam far. There will be plenty more sport soon enough, when the enemy reach the brink. They must be delayed long enough for me to effect another transloca-tion. I'll have them chasing this fortress all over the realm.' Naturally, this was only one option Ephryx had, and the least favoured, but he wasn't about to tell Thrond that.

'Do you tell a king his business in his own kingdom?'

Ephryx curled his lip. 'No,' he said.

'As it should be,' said Thrond. 'I will gather my army. Life has been somewhat tedious of late. I look forward to this battle. I will buy you your time, sorcerer, so you may build your power to remove your fortress from my kingdom. But remove it you will.'

Thrond swaggered out. Another muscle-bound idiot. Ephryx was doubtful Thrond could be killed easily, and he was far more dangerous than Maerac. Still, he mused, we shall see how well his strength serves him when he is trapped forever in the Crystal Labyrinth.

Ephryx pursed his lips in thought. He supposed he ought to thank the Stormhosts for dealing with Maerac. He watched the dragons fighting, immense god-beasts tearing wounds the length of canyons in each other. The celestial dragon was coming off worse. Argentine was youthful as star-dragons measure things, and invigorated by the power of Chaos. That battle would not last much longer. With luck, Argentine would drive off Dracothion and melt the silver before the Stormcasts could reach the lip. Now wouldn't that be a fine sight, and most fortuitous.

He left the bowl troubled. Somehow, fortune did not seem to be on his side. From the great window of his tower he looked out across Thrond's lands. The crucible kingdom was a series of islands in the Silver Sea, each capped by an ornate castle and linked by a complex set of raised causeways and bridges. Ephryx had brought the Eldritch Fortress to rest upon the biggest island. Thrond's own citadel occupied this island also, but jutted out from the side. He had not built it at the summit, for that lay directly beneath the Shardgate. That suited the sorcerer perfectly.

As Ephryx thought of the gate, the window showed him a jagged gash in the world surrounded by a gemstone-studded archway that glowed with a hard, diamond light, for the Shardgate opened directly into the Crystal Labyrinth of Tzeentch and was the chief entrance to this realm for the god's servants. Ephryx could feel the regard of the Great Changer coming from the gate, fixed upon him with a mixture of amusement, pride and malice. The giant crystals around the opening glinted threateningly.

Ephryx shuddered and bade the window show him the work of his slaves as they patched and mended his ruptured castle walls. He had brought his fortress beneath the Shardgate not only to deny the hammer to the sigmarites, but to speed the delivery of all of Chamon to Tzeentch. For that to happen, he needed the Stormcast Eternals to attack one more time, to die and fill his copper skulls with their magic.

Kairos was as likely to stop him as to aid him now, wishing to bring the prize to Tzeentch himself. They were coming to the end of their relationship.

Ephryx crossed his arms. Only a week ago everything had seemed so simple. Now he had Thrond threatening him, Kairos moving against him and Sigmar himself banging on the gate. He had to either fulfil his ultimate ambition or move the fortress by the time the Stormcast Eternals got there, and all before Kairos did whatever it was Kairos wanted to do.

As he thought over his predicament, his frustration gave birth to a fresh smile. Why pledge oneself body and soul to the master of the great game if one did not enjoy playing? The board as presented offered a fine challenge.

A great bellow shattered his train of thought. His window swerved and looked for him, finding the source. Dracothion was departing, his mighty head rising over the low hills of the crucible's rim. Swimming through the aether, he fled ponderously upward, bleeding starlight from a thousand wounds. Ephryx's window followed the Father of Dragons as he ascended high into the sky. There he vanished with a nova flash, and returned to the heavens of Azyr.

Moments later, Argentine's flames roared anew.

* * *

'Form up!' bellowed Vandus. A thin line of Stormcasts bowed outward around the lip of the falls. A horde of Chaos warriors came at them.

'Protect those still climbing!' Thostos shouted.

Calanax roared. Others of his kind answered. Prosecutors alighted on the slippery metal to drag their comrades up from the ladder of swords. Others worked in pairs, wings beating hard as they flew Judicators and Liberators up. A mist had met the Stormcasts as the first gained the lip of the falls, but this was clearing and Vandus had a good view of exactly what they were up against.

The oncoming horde was emerging from a confusion of high towers, walkways and bridges that stretched across the set sea, linking island to island. In the far distance a plug of rock jutted out of the metal, the plateau atop it veiled by multicoloured clouds. The Eldritch Fortress was there. Even as Vandus looked upon it he was sure the great eye atop the central tower was looking at him in turn, as well as something on the far side of the gate that glimmered above. Master and servant regarded Vandus with uncloaked hatred.

Night had come. The scarred face of the Alchemist's Moon was crawling along the horizon, its light glinting from plates of Chaos armour as the horde raced down steps and from wharfs onto the solid silver.

'Ionus!' Vandus called. 'The sea warms already.'

'We do not have much time,' said the Lord-Relictor.

'We must take the fight to them,' said Thostos, and strode forward.

'He waits for no counsel,' complained Vandus.

'Do not blame him. His wrath fills the hollows left by his death,' said Ionus. 'Come, let us be at them!'

The lords of Azyr led the charge. A wedge formation of Stormcast Eternals from half a dozen different Stormhosts ploughed into the foe. The climb had tired them all, but they fought hard, the knowledge that their brothers' lives depended on their valour giving them desperate strength.

Ionus and Vandus fought close by, the magic of the Lord-Relictor and the hammer of the Lord-Celestant reaping dozens of lives. Many of the enemy bore terrible disfigurements and mutations. The army of Sigmar was nearing the heart of Chaos in this land, and its influence was becoming pronounced.

More Stormcasts were coming over the brink, running to reinforce the line of their fellows. A multi-hued phalanx pressed forward, weapons swinging as one engine of destruction. Never mind that they were of different hosts and tempers; all were Stormcast Eternals, and centuries of training had made them brothers. They fought with a single mind.

With the first formation reinforced, a second and a third were brought into being by Vandus' peers and pushed out from the falls.

Thostos forged on ahead. Vandus saw him and his dwindling Warrior Chamber engaged by a crowd of giant mutants, more daemon than man. These beasts bore blades that shone with dark power, and they cut through sigmarite like paper. Celestial Vindicators fell around them, but Thostos' skin was again somehow proof against their weapons, and he killed them with impunity. The changes in his friend were strange indeed, thought Vandus.

Vandus went about the slaughter grimly. For all their misbegotten nature, there was discipline to the Chaos army. Those sections of the Chaos line that fell back did so in good order towards the stairs where they formed deep ranks, keeping the Stormcasts upon the rapidly warming silver, while other Chaos warriors came around their flanks, seeking to cut off the route from the crucible lip.

Slowly but surely, the Stormcast Eternals were being surrounded. The silver underfoot became sticky and yielding, the armoured corpses upon it cooking as they sank into the sludge. The nearest stair was agonisingly close but blocked by black-armoured warriors.

'To the stairs! Decimators! Gather together! Forge a path! Prosecutors, clear the way!' ordered Vandus.

By now the Stormcast Eternals had become more organised, falling into their allotted units as they fought their way forward. Twenty Decimators advanced, heavy feet snagging into the softening silver. With a cry to Sigmar, they charged. The warriors in the front rank struck down the enemy before them, then peeled away to the back of their retinue, allowing the axe of the next warrior to hit, so that they kept up a flowing charge that penetrated deep into the Chaos warriors mobbing the stairs. Prosecutors blasted those enemies trying to reinforce the weakening regiment, and suddenly the Decimators were through. They battled up the stairway, their fellows coming after them. Nearby, Thostos roared out a command and led his own Decimators in a similar endeavour up another stair. Other Lord-Celestants followed suit. Once upon the road they joined forces and pushed on towards the first tower on the network of causeways.

Calanax bounded up the stairs, and Vandus urged him to the edge of the road so that he might see how the battle went. He cursed loudly, for the majority of the Stormhosts were still embattled on the Silver Sea. Streams of molten silver were opening up between the fragmenting surface. Large chunks of the surface sank abruptly as the silver underneath turned liquid, dragging down Stormcast and Chaos warrior alike. The air whooshed and banged to the departing energies of men he could ill afford to lose. A pair of diabolical voices rolled out over the conflict, delivering orders and rebukes in a dark tongue.

'Ionus!' shouted Vandus down to the Lord-Relictor. 'Make haste!' Though scores of warriors had fought to the stairways and beyond, the rest were still intermingled with the Chaos horde. Perhaps a tenth of their number would make it through before the sea baked the rest in their armour.

'There are too many!' shouted Ionus Cryptborn, raising his reliquary, 'I shall forge a path if I can! For Sigmar and Azyr!'

There was a crash of thunder, and a colossal bolt of lightning shot from the skies to slam into the Lord-Relictor. It coursed through him, shooting through the molten silver to turn every Chaos warrior within a hundred paces to scorched meat. The Stormcast Eternals were invigorated by the divine bolt. Finding their passage suddenly unbarred, they surged for the walkways by the hundred. Cryptborn came last, sinking further as he struggled onwards. A giant Chaos warrior clad in golden armour and carrying a huge axe waded after him. Ionus reached the bottommost step of the stair before the surface collapsed and slid under a roiling swirl of molten silver. The Chaos warriors howled in agony as the sea took them.

'Ionus!' Vandus called. 'To me!'

Ionus never made it to the top of the stairs. The giant in gold hauled himself from the silver, steaming with the heat. He swayed upon the bottom step.

'Ionus! Beware!' roared Vandus, but it was too late. The giant leapt, his axe swinging into the Lord-Relictor's head and splitting it neatly in two.

'Ionus!' Vandus cried out. He slipped off Calanax and ran to the stairs. A trio of Prosecutors stepped before him, their sword staffs blocking his way. He made to shove past them but they pushed him back. Below, Stormcasts pressed forwards and the golden warrior was cut down, landing on Ionus' corpse.

The Prosecutors placed their hands upon Vandus' shoulders, gently restraining him. 'No, my lord. You must not go to him.'

A crack of thunder, mightier than all the rest, split the sky. Ionus' mortal form transmuted into a blazing spear of lightning that rushed upwards. Where it pierced the sky, black clouds wheeled and flickered with power.

Ionus Cryptborn departed the realm of Chamon. Vandus watched helplessly as his friend was taken home to Azyr. Then Calanax was there, growling at Vandus in rebuke. Vandus placed his palm flat on the beast's hide in wordless apology for leaving him, and climbed onto his back.

Horns rang. There were two towers close by, one standing athwart the raised road Vandus was upon, and another situated further into the sea on the roadway parallel to him. Upon the second road Thostos and his Warrior Chamber had a group of Chaos warriors trapped. These were being pushed back, screaming as they fell from the edge. Vandus' roadway was almost clear of the enemy and the army was retreating towards its towers. Another horn blared and the retreat abandoned all semblance of order as the Chaos warriors broke into headlong flight.

'Hold!' shouted Vandus. To his relief, the Stormcasts checked their pursuit, and began ordering themselves.

Another horn sounded, shrill and daemonical. The gates to the keeps clanked open, and out thundered tall knights of Chaos upon heavy horses. They rode forward without care for their fellows, and more than one fleeing infantryman was buffeted off the edge of the road. Their lances dropped, and they smashed into the lead elements of Vandus' army. So many died that the Lord-Celestant lost sight of the Chaos knights as a wall of storm magic leapt upward. Vandus and Calanax hastened forward, the dracoth leaping between lesser walkways, support spars and the vile decorations that clung to them.

A clattering of metal wheels upon the road preceded the arrival of heavy chariots, fashioned from steel, each dragged by a grunting, ape-like creature. Their charge spent, the knights wheeled and fell back with admirable grace, leaving lanes free for the chariots to crash into the ranks of Stormcasts. Unable to move aside, Sigmar's warriors instead leapt to the attack, and were cut down for their bravery. Dozens of Stormcasts were tossed high into the air by the impact and the flailing fists of the warbeasts. Scythes on wheels lopped limbs from bodies, while those Stormcasts wounded but not slain were finished by the halberds of the charioteers.

'Is there no end to them?' asked Vandus. He looked for opportunity. There, on the other causeway, a chariot went hurtling at the rear of a group of Celestial Vindicators. 'Can you make the leap, my friend?'

Calanax grumbled deep in his chest by way of reply. He crouched down, muscles bunching in his huge haunches. With a tremendous push he jumped into the air. A blur of bubbling silver passed beneath his belly, and he and Vandus were over, slamming straight into the side of the chariot and tipping it over with an almighty bang. It skidded across the road and plummeted into the Silver Sea, its dray-ape hooting in surprise and fury as it was dragged to its death. Another chariot came at them and Calanax lowered his head like a bull, bashing aside the ape and knocking the chariot onto its side. The charioteers were thrown free, one sliding straight off the edge, the other arresting his fall and scrabbling for an axe. Calanax crept up over the upended chariot, and Vandus swept off the man's head with a blow from Heldensen. The ape-thing ripped at its traces, dragging itself free enough to aim a brutal fist at the dracoth's face. Calanax caught the hand in his jaws and wrenched it free in a spray of blood. The ape howled and staggered before Calanax disembowelled it with a swipe of his claws.

Calanax climbed atop the wreck, raised his head and roared.

Behind them, Thostos and his men were dispatching the remainder of the infantry. On the other road the Stormcasts finally halted the chariots' progress and slew riders and beasts. Lesser walkways swayed as warriors duelled upon them.

No quarter was asked and none given. At great cost, the day belonged to the Stormcast Eternals.

Vandus stood atop a captured tower, and watched his men as they went about the unpleasant business that follows any battle. They walked causeways choked with corpses, tipping the bodies of Chaos warriors into the Silver Sea. The air was thick with heat, and the sea glowed ruddily in the dark. The Stormcasts went slowly, for all were by now mightily weary.

'Eight days' march, four days' climb and a battle,' said Vandus to Calanax, 'and still Lord Thostos paces like a caged lion, eager for the hunt.'

Vandus watched his restless friend. The foxfire of his eyes glowed balefully. Vandus suppressed a shudder, thinking on the fates of Andricus and Ionus. Would they too be changed when next they met? He had assumed that his friendships in this new life would never be sundered by death. How quickly he had been proven wrong.

'As for the rest, they are tired.'

Calanax rumbled beside him.

'Men's strength lies in another place to yours, my friend,' said Vandus. 'And these are not men, but more than men. Even they have their limits, and they must rest.'

He himself was exhausted. His muscles ached. Sorrowful and uncertain, he looked out down the network of pathways and roads. The day had been carried, but the price was almost too high, and Vandus had sincere doubts that he would be successful. First Andricus had fallen, and now Ionus. Only a thousand Stormcasts had followed him up the falls, the rest taken elsewhere by their lords, and of that number a full half had been slain gaining the crucible lip and the first tower. There were dozens of fortifications between them and the island where the Eldritch Fortress sat gloatingly beneath the Chaos gate. Fires burned from the tops of towers, and harsh music and uncouth shouts came from the nearest.

'How do we reach it?' he murmured. 'We have but five hundred Stormcast Eternals remaining. So many are gone back to the chambers of Reforging. I will sorely miss Andricus' guidance in the matters of siege. We are lost and alone in a nation of maniacs.' He looked upward. The night was at its darkest, and the skies were rich with stars. He looked to them a while, and when he spoke again he was less bitter. 'During the Long Calm, I would go to the top of the towers in Sigmaron,' he said. Calanax huffed out a steaming breath. 'I would seek enlightenment there, try to remember who I was, and to find my place in the new world I found myself in.' He looked to his mount. 'I hear the dragonkin ask the stars for sooth often, and that they sometimes reply. Will they answer me now?' Vandus looked upwards and slowly shook his head. 'No. I see nothing. The constellations are all different, and they do not know me. What should I do, noble Calanax? I wish you could speak the tongues of men and share your wisdom.'

Vandus returned his gaze to the stars. The venture hung by a thread. What could he do?

Perhaps... Perhaps the answer lay within himself. He recalled Ionus' words to him about his visions, that they might prove either useful or treacherous.

Could he seek to trigger them consciously? Vandus was profoundly uncomfortable with the idea, but he closed his eyes. He had no clue what he should do. In his old life he had no gift of magecraft. But was his Stormcast body not suffused with magic? Perhaps all he must do was...

He fell deep within himself. His knees buckled. He felt it as if it had happened to someone else, but enough awareness remained that he fell away from the edge of the tower, and then he knew no more of his earthly body.

A flicker of images came. He saw the Alchemist's Moon rising up over the edge of the crucible and climbing towards its apogee. As its light intensified, the great wyrm Argentine twisted and hid its face from the brightness. Silver stiffened and solidified. Baying parties of Chaos warriors poured from the keeps and islands of the land and hunted across the solid surface. The silver was still hot, and steamed in the reflected moonlight, but was made hard.

Vandus' perspective shifted. He saw before him a citadel bigger than any other, and he knew with iron certainty that this was the castle of King Thrond, the lord of this land. It jutted out over the Silver Sea on a natural promontory of stone and metal. As he saw this, what he must do came to him with utter clarity.

He gasped, and his eyes flew open. His skin ran with sweat under his armour. Despite the heat of the crucible, he shivered.

Calanax nosed his master.

The Lord-Celestant slowly sat up, then stood. Again the weakness he had felt before afflicted him. He walked to the parapet of the tower to look upon his warriors.

He knew what he must do. He shouted for attention and began to address his men.

CHAPTER SEVEN

The siege of the citadel

After many travails of blood and sorcery, Vandus' army had reached the centre of Thrond's kingdom. Of the many thousands who had set out from Elixia, just a few hundred Stormcasts remained. Behind them burned a score of keeps and lesser forts. Thrond had fled, his armies overthrown and his citadel empty. The king had taken refuge in the Eldritch Fortress.

Nevertheless, Vandus feared victory might slip from his grasp at this last pass. The Alchemist's Moon was rising and today it would reach its apex, an event that would cause the great wyrm to turn its fires away from the silver sea. Already the moon was sliding past the crucible's rim, its light picking out the rough hills there in bright silvers and deep sable.

'Faster my warriors! We must be quicker!'

Vandus sat upon Calanax on a knoll overlooking Thrond's castle. Around the landward side, Stormcasts worked at the hill, hacking away at the hanging promontory the citadel perched upon. Magical hammers boomed and swords hacked slivers from the metal-rich stone. Thunderbolt crossbows sent crackling jags of energy searing into bedrock, melting the ores therein. Molten metal dripped into the sea and the stone glowed ruby red.

The Alchemist's Moon cleared the crucible, its lower rim parting from the horizon like the end of a kiss. Argentine shuddered and shied away from its weird brightness, and the silver started to thicken.

'Faster!' called Vandus. His eyes flicked back and forth between his warriors and the Alchemist's Moon. So quickly it hauled itself heavenward, flowing as smoothly as quicksilver. At the summit of the island squatted Ephryx's Eldritch Fortress. Its walls ran up to the very brink, jutting over the Silver Sea here and there. Strands of magical force crackled and whooped around the walls. Its copper skulls glowed with evil energies. The air shimmered and ran with multicoloured sheet lightning. Over it pulsed the mighty Shardgate, an irregular gash in the air surrounded by an inhumanly tall archway studded with gigantic crystals.

The stepped walls of Thrond's castle were modest by comparison, a crenellated ziggurat adorned with snarling effigies of his menagerie. It was situated upon a jag of rock standing clear of the island, directly above the Silver Sea.

'You race against two hourglasses. The timing must be perfect for your plan to work, and the sorcerer prepares to shift his fortress once more,' said Thostos. 'Let the sands of one run out, and all is lost. How long can we chase this mage across Chamon?'

'The timing will be perfect,' said Vandus. 'And if it is not, we will hunt him until the hammer is recovered. There is no other way.'

'There is not, I concur. But we have only minutes before this chance is gone,' said Thostos.

'We shall be ready,' said Vandus.

Some deep-set part of the castle's foundations cracked. Stone screeched on stone. A quiver ran through the building, barely perceptible to the eyes of men, but strong enough to shake loose a statue and send it crashing into the sea.

'Halt!' shouted Vandus. He ordered the Stormcasts back from the trench they had hacked into the stone. Judicators aimed their weapons at the weakened section bridge and tensed for the final order.

The moon went higher, eclipsing the stars with its bulk. Magic shivered through Vandus' armour at its waxing might. The silver wyrm's fires had gone out. The sea heaved under a rapidly forming skin.

'Stand ready,' said Thostos.

The moon passed over the Shardgate, and its outline wavered behind the weird magics. The crystals in the gate glittered with colours as they captured the moon's light.

Calanax roared. Vandus dropped his arm.

The assembled Judicators of his army fired with their magical arrows. The missiles transmuted themselves to darts and spears of energy, and slammed into the ground by the base of Thrond's citadel.

A dazzling light burst across the Silver Sea, the moon's glow reflected twenty times over. Deprived of Argentine's fire, the ripples on the metal slowed and stopped. The shadow of the fortress and the island swept around the coast, and the silver stopped its churning.

With a tremendous crack, the stone under Thrond's citadel broke. Showers of rock splattered into the thick medium of the sea. Then the fortress itself hit the setting sea, sending up a tall sheet of thick silver as it splashed down. This washed up the cliffs, onto the fortress walls, curling back onto itself in a massive argent wave.

The shadow passed. The moonlight arrested the ocean, and the wave froze. Droplets of suddenly solidified silver fell from the sky as hard as bullets, rattling on the surface of the sea.

'The fortress is held fast!' shouted Vandus. 'Ghal Maraz awaits! Charge!'

With a shout, the Stormhosts scrambled forward onto the frozen mass of the wave. Digging in blades and clawed fingers, they hauled themselves upwards. The silver was still hot, and the metal burned them as they climbed, but the Stormcasts did not relent. In places it was thin, while in others too smooth or too hard, and a number fell, sigmarite clattering as they skidded helplessly off the metal and down to the sea below. Their departure boomed loudly over the frozen ocean, but still the Stormcasts were undeterred.

Calanax raced up the wave, taking Vandus to the plateau atop the island. Magic crackled and arced along the fortress wall, then gave out with a piercing series of whistles. Frozen silver anchored the walls firmly to the stone. The fortress was held fast.

Vandus got down from the back of Calanax and strode to the nearest gate. He hefted Heldensen and slammed it hard against the grotesque bronze face cast into the surface.

'Bring out the hammer!' bellowed Vandus. He smote the door again. 'I call upon you, Ephryx of Chamon. Bring out the hammer and your end will be swift.' A third time Heldensen clashed into the gate, scarring the metal.

The Stormcast Eternals had gained the cliff top and were forming up. No word came from the fortress. The outer walls were much cracked and damaged from Thostos' earlier assault, and left unmanned.

'Give me your answer, Ephryx!' shouted Vandus. 'You are lost!'

The rest of Vandus' army came after him. Thostos strode to his side.

A crackling sound came from above, a whine building behind it. Vandus stepped backwards until he could spy the Shardgate over the looming tower and walls. The crystal adornments sprayed fountains of sparks and long, bright streaks of crimson fire into the night; they flickered, turning through forms of pure light, patches of darkness, and back to gems. The Shardgate rippled, the roil of energy visible through it coalescing and forming a wide landscape comprised solely of hideous faces. Uncountable voices whispered covetously as unearthly eyes fixed themselves upon Chamon.

'Here is your answer, Vandus Hammerhand.'

The voice issued from the mouth of every gargoyle on the fortress walls. It was old and wise and full of dread power. Malice dripped from every word. 'A tide of daemons to drown in. The hammer is no longer the godling's, but mine. Begone from the gates of the Eldritch Fortress – take tidings of his defeat from here and you may yet live awhile.'

The whine reached a crescendo. A howling wind burst out

from the Shardgate. One after another, the crystals exploded, sending tinkling fragments all over the fortress. When the last detonated in a burst of multicoloured fire, the Shardgate dilated, yawning wider and wider until it filled the sky. A triumphant scream blasted out and the faces upon the other side pressed forward then burst through, the single mass they made splitting into a cascade of daemons that showered to the ground in an unending flood. They were long-armed and pumpkin-bodied, of blue and pink. They laughed and grumbled as they landed, galloping forward in knuckling runs and swinging down the decoration on the outside of the walls, as agile as apes.

'There is a breach in the wall,' said Thostos to Vandus, unmoved by the horde of creatures leaping free from the Realm of Chaos. 'This way.'

Moments later, the first of the daemons slammed into the Stormcasts.

'Your magics are poor, wizard,' said Korghos Khul. He and King Thrond seemed to fill Ephryx's scrying chamber. Khul stank of blood and his eyes were manic in the sockets of the skull he wore as a helmet.

'And you promised me a horde of daemons, but bring me only mortals!' snapped Ephryx. 'Fortunate it is for us all that my magic is strong enough to call up my own daemons.'

He stalked back and forth, mind working madly. His plans were not going as he intended, none of them. The daemon gale would hold the enemy for a while, but for how long? Already, upon seeing the Stormcasts approach, he had resolved to flee once again. But the fortress was held fast. Dare he attempt the translocation to the Crystal Labyrinth now? He fretted over the issue. Despite what he said to the warriors, he had taken no part in the daemon gale, and its advent spoke of but one thing: Kairos.

'My chariots will stop them,' said Thrond. 'We have no need of this blood-crazed madman.'

'Will they now?' Ephryx cast his gaze heavenward in exasperation. 'They did not stop the foe upon the walkways. Your forts did not stop them, your warriors did not stop them, your knights did not stop them!' he said bitterly.

'This remains my kingdom, Ephryx. Watch your tongue.'

'Your kingdom has fallen, you fool!' shouted Ephryx. 'This fortress is all that remains! You complained at my behaviour as a guest, Thrond. Now you are my guest, so I say to you, watch *your* tongue.'

'This is your doing, mage – you led them here,' said Thrond. 'I ought to kill you where you stand.'

'And if they had the hammer, you would already be dead. We are forced upon each other's mercies, Vexos. This is a common enemy. Surely even you can see that Khul's presence here is proof of that?'

'I am here only for the Hammerhand,' growled Khul.

'You invite the servant of the Blood God into my lands when I could deal with these invaders myself. We will live to regret this–'

'Silence!' screamed Ephryx. He jabbed a clawed hand at Thrond and the king went as rigid as a corpse. When his muscles relaxed, his eyes glowed a watery green and he was indeed silent. His head tracked Ephryx's pacing as loyally as a dog's.

'Leave the one called Vandus to me. His head is mine,' said Khul.

'By all means!' said Ephryx. 'Now get to the defence. In the absence of more powerful allies it will be you facing their hammers. But not alone. Thrond, get your chariots to the breach.'

'Yes, my master,' intoned King Thrond. 'I obey.'

The two warrior lords departed: Khul quickly, eager to be at the slaughter, with Thrond plodding after as sluggishly as a sleepwalker.

Feathers rustled in the shadows. A dry smell of birds and magic wafted across the room on a draught stirred up by broad wings.

'Kairos!' said Ephryx. He fought to keep fear from his voice, smothering it in a shrill haughtiness. 'Why must you lurk so? You could have come forth and dazzled these wretches with your magnificence and saved my temper.'

Kairos emerged from an alcove much too small to have contained him. He looked down on his acolyte with detached amusement.

'You cannot make them do your bidding? Must I do everything myself? You are a poor servant, Ephryx.'

'All this is but a distraction!' said Ephryx. 'The daemon gale will hurl them back.'

'Will it?' said the daemon's right head. 'It was I that summoned it, though you told the bloody one otherwise. Alone it will not be enough. I shall bring up an Arcanabulum. You will have the honour of casting the Lunar Reversal, that we may escape the crucible's grip and ascend to the Shardgate.'

'The Lunar...' Ephryx's face dropped. 'You will attempt the translocation now?'

'When else, small-horned dabbler?' said Kairos' left head. 'Did you intend to flee at our moment of triumph?'

'Will I not die attempting it?'

'Perhaps,' said the right head. 'If you don't, then I will have nothing left to teach you.'

'Perhaps not,' said the other. 'If you die, well, the same will also be true.'

A stab of cold terror raced down Ephryx's spine. He had spoken those words himself once, long ago. 'What have you seen? What is my fate?'

Kairos held up a taloned hand, bringing it up and round in a grand gesture, finishing as a clenched fist before the sorcerer's face. 'You of all people should know that your fate is unimportant. Sigmar once learned that even he is not beyond Tzeentch's influence. What makes you believe your fate is your own to choose?'

Kairos' index finger flicked out. Ephryx made to move but found he was immobile, transfixed by Kairos' stare.

'With the daemon gale come my brothers of the Nine. They gather now to call the Shardgate down. It is too late, I think, to bring all of Chamon to our master, but the hammer shall be his. Tzeentch himself will grant us many boons for that.'

Kairos tilted one head to one side, the other the opposite way. 'See? A simple plan. One even you cannot disrupt for me. The spell you cast upon Thrond, I taught you that, no?'

Ephryx was unable to answer.

'Of course I did,' said Kairos' other head. He pressed his long talon into Ephryx's left eye and Ephryx felt his will drain away from him. First went his control over Thrond, then his desire to triumph, until all was replaced with a cool indifference. Beneath this numbing blanket existed an ember of defiance, but it was small and cooling. Green light pulsed from Ephryx's eyes.

'It is high time we reminded Sigmar who is the master of the spheres,' said Kairos Fateweaver. 'You will aid me, little puppet, whether you wish to or not. Your days of freedom are done, Ninth Disciple of the Ninth Tower.'

Kairos walked to a blank spot on the wall with a shambling gait, as if the form he wore were not entirely to his satisfaction. The Lord of Change spread his arms and the wall flowed apart, revealing a staircase that wound around and down through the thickness of the great tower. The outer walls were pierced by many windows that let out onto the howling storm of Chaos outside. Through them the sorcerer could see the vortex of energy spiralling around the fortress, carrying daemons on its winds. Thunder cracked and banged, fighting against the intrusion. Kairos clacked his beaks in laughter.

'The storm god tries to bring his wrath to bear, but he cannot! All he can do is watch helplessly as we snatch away his true power. Your allies did better than you think, ninth fool of the ninth idiocy. They killed the rain-callers and the nursemaids among the foe, and they cannot call more of Sigmar's lackeys down to earth.' Kairos eyed the stairs. 'You first, I think,' he said.

He jiggled one hand in a mockery of a puppeteer.

Ephryx danced stiffly towards the stairway, unable to stop himself. He raised his arms up before him, straight as brooms. Strangled arcane phrases spilled from his lips.

'That is good. Wage the war for me,' said Kairos.

'While I think,' said the other head.

And so Ephryx was carelessly worked by the Lord of Change as they went down and round the mighty tower, heading towards the secret inner keep. Ephryx called up daemons by the score as Kairos muttered and argued to himself, his heads disagreeing on most petty of matters.

Although he could not move without Kairos' direction, Ephryx caught glimpses of the battle from the corner of his eyes. Stormcast Eternals had come easily into the ward of the castle via the unrepaired breach. They fought through Thrond's chariots, his own traps and hosts of daemons. They were mighty, he had to admit. Being so enslaved robbed him of anger, and he viewed the furious battle outside in a detached, calculating manner. Each twist of the stair brought him a new view: winged warriors snatched from the air and magical flames incinerating the enemy by the dozen. Lords transformed and destroyed.

Warrior by warrior, the Stormcasts were being whittled down.

Kairos and Ephryx reached the bottom of the stairs. The tower encased a domed keep of stone, and the tall gash in the tower let in the light of battle to fall upon it. From the centre of the keep glowed the painful brilliance of Ghal Maraz.

'Come brothers, we have great works to accomplish!' Kairos croaked.

Through the gap in the wall came a procession of eight Lords of Change. They shuffled through, as slow as elderly men. All were different, their staffs marked with esoteric symbols even Ephryx did not know. Here was one with plumage of bright magenta, there one with four eyes above a hooked beak. One was fat, while another was skeletally thin. One was covered in scintillating plumage, another's form flickered and blurred. They bowed to their lord as they passed, and Kairos greeted them all by name. Such names as hurt the minds of men, even those as well-versed in the arcane as Ephryx. Names like that should only be learned after great preparation, but Ephryx heard them all in relentless order. He was locked upright, unable to move. Inside the prison of his skull, he screamed.

The eight stepped by, croaking obscure mandalas or bandying ineffabilities with each other. Their chatter was the chatter of madmen and geniuses; they were the sages of insanity, and reality itself rebelled at their presence.

The foremost Lord of Change raised his staff, and the inner keep's doors shattered into colourful motes that swarmed upon the air. The lead cairn that had contained Ghal Maraz inside the keep had been much battered, and the light of the hammer flooded out stronger than ever before. The Lords of Change were unconcerned by the light. At another croaked command the cairn exploded, scattering lead bricks across the chamber and revealing the hammer itself. Ephryx was exposed to its radiance in full. Some device of Kairos' protected him, but the sight of Ghal Maraz to him was agony beyond agonies. Sweat dripped from his face, and he emitted a strangled scream.

The nine Lords of Change shuffled inside. As the last entered, the particles of light gathered themselves, and gates barred the way once more.

'There, the first piece is in place.' One of Kairos' heads swung to address Ephryx directly. 'Now for the second.'

Kairos raised his hands and extended his long necks. A yellow and green nimbus flickered around his staff. The Lord of Change said nothing, only held his arms aloft for a moment, then lowered them slowly.

'It is done.'

The ground heaved. The space around the inner keep became hot as a forge, and the stone of the ground glowed white with heat. From this bubbling pool rose up a complex machine, plucked from the hidden workings of reality, its spars and cogs dripping molten rock.

'To work, Ephryx,' said Kairos. 'I am afraid you must perform this rite. I do not wish to suffer the energies myself.'

'Quickly now,' said Kairos' other head.

Ephryx stepped close to the machine as it fully emerged. His clothes smouldered. His eyes watered, but he could not close them. The machine and the ground were cooling, and it was this alone that saved Ephryx's skin and sight.

'Begin the reversal!' said Kairos.

Ephryx set his body into motion. He knew the spell, of course, and locked inside his body he cursed himself for the curiosity that had set him to learning it.

At the black-worded incantation, the machine began to work, turning against the way its creator intended. Although physically divorced from the world, it retained a connection with it, and as it screeched into life reality grumbled around it. The natural order of things was flung into reverse.

'Glorious! Glorious!' cackled Kairos. 'Magic infuses everything, a heady mix of so many colours and winds! Feel it, Ephryx – this is true power! Further, further! Make the silver flow away, so that we may greet our master in person.'

The ground shook, the tower encasing the keep swayed. With a groan of tortured metal, Ephryx's dwelling sheared away from the tower's stalk, revealing the Shardgate blazing directly above.

'That's the way, small sorcerer,' said Kairos indulgently.

Ephryx's limbs ached. Age ran cold claws over his bones. He had lived for hundreds of years and his powers promised thousands more, but the Arcanabulum ran roughshod over the laws of nature and magic both, and the sorcerer withered as he chanted. His spine twisted and his horns lost their lustre, becoming flaky and dull. His hands clawed with arthritis. All the while, Kairos croaked and clattered his beaks in laughter, and true hate bloomed in Ephryx's heart.

'Success! Ha! Well done!' shouted Kairos.

The moon ground to a halt and slowly, reluctantly, began to slide backwards. It went back past the point of apogee, and with a sudden rush, the silver holding the fortress liquefied and ran back into the sea.

CHAPTER EIGHT

The will of Tzeentch

A cackling daemon ripped the head from the Retributor at Vandus' side. His body vanished into a blaze of light that reached for the churning clouds, only to veer sideways and be dragged into the fabric of the Eldritch Fortress. Vandus shouted out his anger, smashing the pink daemon down with his warhammer. It burst, and from the gory remains climbed two smaller, blue daemons. Where the first had laughed and howled, these scowled and grumbled as they fought.

Vandus slew these two also, and spurred Calanax onward. Thostos fought nearby, an unstoppable tornado of hammer and sword. They were through the breach, into the first courtyard. Many ways led off the ward, leading into a labyrinth of passages and walls, but ahead the route was clear. The walls were riven by magic and war, and the tower's base was visible to him through a further gap.

Vandus pushed his way on. The Stormcasts were dwindling

in number, but remained in good order. With Liberators in solid lines, Judicators behind, Retributors and Decimators working in small groups to bring down the worst of the daemons and the greatest champions.

There was a screech like that of tortured metal. The Shardgate pulsed ever quicker. The ground shook and the top of the tower fell down. Incredibly, the moon was reversing its course.

'We do not have much time!' shouted Vandus. 'Onwards, before they steal the hammer from us!'

With a ringing of trumpets, the Stormcasts pushed forward to the gap in the next wall. They poured through, routing the few warriors of Chaos that dared stand before them.

Vandus felt a surge of relief as they crossed the second courtyard, but then the walls rippled and became convoluted, trapping two score of his men within. The courtyard became smaller, then opened up at one end.

A fresh foe waited behind – a huge warlord with a skull for a helm and a daemonic hound beside him. He bore a daemon-weapon, a two-headed brass-bound axe the size of a mortal man. A band of massively muscled warriors attended him, eyes bereft of reason, teeth stained brown with the blood of the innocents. They stood tensely, a rabidity coming off them as a wall of iron-tinged heat.

'Khul!' said Vandus.

'I have come for you, Blackfist. You are the last of your tribe. You think yourself my equal, raised up by your puny god.' Khul swept his axe around to point at Vandus. It trailed streamers of unlight. The fabric of reality tore upon its edge. The air shed droplets of blood and screamed. 'You are nothing! Craven! Fleeing into the arms of Sigmar when I proved stronger. I will destroy you and offer up your skull to Khorne as I gave the skulls of your wife and children to him!'

Vandus was nearly overcome by the urge to rush at Khul. Hatred boiled in every part of his being. The ghost of the man he had been demanded vengeance. Calanax felt his wrath and stamped and snorted.

Perhaps Vendell Blackfist would have broken from his men, his anger overcoming reason and sense. But Vandus was Vendell no longer. He fought down his fury and shouted out an order to his few remaining warriors. 'Defensive square!' he bellowed. Horns rang, and his men ran quickly into a formation opposing the mob of Khul's warriors.

Khul laughed hollowly, a madman's humour, sick and shot with bloodgreed. 'Coward. Very well. Hide behind your golden weaklings. No matter how much magic Sigmar has imbued you with, it will not help you.'

The tribesmen around Khul gripped their weapons and growled, barely holding their anger in check.

'Blood for the Blood God! Skulls for the Skull Throne!' shouted Khul, his words so thick and crazed they were barely discernable; a raw cry of unfettered rage.

With an animal shout, the warriors of Korghos Khul surged forwards.

The Bloodbound crashed into the shieldwall of the Liberators with shocking force, only to be thrown back. A bloody toll was levied by the Judicators behind the Liberators, the last Prosecutors picking off Khul's elite deep within their own ranks, while Protectors plugged gaps in the line. Again the Bloodbound charged, and again. Vandus and Thostos fought side by side, slaughtering the followers of Khorne by the dozen wherever they went. Soon enough, Vandus realised that no man of Khul's dared raise a blade against him, and he used this reticence to his advantage.

But Vandus' Stormcasts were fatigued and diminished in number, and the Bloodbound of Khul fresh and numerous. One by one the Protectors were slain, and the Prosecutors dragged from the air. Before long, the ranks of the Stormcasts were in tatters and the battle had descended into a swirling maelstrom of individual melees.

At this moment, Korghos Khul chose to strike. He burst through his own men, his great axe parting their souls from their bodies in his eagerness to bring down his enemy. The daemonic hound at his side leapt at Thostos. The strange magic infusing the Lord-Celestant saved his flesh from the creature's teeth, but he was knocked sprawling and clanged off the cobbles of the courtyard.

Vandus and Calanax faced Khul alone.

'Now you will join Khorne, Blackfist, as a skull to be ground beneath his feet,' snarled the Chaos lord.

Vandus and Calanax were forced back by Khul's ferocious assault. Their weapons banged and flared from one another as each lord strove to bring the other low. Through Vandus' concentration on the fight came the realisation that he and Thostos were alone, beset on all sides by the Khul's Bloodbound. No weapon could harm Thostos, and the followers of Khul drew back from the duel between Vandus and the Khornate lord.

Still Vandus was being forced backwards.

A clatter of wheels came from behind. From the corner of his eye Vandus saw Thostos leap, and heard a bestial cry as something died. Then Khul barged Vandus aside, knocking him sprawling from Calanax. The Chaos lord's axe slammed into the blade of another, staying it from slaying Vandus.

'I said the Hammerhand was mine, Thrond!' roared Khul.

'My kingdom. Who are you to demand the head of our foe?' Thrond asked.

'Wizard's puppet. You dare defy me? I shall add your head to the tally!' Khul's fury broke like a dam and he slammed into Thrond, knocking him from the back of his chariot. The two Chaos lords wrestled upon the blood-slick cobbles.

Thrond's warriors let out a cry and turned upon the Bloodbound. The far side of the square erupted into fresh and furious battle.

Vandus stood, Heldensen at the ready. The Bloodbound parted before him, teeth bared. Their muscles stood out from their necks and their eyes glared. They strained like dogs on a leash, but they would not defy their master. They would not attack him. He was Khul's alone to slay.

Thostos came to his side.

'We must kill him!' said Thostos. The desire for revenge burned coldly in his baleful eyes.

'Do you not think I wish to slay him?' asked Vandus. 'Our duty lies elsewhere.'

'Where is your desire for wrath and ruin?' Thostos' voice reverberated strangely behind his war-mask.

'There is a time for vengeance. This is not it. One petty revenge can upset the chance for ten thousand greater victories. Come.'

Reluctantly, Thostos backed away from the horde.

'This way!' said Vandus, and pointed to a gateway barred by

a portcullis. Calanax rejoined them, forcing his way through the melee. The Bloodbound of Khul would not fight him either.

'Strange luck,' Thostos said as Vandus remounted.

'Let us pray it holds,' said Vandus. Most of the warriors had backed away, going to join the fight with Thrond's knights. A few remained, unsure. Vandus held his hammer in a guard, ready for them, but still they did not attack. More and more of them were glancing over their shoulders to the duel between Thrond and Khul.

Thostos broke the portcullis into pieces with one swing of his hammer and rushed through. Vandus came behind him on Calanax. No warrior of Khorne dared follow him.

'The hammer is close!' Vandus shouted. Before them was the tower of Ephryx, its side rent apart. Light blazed through cracks.

A deafening shout made him turn. Riding upon the platform of another chariot came a warrior Vandus recognised, Khul's lieutenant, the bearer of the icon that had summoned the Realm of Chaos into Aqshy. The bloodsecrator carried his icon with him, blood boiling from Khorne's rune in a crimson fog.

'We sell our lives dearly, then,' said Vandus.

Thostos snarled.

From the other side of this courtyard, daemons came capering. The two Lord-Celestants were surrounded anew.

'I will slay you! I will cut your head free! I will spit on your corpse and dedicate your skull to Khorne,' shouted the bloodsecrator. Spittle flew from lips bitten raw.

'Khul has claimed my head,' said Vandus. 'Do you dare his wrath?'

'Khul is weak! Sigmar is weak! Blood for the Blood God! The Lord of Skulls cares not from whence the blood flows.' The bloodsecrator grinned savagely, exposing black teeth filed to points. 'Do you hear that, feeble one? Your power is nothing compared to mine!' He slammed his weapon against his heavily muscled, scarred chest and raised his icon to the clouds boiling impotently in the sky. 'Do you hear? You are weak, Sigmar! Weak!'

In reply a mighty thunder boomed. The sky split with a bolt of blue as wide as a tower. It struck the wall, then again, opening up a fresh breach. The metal of the wall exploded. The breaches revealed the sea and the broadness of the crucible. Clouds raced around its rim, and light played there, bright and godly.

More lightning bolts slammed into the earth. The bloodsecrator and his tribesmen recoiled. From out of the light stepped a figure bearing an icon of his own, topped also with the emblems of death.

'It is you who are weak, to fearfully sell yourself to the murder god,' said Ionus Cryptborn.

A bolt of pure magic shot from his hammer and blasted the chariot. The metal of it withered, the draught beasts were slain, and the bloodsecrator was cast from it and lofted through the wall, where he fell flailing into the Silver Sea far below.

Light faded. All around Ionus stood a host of Stormcast Eternals.

'Ionus! You are returned!' said Vandus. 'How did you manage it so quickly?'

'I told you, my friend. Death has little hold on me,' said Ionus.

Singing their praises to Sigmar, the Stormhosts charged.

The renewed crusade fought on, smashing daemon and mortal alike, until Vandus and Thostos forced their way through the fracture in Ephryx's ruined tower and into the space it contained. A bizarre machine sat there, creaking and pinking as it cooled. There was the hidden keep, light burning from its riven walls.

'Ghal Maraz…' said Vandus breathlessly.

'The sorcerer, Ephryx,' said Thostos. The heat of emotion entered his voice, his deadened soul awakened by hatred.

The sorcerer had become ancient, bent with age. He hobbled as quickly as he was able from the machine, towards the iron doors of the inner keep. As he passed within, a wall of fire leapt up, encircling the keep. The sorcerer's bodyguard moved to interpose themselves between the gates and the vengeful Stormhosts.

In the sky, the Shardgate was sinking, the infernal energies spilling from it now caressing the tower's stump.

'We are running out of time,' said Vandus. But Thostos had already rushed ahead, a group of returned Celestial Vindicators at his heels, and was slaughtering his way through Ephryx's bodyguard. Vandus went after, Calanax bowling over four of the hulking warriors.

'Retributors, to the gates!' ordered Vandus. Calanax forced his way through the bodyguard, Vandus smashing them to the ground with Heldensen. In short order there were no more Chaos slaves to slay. Protectors held the breach into the tower, preventing others from assailing the lords. Outside, bolts of celestial energy rained down.

'Hurry!' urged Vandus. The Retributors banged rhythmically

on the gates with their lightning hammers. The flames crackled, the warplight racing over the vile carvings that covered their surfaces. The fire went out and the warriors attacked. The gates shook with each impact, but did not shift. The Shardgate continued its descent.

There came a louder bang, and the gate shuddered differently, shifting on its mountings. A wide crack sprang across it. Blue light shone out and the Retributors called out joyously. They struck harder, until another crack, then another, crazed the surface of the door.

Together with the light came the sound of chanting, words so evil they crashed around his skull. Vandus fought against the pain though blood ran from his ears.

With one last impact, the doors burst inward in a storm of iron shards. Vandus and Thostos ran in, drawing sustenance from the holy light that bathed the chamber.

The whole of the inner keep was one large, domed chamber with but two apertures: the gate, and a slit window glazed with amethyst in the eastern wall. A rubble of lead bricks was scattered across the ground. Above it, chained by blood iron and bonds of pure magic, floated Ghal Maraz, Sigmar's own hammer, and relic of the world-that-was.

A coven of nine daemons sought to take it for their master, and it was from them that the chanting came. They turned one by one to glare at the Stormcast Eternals, wizened faces full of hatred and amusement, knowing faces that carelessly harboured the wisdom of ages. There were eight of lesser order, great in their own right, but not so powerful as the ninth, a two-headed horror, taller than the rest and shrouded in dark majesty.

'You cannot stop what has become. The end is in sight! Come in, come in! All are welcome in the Crystal Labyrinth of my master,' cawed the two-headed greater daemon.

The Eldritch Fortress lurched, sending the Stormcast Eternals staggering. Slowly, it began to rise towards the Shardgate.

'Get the hammer!' yelled Vandus. 'Bring them down!'

The Stormcasts charged. The greater daemons came down to do battle, and all the while Kairos laughed.

Vandus hurled himself at a Lord of Change. To his left, five of his warriors were cut down by a bolt of dark fire. Others exploded, disappeared or were transformed. The air wavered and the scene changed. Vandus staggered, finding himself in a quiet forest. He spun about, looking for his foe. A sudden coldness gripped his legs, but when he looked he could see nothing amiss. 'Do not trust your senses,' he said to himself. 'They cannot help you. Trust Sigmar.'

He shut his eyes, letting the vision-fugue come down on him. In his mind's eye the interior of the chamber overlaid itself upon the forest. The room was ablaze with magic. Some of his warriors staggered about, as lost as he. Only the Celestial Vindicators seemed unaffected, and in his state of altered perception, Vandus could see how the fury in them burned hot enough to sear away the magic set against them. A bird-headed daemon shrieked as enchanted blades cut into it and laid it low.

His own opponent stared at him with dead eyes, its hand waving up and down slowly. Cruel humour was writ upon its features.

It does not know I can see it, thought Vandus. With a great effort of will, he called upon his distant body to obey him.

With a mighty heave, he swung Heldensen. His limbs felt feeble, as if they moved underwater. Heldensen sped true, smashing the daemon in the face. Its head snapped back and, with a blast of warplight, it fell dead upon the floor.

The glamour was lifted by the daemon's expulsion, and Calanax pressed forward towards the hammer. The Shardgate was forcing its way through the domed ceiling, still descending as the fortress rose up. Chunks of masonry fell down, and the whole keep rumbled.

'Thostos, the hammer!' called Vandus. Calanax pushed onwards, fighting through a swarm of leaping daemons that twisted into being from jets of fire projected by a Lord of Change.

'The chains!' shouted Thostos back.

Vandus nodded in acknowledgement. He stood up in Calanax's saddle, swinging his hammer at the first of Ghal Maraz's restraints. Several links burst. Fizzling magic, they fell away. Thostos cleaved through one, then two, with his runeblade. Vandus rode swiftly to the next, then the next.

'You cannot triumph! This hammer belongs to Tzeentch!' crowed Kairos.

The greater daemon stalked across the floor and levelled his staff at Thostos. From the top of the rod spouted a gout of magical fire. When it touched the Celestial Vindicator, his magic aura seemed to transmute his flesh into pure sigmarite, but the fire burned hotter and hotter, and Thostos' body began to run. With heroic effort, Thostos cut through another chain, one of pure light that vanished as Thostos' sword passed through it. Stormcasts ran to Thostos' aid, but Kairos sent them sprawling with a thought, and the Lord-Celestant remained trapped in the searing fire.

Vandus rode to the next chain and shattered it. The noise attracted the attention of Kairos' left head.

'Ah, ah, I think not,' said the Lord of Change.

'It thinks it can outthink me!' said the other head.

'Kairos Fateweaver!' said the first head. He advanced on Vandus. The fire winked out and Thostos fell to the side.

'The Great Oracle, to whom no secret of past...' said the first head.

'...or future...' said the other.

'...is any kind of secret at all,' they said together.

The end of his staff glowed with awful light.

'Now,' said the heads together, 'let us change you into something fitting–'

A bolt of light streaked from the side of the room, catching the Lord of Change on the arm. Kairos' heads snapped round, and Ionus Cryptborn sent another blast at the daemon.

In the corner of the room, Ephryx blinked. The green light went from his eyes as Kairos' control of Ephryx was shattered, his master embroiled in a magical duel with the skull-faced warrior.

'Kairos,' he said. His aged voice was a dry whisper. The sorcerer bent painfully to the floor and took up a fallen staff of change. Its violent energies coursed through him, warping his flesh and soul, but he hobbled forward toward his treacherous master. The Shardgate, the hammer, the invasion – all had become of no consequence. He was consumed by his hatred of Kairos.

Raising the staff in palsied hands, Ephryx swung at Kairos' back. The head of the staff barely scratched the daemon's skin, but it was enough.

Kairos flung back his head and screeched from both mouths. Rippling energy engulfed him. His physical form sped through a dozen transmutations: a tusked skyray, a moonfaced puppet jerking in multicoloured flame, a pink-skinned lesser daemon, a statue of coal and a chirring song bird.

Ephryx sank to his knees, all his strength gone.

'You didn't see that coming did you, you preening peacock.'

'Vandus, the hammer!' said Thostos, his voice a gurgle.

Vandus stood upon Calanax's back and launched himself at Ghal Maraz. He flew through the air, hand outstretched. A Lord of Change reached out for him, only to be blasted back by a bolt of lightning from Calanax. A second fell to a magical attack from Ionus. Time slowed to a crawl. A thousand futures depended on this moment.

Vandus' fingers closed upon the gleaming haft of the hammer. The last chain fell away, and it came free. His mind flooded with memories that were not his own, images from times and places far away, and a world long gone. Then he was falling and rolling. He came up easily, and he held the power of a god in one hand.

Kairos Fateweaver leaned over him, the last effects of his transformations flickering over his faces as he regained control of his form.

The daemon lifted a hand and a glow of power formed around it. 'I do not think that is yours,' he said.

'Nor is it yours,' said Vandus.

Before he had even formed the intent to move, Ghal Maraz streaked forward with the power of a comet. Vandus was only the means to the end. The weapon used him to exert its will.

Ghal Maraz smashed into Kairos' shoulder, sending the arm spinning free in a spray of mashed flesh and daemonic ichor. Kairos shrieked, twin screams from both mouths.

The hammer arced round, dragging Vandus' hand with it. It powered into Kairos' left head, caving in his skull and sending it crashing into the right. Kairos toppled forward cawing in pain. Vandus stepped back, and the hammer swung up and down, crushing one head into a bloody paste upon the floor, then the second.

Kairos' body convulsed, making a scream-like a whistle. He juddered, vibrating so quickly his outline was a blur. He convulsed, inwards, outwards, then with a sorry pop he transformed into a smoky crystal.

Vandus brought his boot heel down hard on the gem, crushing it to glittering powder. The Shardgate was now only feet above Vandus' head. He held Ghal Maraz up in defiance.

'See this, Great Changer! This is Ghal Maraz, Sigmar's weapon of old! It is in my hand, and shall soon be in the hand of the God-King. Fear it, for as it slew your servant, so one day shall it slay you!'

Lightning burst from the hammer. Wherever it landed, it struck down a servant of Chaos. The roof of the keep was flying apart, the tower coming to pieces around it. The fabric of the Eldritch Fortress was rooted in the power of the hammer, and now that Ghal Maraz was free, it disintegrated, the pieces flying upwards into the Shardgate where they exploded into showers of silver sparks. The skulls around the walls burst. A furious howl raged from the Shardgate, sending the incarnate Stormcasts reeling. It went on and on, then changed pitch, becoming wild laughter.

The Shardgate winked out. An echo of the laughter remained, and for a moment the bare floor of the keep hung in the air over the site of the Eldritch Fortress. Ionus, Thostos and two dozen more Stormhosts stood upon a mosaic that depicted Sigmar in his glory, the last remnant of Elixia's Great Monument. The sorcerer Ephryx lay dead upon the God-King's face. Then the floor tilted and dropped towards the naked summit of the island, coming apart as it fell. Upon the bare stone its fragments shattered, scattering the Stormhosts all about into the ranks of their brethren. Of their foes there was no sign. All were gone, taken up by the Shardgate.

Vandus lay sprawled upon his back, looking upwards. The Alchemist's Moon had resumed its true course, and as it passed overhead, a new light was revealed. A brilliant, pure radiance that banished every scrap of shadow from the island. A twin-tailed comet burned across the heavens.

Vandus held aloft the god-hammer, saluting the arrival of the Sigmarabulus. A great peal of thunder split the sky.

The Stormhosts fell to their knees, and were surrounded by a blaze of light.

Ghal Maraz was reunited with its master, and the war began in earnest.

ABOUT THE AUTHORS

Josh Reynolds is the author of the Blood Angels novel *Deathstorm* and the novellas *Hunter's Snare* and *Dante's Canyon*, along with the audio drama *Master of the Hunt*, all set in the Warhammer 40,000 universe. In the Warhammer World, he has written the End Times novels *The Return of Nagash* and *The Lord of the End Times*, the Gotrek & Felix tales *Charnel Congress, Road of Skulls* and *The Serpent Queen*, and the novels *Neferata, Master of Death* and *Knight of the Blazing Sun*. He has also written many stories set in the Age of Sigmar, including the novels *Fury of Gork, Black Rift* and *Skaven Pestilens*. He lives and works in Northampton.

Guy Haley is the author of the Horus Heresy novel *Pharos* and Space Marine Battles novel *Death of Integrity*, the Warhammer 40,000 novels *Valedor, Baneblade* and *Shadowsword* and the novellas *The Eternal Crusader, The Last Days of Ector* and *Broken Sword*, for the *Damocles* collection. He has also written *Throneworld* for The Beast Arises series. His enthusiasm for all things greenskin has also led him to pen the eponymous Warhammer novel *Skarsnik*, as well as the End Times novel *The Rise of the Horned Rat*. He has also written stories set in the Age of Sigmar, included in *War Storm, Ghal Maraz* and *Call of Archaon*. He lives in Yorkshire with his wife and son.

WARHAMMER
AGE OF SIGMAR

THE REALMGATE WARS

HAMMER OF SIGMAR

DARIUS HINKS · C L WERNER

An extract from

HAMMER OF SIGMAR

taken from *Stormcast*

by Darius Hinks

The hammer falls.

Vengeance tears from my throat, ringing through the bloodless metal of my mask. 'God-King!' I cry in a voice that is no longer my own.

'God-King!' howl my lightning-born brothers as the tempest hurls us from the sky.

The ground gives as we land but Zarax rides on, ignoring the odd, yielding terrain. I cling to her scales, as blind as a newborn. The others are close behind and I hear their metal boots pounding across this broken, benighted land. Weapons are drawn, oaths are howled and I take my first breath of mortal air. Sulphur pours through my mouthpiece and I gulp it down, relishing the bitterness.

The storm thins, revealing plumes of smoke and embers. I whisper to Zarax and as she slows I sense the others gathering around me. I almost pity those we have come to destroy. Who could dream of such an enemy?

The smoke drifts, revealing glimpses of a tortured landscape. We're heading down a glistening, crimson road that seems to have been carved from a flayed corpse. Sigmar's tempest has landed us on a butcher's block of body parts and thrashing, broken wings.

It's a shameful sight but I don't avert my gaze. I must be vigilant, aware. I must understand this place quickly.

I look harder and realise that it's not a road, but a bridge of meat and chains, hazy with flies. Its span is vast beyond measure, stretching miles ahead before disappearing into a crimson wall of smoke. Over the side I glimpse wisps of cloud and realise we're far above the ground. Shrieks fill the air and I see that the bridge is alive. The whole structure is made of living birds – thousands of them, broken and burned together by hot irons and fixed to a mesh of thick, oily chains. It's the stink of their ruined flesh that fills my lungs. It's their thrashing bodies I'm riding across and their pain I can hear.

I want to roar in outrage, but I bite down my fury and keep my voice level.

'Advance,' I say, rising up in my saddle and turning to face my army.

My heart races as I see what I command. The storm has spawned a golden host. Even in this stinking, bloody wound, they are a vision. Every one of them is clad entirely in gleaming armour, still crackling with the fury of the storm. Pennants trail above glinting, haloed helmets, bearing the divine sigils of Sigmar and the Celestial City. No army ever looked so glorious, so *dignified*. And Sigmar has entrusted it to me.

The vanguard is a seamless wall of shield-bearing Liberators; numberless ranks of heroes, marching towards me in perfect unison. Then come the retinues of paladins – striding goliaths that dwarf even the Liberators, clad in blessed, god-wrought suits of armour. Some carry great, two-handed hammers that look like they could topple city walls, while others wield pole arms – long, gleaming glaives with lightning in their blades. In the rearguard are my divine archers – hundreds of Judicators, moving with the same precision as the rest of the army, readying their shimmering bows. High above, riding the thunderheads, are our winged guardians, the Prosecutors: radiant, inviolable and more dangerous than the lightning.

I almost laugh. *Stormcast Eternals* – the God-King's unbreakable fist. Removed from the golden halls of Azyr, we shine all the brighter.

I turn back to the bridge and see the sky for the first time. It's almost entirely obscured by rock. A vast sphere of smouldering ore, hundreds of miles in diameter, hangs directly over our heads. Such a star-burnt hulk can only be a moon, dragged from the heavens by divine will. It's moving towards us, shedding sparks and boulders as it glides majestically through the clouds. The sky ripples in its wake like water in the lee of a ship.

'Lord-Celestant.'

I look down from Zarax's back at Lord-Relictor Boreas. I can barely recognise my brother's dry tones. His arcane duties have left their mark on his speech, just like every other part of him. As I was being drilled and remade in the Celestial City, Sigmar sent my brother through death and beyond. Eternity echoes in his every word.

Unlike the rest of us, my brother's mask resembles a bleached skull, and I find myself wondering what lies behind. Would I recognise his face? Unlike me, he has endured Sigmar's fire a second time. He knows what it really means to be immortal.

The rest of my captains stand back in respectful silence as he approaches.

'What are your orders, Lord-Celestant?' he asks, speaking formally, giving no hint of our shared past. He glances at the heavens. 'This was not prophesied. None of my auguries indicated that we would land here, on this bridge of birds.'

I look back down the road, blanking out the thrashing wings and the insanity hanging overhead.

'The tempest can't have strayed too far off course, Boreas.' I nod back down the bridge. 'We've clearly found our foe.'

There are figures emerging from the fumes – a barbaric, crimson-clad rabble scrambling along the bridge, pouring from the smoke like blood from a wound. The moonlight shows them in sickening clarity. They wear jagged, red and brass helmets and their bare chests are lashed with scarred muscle. They carry repulsive, brazen idols and axes as tall as men, scored with foul sigils, and every one of them is draped in skulls and glistening with blood.

'Bloodreavers,' says a voice edged with hate. 'Finally these snorting dogs will receive some justice.'

I turn to face the speaker. 'Liberator-Prime. There can be no victory without discipline.' I nod at the lines of Liberators marching towards us. 'They will follow our lead, Castamon. Show them what Sigmar expects.'

He nods, humbled. 'Lord-Celestant.'

I turn back to the bloodreavers. As they run they fill the air with a dreadful din. They are trailing something that clangs and clicks along the chains of the bridge but at this distance I can't make out what it is.

The rest of the Liberators clatter to a halt around us, moving with such well-drilled precision that they could be on a parade ground.

I point my hammer at the bloated moon and raise my voice.

'Remember this, Stormcasts: nothing is forsaken. Look deep enough into the darkness and you will always find Sigmar looking back.'

They remain motionless and silent, but I feel their battle-hunger; it radiates from their gleaming armour.

'Lock shields,' I say, and there's a deafening clang as the vanguard snaps into place. The entire army moves as one, bodies, shields and armour, fitting together to make an impenetrable bastion of sigmarite.

Struggling to suppress my pride, I raise my warhammer, Grius, to the crimson heavens. It flashes in the moonlight, and Zarax lets out a roar. As the dracoth rises beneath me she opens her reptilian jaws and unleashes pure white fury at the clouds. The air crackles and spider legs of electricity dance across my armour.

I give the signal to advance and as we meet the enemy lines I become one with my expressionless mask – an emotionless implement of Sigmar's will. Anger is forgotten. Grief is suppressed. Everything falls away: the sound of shields rattling on greaves, the torment of the bridge, the lunacy of the moon – all I know is this moment. I feel the long, slow arc of my life reaching its culmination. Finally, I face the monsters I was born to slay.

Gold and crimson collide. There is an explosion of grinding metal as the vanguards meet. Sparks glitter in the darkness, axes clang against shields and bucklers smash against armour.

The lines of Liberators hold steady and I order them onwards. Their shields lock tighter with every step and they drive the enemy back across the bridge of birds. Even from a few rows back I can barely breathe for the stink of the bloodreavers, a ripe stench even more powerful than the sulphurous moon. They fight like wounded animals, snorting, spitting and howling as they throw themselves against the Liberators' shields, trying and failing to break our line. I glimpse deranged faces, eyes rolled back in sockets, delirious with rage. They're more stampede than army.

'Drive them back!' I shout as the bloodreavers' frenzy grinds us to a slow plod. 'Drive them back to whatever dark vaults spawned them!'

They begin to drop, felled by lightning hammer-strikes, golden flashes that lash out from behind shields, crushing armour and bone. It seems that victory will come before I even have chance to gauge the strength of my army.

I hear a cry of pain from the shield wall.

I peer through the serried, golden lines and glimpse one of my Liberators clutching at his throat. His armour has been rent and there's blood, lots of blood, rushing between his fingers. He vanishes from view as the phalanx closes around him.

His choked screams scrape around my skull and I drive Zarax forwards, keen to be done with these animals. Even the dracoth cannot easily wade through such a crush, so she unleashes a gout of lightning, tearing a channel through the enemy ranks. The smell of cooking meat intensifies the stench.

A bloodreaver bounds over the shield wall. He vaults several rows, screaming hysterically, and lashes out with a pair of jagged axes. Another Stormcast staggers as the bloodreaver crashes into him.

Before the Liberators can respond, a paladin strides casually forwards and brings down his huge, two-handed hammer. He moves with a languid, easy grace but his blow lands like a thunderclap. The bridge rocks and blinding light envelops us all. Even Zarax stumbles.

When the glare fades, the bloodreaver is gone and the paladin has calmly resumed his place. If it weren't for the gore sliding down his breastplate there would be no sign that the Chaos creature had ever existed. I take note of the Stormcast's markings.

'Retributor Celadon,' I shout, disguising my pride beneath a stern snarl. 'Wait for my command.'

More of the howling curs manage to scale the shield wall, disrupting our faultless lines. It's becoming harder to match the dispassion of my mask. Anger boils through my limbs. I clutch one of my honour scrolls and recite the Oath of Becoming.

Dozens of the bloodreavers are falling to the Liberators' hammers and swords but I hear Stormcasts crying out too. Such noble beings were not made to succumb to such soul-sick dogs and my patience starts to fray. The crush of bodies becomes oppressive. My eyes blur with sweat and my muscles burn with the effort of holding myself back.

Another Liberator falls and a whole section of the shield wall gives.

The bloodreavers seize their chance and wrench the gap wider with a flurry of axe blows.

I signal to the paladins, finally giving them permission to advance, and they surge forwards, led by Celadon's brutal blows.

'Close ranks!' I roar, rising up in my saddle and ordering the Liberators back into position as the paladins storm ahead. They try to obey but the bloodreavers are becoming even more feral. They fight with no structure or reason. Something is driving them into a boiling frenzy. It's bewildering.

Another Stormcast cries out in pain and I will take no more.

'For the God-King!' I roar, launching myself from Zarax's back and into the enemy, joining the wave of paladins.

Ranks of warhammers rise behind me, along with a chorus of battle cries.

The fight begins in earnest.